Scott's Tulsa II

Spies, Ballplayers, & Murder

A WYATT SCOTT NOVEL

BY

S. L. CHALMERS

TABLE OF CONTENTS

For this second Wyatt Scott novel and the remaining two, I render my deepest thanks to Terry Collins for editing, suggesting, encouraging, and supporting my writing through many years. He was a constant source of inspiration and a grand friend. I miss our laughs and conversations.

CHAPTER I

An Assassin and Janet

A Japanese business executive sat in the next to the back row on the left side of a sparsely populated train car of the Oil Flyer, which operated nightly from Kansas City to Tulsa. He sat properly, if not stiffly, gazing out his window at sporadic lights amid the Oklahoma darkness. At the front of the car, two drowsy salesmen yawned and alternately consulted their watches, while a matronly woman sat engrossed in a novel of Civil War romance. A solitary man, carrying an out-of-place raincoat on a clear evening, entered the car from the one behind. He slipped into a seat in the last row behind the Japanese gentleman. He wore his hat low and his gaze lower.

From under his raincoat, the man produced a revolver with a noise suppressor threaded onto its barrel. Keeping it down, he pointed the gun toward the seat. The Flyer chugged along the tracks. It passed Claremore, Oklahoma, when two piercing whistle blasts raged from the engine. During the second shriek, two shots hissed out of the muffled barrel, and a pair of holes appeared in the seatback. The Japanese man slumped against the window with two huge wounds through his torso. The high-powered bullets exited his body and burrowed into the cushion of the row beyond him. Blood poured from the man's back and chest, soaking his seat with the residue of murder.

The assassin reached over the seatback and withdrew the man's wallet and passport from inside his coat. Ignoring their bloody corners, he stuffed them inside his own jacket. In the victim's side suit pocket, the man found a clean slip of paper. He studied its contents. After a few moments of deliberation, he slipped it back where he found it. He righted the Japanese man's hat and tipped it to cover his eyes. His cold-blooded work done, the murderer crept out of his seat and returned to the car from where he had come. The Flyer persisted on toward Tulsa with half an hour left on its journey. The passengers in front continued with their modest pursuits, hearing nothing and unaware of what transpired behind them.

* * *

Wyatt Scott rocked in his office chair, staring at the pile of bills he had avoided for days. Those bills presented no burden, but the time and sorting they took annoyed him. The five hundred dollars from the millionaire, Albert Campion, to escort his brother-in-law Sleener out of Tulsa, while not well-earned considering the man's murder, had been safely deposited in Scott's checking account. His payment from Catherine Folger, equally short of overall success due to Sleener's murder, added another two-fifty to his living expenses. The two sums, being far more than required to bring him current on his debts, would also keep him in the good graces of his bootlegger.

The worrisome and excessive fee from Queena Capps remained in the envelope she gave him. He hid the cash inside the shell of his console on the phonograph side, away from the vacuum tubes of the radio and safe from overheating and fire. Well-earned or hush-money, the verdict remained in doubt. The last act in an alley off Sixth Street and the unsanctioned justice likely dispensed against the murderer, KTOO Joe, gave Scott no serious qualms. The future repercussions for all involved worried him still.

While his mind roamed, sorting his small debts fell into autonomous movement. He wrote six checks, addressed envelopes for each, and affixed stamps. The irksome details of business completed, Scott decided he could make his way home for records spinning out tuneful loneliness from sad torch singers or muted trumpets warbling soft jazz. Several sips of Cutty Sark would complete his evening. With the envelopes on his desk, he left his office.

Darkness had won out against the protracted summer day. The LaSalle waited in an unfamiliar parking position on Boulder Avenue in front of the Pythian Building. Not a spot where Wyatt would park during the day because plugging the damn meter annoyed him more than the expense. Scott hated providing any financial support beyond his legally required taxes for what he considered the city's piss-poor performance at local governance.

Scott swung around the parking meter designated for the empty spot behind his convertible. Before he completed the arc, the parking meter exploded. Shrapnel of pennies, nickels, and dimes sprayed him and littered the sidewalk. He dived behind the LaSalle, abrading his suit coat on the sidewalk. A subtle, but discernible 'pop' barely preceded the 'whoosh' of air from his car's curbside rear tire. He pulled his Colt and primed it.

Scott couldn't fathom who could take such potshots or whom he might have crossed that possessed a silenced gun. Eyes searching, head twisting, he stayed low behind the fender's protection. From his limited vantage point, he saw a streetlight spread its circle at the corner, a window or two show against the shadowed buildings, and a distant traffic light jumping to green. No human forms emerged along the east side of Boulder. He listened intently; his ears being his most reliable sense behind the safety of the LaSalle. He heard the clanking first, then saw the trolley car coming from Fourth Street onto Boulder. The trolley sparked along its overhead line as it passed by the LaSalle. Seeing an option for retreat, Scott bolted from the shelter of his Cadillac, running with the trolley between him and the direction of the shooter. He kept pace until the trolley curved away, then he hustled into the blackness.

* * *

In the unassuming office of Detective Art Cleveland, Wyatt Scott trod from the blank side wall, past the empty coat rack, to the opposite wall where a city-issue, cheaply framed photo of the mayor smiled with the usual enthusiasm politicians show for cameras. The neat, uncluttered office included an empty trash can, a desk photo of Cleveland's wife, and a typewriter on the edge of his desk, which sat rather too distant for the presumptive owner's use. Seated in his desk chair, Cleveland followed the pacing Scott with his eyes, while otherwise remaining remarkably still.

"Damn!" exclaimed Scott just as he swung from the mayor's image back toward the blank wall. "Who and why?" He didn't look at Cleveland as he continued. "Silenced gun; professional quality work." He bobbed his head, looking at the floor as he paced.

"You said you didn't see anything. Not even where the shots came from?" Cleveland recapitulated the circular conversation in which they had been engaged for the last five minutes.

"Not the exact spot. Just across the street, east side of Boulder." Scott spun again to pace back toward the picture wall. "Exploding parking meter was the first damn thing I heard and saw. Stupid gadget probably saved my life." Scott pivoted toward Cleveland before an impish grin joined his sardonic eyes. "Your guys probably made thirty, forty cents when they inspected the scene."

Cleveland did not rise to the bait, replying, "I bet they did."

The sarcastic moment lost; Scott drifted back to the redundant recounting of the attempt on his life. "Air coming out of my tire came next. There were no other shots that could give him away." Scott stopped in front of Cleveland's desk. "I never saw a muzzle flare. Didn't hear the first shot at all. The second made a pop."

"Silenced guns are pretty rare." Cleveland swiveled a little in his chair and leaned forward on his desk. "Your CIA pals have any special beef with you?"

"Too clumsy for anyone from that group. It's not impossible they want me dead, but they would not be so overt. An accident, my suicide, drowning when my car went into the river – those are more their style." Scott detailed his expectations of Fielding, Pierce, or any of the CIA factions. He did so calmly with a matter-of-fact expression, which surprised him after he had defined their likely methods of his murder.

"We didn't find any shell casings across the street. The shooter collected them, even in the dark."

"Professional, like I said." Scott spun away from Cleveland and back toward the smiling, and increasingly annoying, image of the mayor. "I suppose he could've used a revolver. Even so, professional, and thorough."

Cleveland rubbed his chin. The situation apparently brought a cliché to his thoughts. "Mobster possibly. You crossed any of them?"

"No. None I am aware of." Scott nodded his head. "It seemed like a pro hitter though. You have any running around Tulsa you keep tabs on?"

"Not really. K.C. mob dabbles, but our little hamlet is too insignificant for them. Besides, the small-time competition from our many local bootleggers would waste their time." Cleveland paused. He grew a smirk akin to Scott's earlier one. "And you understand about Tulsa's prostitution being far too independent to let them muscle in."

Scott nodded his appreciation of Cleveland's subtle spur. He gloved the sarcastic barb but didn't have the inclination to throw it back to Art. Wyatt's roaming began wearing on him. He edged near Cleveland's guest chair.

"We recovered the bullet that flattened your tire." The detective offered Scott some positive, tangible information after his gibe. "The other one makes up a metal hodgepodge mixed in with pieces of parking meter and bits of coins – no chance we can tell what's what."

Scott sat in the chair facing Cleveland. "I suspect unless you match something from Kansas City or Chicago, you won't find the gun in Tulsa." Scott tossed a smile Cleveland's way, showing some gratitude mixed in with the tension of their roles. "Just not many professional killers plying their trade here in the Oil Capital of the World."

Cleveland dodged the smile and reverted to police basics. "No. Just the same, we'll see what word comes from out of town."

"Sure." Scott leaned toward Cleveland and looked him in the eyes. "Thanks for coming in, Art. The night guys didn't want to call you at home, but I knew better than to ask for Morgan after supper."

"It's fine. I serve the Tulsa public." Cleveland scooted his chair back and smiled for the first time. "Besides, it's nice to have a mystery where you're not two steps ahead of me."

"I am perplexed. And being the victim puts some urgency into it." Scott pushed his chair back and stood.

Cleveland did likewise. "I'll get in touch with you when I get something definite back from the lab about the slug.

"Thanks." Scott made his way to the door.

"I'd have your army-issue cannon out and cocked when you open your door," cautioned Cleveland.

"I'll have it handy." Scott left Cleveland facing an interrupted night of sleep and a fresh case. Cleveland left him with no answers and a worrisome future.

* * *

Janet Martindale stripped her white nurse's shoes from her aching feet. She fell back against the cushions of her patterned beige sofa. She rented a tiny bungalow south and east of downtown Los Angeles. A tidy, feminine place with postwar contemporary furniture, it provided the cozy nest she needed when retreating from the sickness and death her job threw at her. She rubbed her worn dogs through the white hose of her uniform. A dot of blood stained her white skirt, while her traditional white blouse escaped the evening's trauma.

A knock on her door interrupted her foot soothing. Mumbling to herself and thinking words her mother would blush over, she forced her sore toes to hike to the door. On the other side of her screen, M. B. Fielding, former colonel and prolonged nuisance, waited with his standard impatience. Once she saw the visitor, her eyes adjusted from surprise to annoyance.

"What do you want this time of night?" Janet accused more than asked.

"The same as I've wanted all along: answers." Fielding grabbed the screen door handle. "May I come in?"

"I suppose if I say no, you'll tear the screen off." Janet stepped back into her home, allowing the CIA man entry space. "Your memory must be failing, M. B. Last time I told you all I know. And I told you to leave me alone. Nothing has changed."

"Using my initials. That's a step up from just my last name." The spy chief stepped into Martindale's living room.

"No. Since no one knows your real name, I have my own for those initials – Major Bastard is what I think when I use them." A defiant sneer punctuated her comment.

"No matter," he grunted. "Someone in Alaska did spy for the communists." Fielding circled around her living room, scouting the few pictures on the wall.

"Alaska was a thousand years ago. I left it behind for a better world. Too bad you didn't, Colonel Fielding."

"The Alaska OSS world and the communists followed us. I think you know more about what happened than you let on."

Janet sat on her couch. She brought her right foot to her left knee and restarted the foot massage Fielding interrupted. "This is getting tiresome. I haven't a clue about who. I imagine there were as many spies there as there were Eskimo fishermen. Hell, for all any of us know, you were the spy, and you covered it up with this obsession." Janet dropped her right foot and pulled her left onto the opposite thigh to give it attention. "You've been chasing this ghost for three years now, and all you have are empty accusations. Less tolerant people would tell you to put up or shut up with your pestering. Me, I just believe you're a ratfink and no goddamn good at your job."

Fielding's face flushed red for the first time. "Nurse Martindale, you crossed a line with that remark!"

"Buster, you are in my house. The lines are *mine*. And they got crossed a long time ago." She released her left foot. She brought it back against the floor and leaned forward. "Here's what I think; you have a serious conundrum with this. You admire Wyatt Scott, but you also suspect him of being a spy, and you can't have it both ways. There is nothing to prove he is and no evidence to exonerate him. While the mystery spy being me would please you to no end, there isn't any evidence against me either. It's driving you nuts."

"It's worth my time and effort to find the damn spy and put things right no matter who."

"Maybe. Even if that's the case, I know what really grinds your gears. You need Wyatt more than he needs you, and you hate it more than anything. We have that much in common." Janet's mouth grinned, but her eyes told a different story. "He will never be your lapdog, and he will never be my fiancé. The difference is I am learning to live without him. I suggest you try to do the same."

"Scott knew the secrets. You slept with him. You kept company with him. You knew Scott," Fielding pushed the facts as if they mathematically combined to equal an answer. He crossed his arms, affirming that his statement carried the final weight.

Janet stared down Fielding. "I tell you; I didn't know anything about what you worked on or any of your secrets." Mirroring her argumentative guest, she folded her arms across her chest. "I can't say what anyone knew, but *nobody* knows Wyatt Scott, least of all me."

"If only I could be sure of ...."

"You can be sure I don't care," barked Martindale. She uncrossed her arms and squared them toward Fielding. "Not about Scott, not about your unknown secrets, or your grandiose old days of bossing us around in freeze fuck Alaska."

Apparently surprised by Janet's vulgarism, Fielding dropped his arms and stared. "There *was* an agent in Alaska who worked for the Soviets against us. I'm certain of it. Mark my words, I will get to the bottom of this!"

"You flogging that old dead horse tells me you have a mental problem, nothing more." Anger and exasperation lost to exhaustion and sadness. Janet rubbed her face. "I lost a patient tonight on my shift. A little girl. She was sickly and frail her whole short life." She dropped her head. "Working with kids is wonderful when you save them. When you can't, you still must go on." Martindale stood. She straightened her skirt. "So, I'm going to fix myself a drink. I won't offer you one because you won't be staying. Then I am going to finish rubbing my sore feet and cry a while before I go to bed. And you, Major Bastard, on the way out, don't let the door smack you in the ass."

"Very well, Janet. Mark my words, I will get answers."

"You get whatever you can find. It won't involve me." Janet gave her back to Fielding and sauntered to her kitchen.

Fielding watched. As she disappeared beyond her kitchen door, the frustrated spymaster marched to the screen door. He shoved it open, fiercely enough to crash against the side of the house. The bang rolled across the lawn and back inside to the kitchen. Janet Martindale poured liquor. Former Colonel Fielding pushed into his government car, thwarted.

* * *

Despite the late night and brief sleep, the summer sun dragged Scott from his bed early. He brewed coffee, scrambled eggs, made toast, and carried his plate to the dining table. He parked the platter next to a tall glass of water, a cup of black coffee, and a neat little whisky pick-me-up. The dining table supported a single setting of stainless-steel utensils, as opposed to the more elegant settings of sterling silver in the sideboard drawers, which had remained sealed away in their case since Scott cleared his parents' belongings from their house. He groused about too much trouble to continually clean the silver finery, but the truth was they evoked more sadness and pain than elegance.

As he pulled his chair out to sit, the telephone rang in the living room. Scott gave it a quick, piercing glance. After the second ring, his fear of the phone continuing interminably outweighed postponing his breakfast. He grabbed the whisky for succor before abandoning his table to answer the nettlesome and insistent telephone.

He manned the receiver and spoke. "Scott."

Through the phone he heard, "Wyatt, it's Janet."

More than a little surprised, he hesitated before recovering enough to reply, "Janet. Hello."

"I had a visit from your old buddy, Colonel M. B. Fielding, last night. I didn't invite him, and it wasn't a social call."

Her sharp tone bordered on punitive. It did not take a detective to note the legion of expletives marching unspoken between the layers. "What did the bastard want? He knows how you feel about him."

"Yeah, and I reminded him too." She paused and calmed a bit. "He's still looking for a commie in the woodpile. I knew nothing about the spy crap you boys worked on." Her anger tipped toward injury and hurt. "He all but accused me of...being a spy." Her voice broke as she trailed off.

"Pure nonsense. You weren't privy to anything sensitive. How was this espionage supposed to have transpired?"

"Pillow talk."

"Say again?"

"He more than implied that I was a great Ruskie seductress, and you likely whispered sweet military secrets in my ear intermittently with headboard crashes against the wall."

"Jee-zus, Mary, and Joseph! What did you say to him?"

"I told him the truth. I said we were intimate...but never close."

"Ouch!" Scott pulled the phone from his ear and stared at it for the impudence of the remark before transferring it back to the proper position. "A harsh assessment of our time together."

"Well, if we *were* close, why am I in California and you're in Tulsa?" Fury, injury, and despondency formed the cocktail of her tone.

"I thought it was settled," lamented Scott.

"It...is." Resignation and ache registered as she trailed off.

"Well, water under the bridge," Scott coughed and swallowed some pride along with the phlegm.

"An ocean!" Her biting tone unmistakable even through the tiny Bell speaker.

Scott drew himself back from their personal history. "I'm sorry Fielding pulled that on you." His regret was genuine. He hated to see Janet abused by anyone, the more so when Fielding did it.

"Yeah, well, he *did*." She drove the fact like a dagger, shredding his words of contrition.

Scott tossed down a swig of his whisky. The taste and the burn offered comfort, but no new thoughts on where to take the conversation. He sipped again and started fresh. "Aside from Fielding, how are you?"

A sigh found its way along the copper wires from California to Scott's ear before Janet replied, "Better. I'm at Children's Hospital. It's older than St. John, but kids don't have war stories to tell."

Her sarcastic lilt notwithstanding, Scott smiled at the shift in subject and tone. "Most of us are storied out. I'm glad you're at a hospital. Maybe you can meet a nice doctor and make your folks happy."

"I want to make *me* happy. Doctors, like private eyes, never seem to have any time. Got my fill of that in Tulsa," grumbled Martindale.

"Sure enough," he replied flatly.

A long pause with merely ambiance being transmitted forced both parties to reflect. Scott knew Janet wanted more from him. He posted letters of apology and self-recrimination after she left – hollow pleadings without the offer of forgetting the past, but Alaska owned his thoughts if not his soul. As the connection time elapsed, only Pacific Bell benefited.

Janet broke the spell of silence. "Say 'hi' to Bugler for me." Janet raised her pitch a little and dropped the tension in her voice. "He always thought I was aces."

Scott noted the change and appreciated it more. "He did, and he was right." Wyatt wanted to make amends for his past intruding on her, even if it meant dealing with Fielding. "Janet, I'll speak to Fielding."

"Fine. You and M. B. can yap all you want about spies or rehash Brock and Harris. Just tell him to leave me the hell alone!" The man and the subject brought antipathy back to her speech.

"I will put things right," proclaimed Scott. "That's a promise."

"I remember your promises."

The words slapped Scott harder than her hand could have. She had every right to them. He deserved them. They still hurt. "Yes. My past is messy."

A tiny cough and a gigantic sigh flowed from California to Tulsa before Janet spoke to conclude the call. "Goodbye, Wyatt. Phone if you ever make L.A."

"I will...if I ever do." Scott hung up. He slugged down the remaining Scotch. He didn't want to, but he drifted back to nineteen forty-seven and his last night with Janet Martindale.

* * *

More than a year before, Scott entered his bedroom with two whiskies on ice. Janet drew a long, slow pull from her cigarette. Propped up against the headboard, her bare breasts rose with the filling of her lungs and dropped with her exhale. A rogue ice cube rattled in one drink, disturbing the background ambient. Scott handed a glass to Janet. She took it and rubbed the chilly surface along the side of her face. She continued down to the top of one breast, then across to the other. Her gaze never left Scott as she cooled her body and accentuated her sexuality. Finally, she stopped using the glass to cool herself and sipped the tawny Scotch.

His own nakedness covered by his silk robe, Scott sat on the corner of the bed. The act was a first statement without words, distinct and different from climbing in beside her where his passion and instinct wanted him to be. Janet replied with a second sip of whisky. She followed with a final draw on her smoke before she stubbed it out, half-finished, in an ashtray on the nightstand.

Janet sipped her drink dry. Wyatt watched the ice settle back to the bottom when she righted the glass. He did not want to be the first to speak. It being his apartment, his home field; she batted first whether she knew the rules for home and away or not. Top of the inning and the first pitch, Janet swung for the fences. "I'm going back to California."

Scott didn't need to see the ball clear the fence; the sound told him. Her tone sailed pure without lilt or question. It spun with finality, leaving nothing to appeal. He made the pitch; pitches over the months; hell, over the years. He bore the responsibility. She wanted him; wanted him forever, but she didn't need him. He needed her. It would not have taken much to avoid this loss. He set it up. Wyatt became the pitcher-of-record. "Can't blame you given the guy you have here."

"Yeah. He has a vision problem. Sees the past clear as crystal but can't see a thing today." She stood. Her full feminine beauty on display. "I need a shower." She headed for the bathroom.

Her athletic figure reminded Scott of the prize his ambiguity had lost him. He stared at the door as she stepped through and closed it. He dropped his robe on the floor of his closet. Scott performed the ritual of clothing himself. Getting dressed made sense. Nothing would change now. Her declaration meant that she had purchased a ticket. He would drive her to the train station. Neither would make a scene. Her pride would not allow it. His guilt would stifle any explanation.

CHAPTER 2

MORGAN AND HIROSHI

Late in the a.m. and certainly not bright-eyed and bushy-tailed, Scott made it into his office. He opened the door, and before he hung his hat on the coat tree, the morning turned sour. Waiting behind Wyatt's desk sat Lieutenant Morgan, Cleveland's boss. His feet crossed on top of the desk; he leaned back in Scott's chair and folded his arms. He had kept his hat on his head and completed his ensemble by wearing the smirk reserved for those with more power than class.

"Tell me, Scott, are you a magnet for murders?" questioned Morgan, in lieu of a morning greeting.

"If you're still on about the whore killings, I've told you all I know." Scott stood without approaching Morgan.

"I don't believe that for a minute, but I wouldn't spend my time coming to the Pythian Building to hear more of your evasions on that." Morgan drew his feet from the desk. He straightened into a rigorous, judgmental posture and placed both palms on the desk. "I got a brand-new killing, and you're the major clue."

"Clue? I figured you might be here because somebody tried to clip *me* last night. I'm the victim, not a clue."

"Yeah, I heard about that. They missed you, so it's this real dead guy I got that interests me." Morgan reached into his pocket and removed a slip of paper. He extended it toward Scott without explanation.

Wyatt ambled near the front of his desk and took the note from Morgan's outstretched arm. He read it. He turned it over and back again. Another quick glance, and he tossed the paper on his desk. "My name and address. And?"

"*And* it was on the dead guy we found on last night's Flyer from Kansas City."

"I don't know anybody in Kansas City," offered Scott.

"Dead guy's not from Kansas City. We're not sure where in hell he's from. But he's a Jap sure enough. You got connections with any Japs?"

"The guy had no I.D.?" inquired Scott.

"No I.D., just that note, about fifty bucks in cash, and an Oilers' game schedule. Oh, and two fat gunshot wounds in his back." Morgan rose behind Scott's desk. "So, leaves me asking again, why's he coming to Tulsa and looking you up?"

"I wouldn't know. Other than a handful of POWs, I haven't seen a Japanese since nineteen thirty-four with the Babe Ruth tour." Scott spent a glance toward his wall of memories and pointed that way for Morgan's benefit.

"You think this dead Jap is a ballplayer?" asked the Lieutenant.

"I barely met any of the players. Only person I knew was our official guide. They called him a guide, but he worked for the Imperial government as a babysitter for the players and spy on their actions back in thirty-four."

"This Jap from thirty-four got a name?" asked Morgan, more complaining than inquiring.

"Hiroshi Ishikawa was the man's name."

"Jap sounding name all right." Morgan looked down at the desk and slowly repeated the sounds. "He-ro-she." He looked back up at Scott. "This Hiroshi call you or write you about visiting?"

"No. Haven't heard or seen him since I left Japan in nineteen thirty-four. I have no idea if he even survived the war."

Morgan cleared his throat. He eased back a degree from the desk. "Just to be clear, you don't communicate with any other Japs, and you don't know anything about this?" If Morgan's skepticism functioned any keener, it would rate its own badge.

"That's right. I don't know!" Scott's frustration with Morgan threatened a breakout from his considerable restraint.

"I know that all you tell is not all you know." Morgan eyed Scott.

Despite the negative, aggressive deportment hurled his way, Scott calmed his tone. "Was the victim the only one on the train car?" He hoped a shift toward facts and detective work would make Morgan think rationally or, if not, send him packing.

"No, but he sat in the back; next to the last row." He glared at Scott for asking a question of the inquisitor. "Nobody saw or heard anything as far as we can tell."

Scott swung beside his desk on the door side. He took a thoughtful step farther. "How did you find him?"

"A porter at the depot found him while cleaning up just before dawn." Morgan folded his arms. "We talked to the conductor as soon as we got there. Finding any passengers after they left the train wasn't in the cards."

"No one heard the shots. The same night, somebody took two shots at me with a silenced gun. Even the Tulsa police might consider that more than a coincidence." The sarcasm that tinged the statement fell short of Scott's usual standard.

"Coincidence, uh-huh. Though some of us think you're slick enough to create a couple of hard misses to cover up you killing the Jap."

"Us is plural, Morgan. I believe you meant to say, 'I.'"

"Just because you have Cleveland fooled, shamus, don't think the rest of us believe your clean-guy image." Morgan stepped around the desk. He went out of his way, brushing Scott's shoulder as he marched to the door. After opening it, he squinted back at Scott. "I plan on solving this damn murder. I'd be happy to pin it on you. No matter though, I'm going to solve the thing."

The door rattled when Morgan slammed it shut. Once Scott disengaged from his conversation with the irritating Tulsa cop, he moved to his wall of memories. He noted Hiroshi, who seemed old to Wyatt when he knew him in Japan. The pictured man looked nothing of the sort now. Scott never imagined mourning Hiroshi's death, yet with the war over and nothing except fond memories of his trip to Japan, he felt regret that he didn't get to greet the old acquaintance, who had apparently come to see him.

* * *

The elaborate multistory lobby, sitting areas, tiny hidden stairs, the grand entrance, and the general H-shape of the Imperial Hotel in downtown Tokyo confounded young Wyatt Scott. For two days, he roamed it near and far, up and down, and stair-by-stair. On a beautiful fall day, he didn't know where he might go without Berg goading him. Scott circled around to the lowest floor of the massive main lobby. He drifted into the section called Peacock Alley. He slid into a chair at one of the various two-person tables that ran along the walls, causing a courteous waiter to float his way. Wyatt smiled and waved him off. The man bowed before gliding toward the main lobby.

While still focused on the smooth maneuvers of the waiter, Hiroshi Ishikawa slipped from behind him, taking the open chair. "Scott-san, did you miss your bus?"

Surprised by his guide's stealth, Scott missed a beat before he recovered. "No. Coach Mack didn't need me for this practice. It's going to be short and sweet."

"Ah, then you have time for yourself." Hiroshi smiled and nodded.

"Yes, if I don't get lost again going round and round this hotel."

"It is a beautiful building, intricate in detail and creative with light." Hiroshi twisted in both directions to embrace the architecture and show his appreciation. "Young Scott-san, do you appreciate the design and the intricacies?" prodded Hiroshi.

"I realize all the stairs and offshoots from that huge lobby are confusing," replied Scott.

"The ground-floor lounge ties all sections together. The vaulted ceiling and stained-glass mosaic bring light to expose the work of our craftsmen." Hiroshi could not hide his pride in his countrymen's work. "Besides its beauty, the Imperial Hotel is unique in its tenacity. Just weeks after it was completed, Tokyo had the most horrible earthquake. Every building nearby toppled to the ground. Do you understand why this building remained intact?"

Scott shook his head. "An ancient Japanese god protected it?"

Hiroshi laughed out loud. He held for a moment, calming himself before he continued. "No, no. It was modern engineering. Your American architect, Mr. Wright, designed the supporting members to float on the clay."

Scott stared blankly. "Float, you say."

"Yes. Mr. Wright knew about earthquakes from San Francisco in your country. His clever design was crafted perfectly by my country-men. We are not afraid to learn from Americans. You might do well to learn from us, Wyatt-san." Hiroshi smiled and bowed slightly.

"Moe insists I learn your language. He says it is important to know it and your culture. It shows respect."

"Mr. Berg is a wise man. He is also worrisome for Hiroshi." The guide scanned the long room before finishing his interrogation of Wyatt. "I hoped you could tell me his plan."

"Hiroshi, there's not any plan I know of, and I don't think Moe has one. You worry too much about him. He's just a different kind of guy. He's so smart he needs to keep his brain going."

"I worry about what he is doing and what that means for Hiroshi. Moe-san is not a bad man, but he is very bad for me."

"Look, I don't know anything, and I wouldn't get him in trouble if

I did. If I could help you, Hiroshi, I would. I'm just a guy on my own today."

Hiroshi bowed his head. When he looked back at Scott, he smiled. "My apologies, Wyatt-san. I shall be your gracious host." He got up. "Come, let me show you charming Tokyo, that which is not forbidden."

Hiroshi escorted Wyatt past the reflecting pond and along the drive from the Imperial Hotel entrance. This excursion headed away from Hibiya Park and the Imperial Palace on the other side of the hotel. As Hiroshi continued, they passed beyond the cab stands and nearby shops Scott saw with Berg. They continued this new trek beyond the Imperial Theater, where Hiroshi pointed at the intersection of Z Street.

"Now Wyatt-san, we shall walk the streets of Tokyo together. You will witness the daily lives of my countrymen."

They swung onto Z Street. It bustled with Japanese citizens moving briskly about their business. The men wore Western suits, while the women included both traditional dress and Western style clothing. Cars cluttered the street, with a splash of rickshaws folded in. Chevrolets and Fords maneuvered through the turmoil. Scott regarded the scene more intently than with Berg, who always hurried through to their specific destination. The oncoming pedestrians gave way to Scott and Hiroshi with bows of recognition.

"You see, our people live their lives the same as you Americans." Ishikawa waved his arm at the teeming street while they continued strolling. "We must work harder because we do not have your rich resources of oil, copper, and iron."

"People want to live their lives the same everywhere, I suppose."

Scott addressed Hiroshi as he continued walking. "Your people are more polite than Americans."

Hiroshi smiled. "It is our way. Formality and respect are very important to us. We are a venerable civilization. It is good and bad for Nippon. We respect our long past and honor those souls that came before, yet that makes change more difficult. America is young. You change, invent, and drive to the future. We need some of that Yankee future."

From behind the touring pair, a new Cadillac LaSalle passed them as it motored down Z Street. Scott jumped as he glimpsed it. He tapped Hiroshi on the shoulder, startling the reserved man. He pointed at the convertible as it rolled away. "That's a Cadillac LaSalle! I plan on getting one of those with my baseball bonus money."

Ishikawa strained to view the fading car. "It is wonderful, Wyatt-san. You are as fortunate to have baseball as it is to have you."

The compliment flew past Scott faster than the LaSalle had. He watched the automobile diminish with distance until it left the road, turning onto another. He kept his joyous expression even after the Cadillac had slipped away.

"You know those automobiles are made in Japan." Ishikawa interrupted Scott's rapt attention to the LaSalle. "We produce tens of thousands of them every year." Pride in his tone painted the factual statement of Ford and Chevrolet production in Japan.

"That so? You folks are full of that Yankee future." Scott whistled. "You buy yourself one of those buggies and we can trade pictures by mail."

"Hiroshi is only a civil servant. I do not have a baseball bonus. You Americans are blessed beyond others."

"You sound jealous, Hiroshi-san."

"No. I am a part of Nippon, and it is a part of me." Ishikawa spread his arms in a gesture to encompass all in sight. "I only observe that your country starts with more than others. America drew a walk to first base and then given second and third. You only need a bunt to score. We need a home run."

Wyatt didn't like the characterization. "Americans work hard too. Right now, we have the Depression. New York and Philadelphia look poor compared to Tokyo."

Hiroshi smirked. "You see Tokyo's Park Avenue or Wall Street. We do not place our poor citizens on display. Dignity is most important in our culture."

"Our Wall Street got messy. Did your businessmen commit hara-kiri when the market crashed?"

"Seppuku is about honor, Wyatt-san, not money. One's spirit must starve with only money for supper." The minder waxed philosophical.

"Well, it comes in handy for buying food for supper."

"You are here now for money and not the spirit of baseball?" questioned Hiroshi.

"Not for money, no. I don't get any on this trip, just room and board. I do get to travel, explore, and be with the greatest ballplayers in the world."

"Ah. You visit here for the adventure of Nippon and the spirit of baseball. Remember what you love and enjoy in that spirit."

Scott halted and grinned at Hiroshi. "You are a lot like Moe. You're both philosophers.

Hiroshi pulled in a deep breath and nodded. "In another age, we would be brothers in spirit. I think he senses the coming peril."

"What peril? What's coming?" Wyatt showed the puzzlement of innocence and inexperience.

"A time when spirit is less than money and people less than cattle."

"Good Lord, Hiroshi, show me your smiling faces, not your gloomy fear."

Ishikawa laughed an out of character bellow, which shook his body. "Right, my young friend! We are here now. The day is lovely. Let me show you laughing Nippon girls who think American boys are exotic animals to behold. They will delight you, and you will delight them."

The now jovial guide secured Scott's arm in a surprising display of physical contact. They continued along Z Street. A pair of girls in school uniforms spotted Wyatt with his guide. As Hiroshi predicted, they clasped their hands over their mouths and giggled through their fingers.

CHAPTER 3

Fielding and Alaska

The piano player plunked a soft tune as background for the dining and dancing patrons of The Tulsa Club. As C. A. Sanborn, the manager of the club, circulated among the tables, he passed Albert and Charlotte Campion drinking and observing from their table. The mayor and his wife shared a table with the Police-and-Fire Commissioner and his wife. Sanborn nodded politely to the foursome before continuing his promenade and smiling at table after table. He wound far and wide through the capacious room, passing the Folgers, who dined on lobster Thermidor, before circling near the bar. The bartender busied himself preparing drinks for a waiter who stood at the bar's drink station. Sanborn smiled at him but made no overt gesture toward the only two gentlemen availing themselves of the barman's domain.

At the farthest end of the bar, against the wall where no direct light shone, Wyatt Scott sipped his Cutty Sark. Next to him, and ignoring his drink in favor of chain-smoking, sat his former army colonel,

Fielding. Further obscuring the pair, Fielding's smoke hung over them like a fog.

"You go all the way to L A to give Janet trouble, then come back to Tulsa asking to see me." Scott focused on his drink and swirled the ice and whisky in his glass. "Let me be clear. If you want any cooperation from me, leave her the hell alone!"

"I saw her merely in pursuit of my spy in Alaska." Fielding sipped at his drink with the same hand that held his cigarette.

"I don't care if you think you'll find Stalin in her bathroom, leave her the hell alone!" Scott glared at Fielding.

"It's my job figuring out what the Soviets are up to." Fielding stared into the backbar mirror, making no effort to view Scott.

"Alaska is over. The Soviets don't give a shit, just you!" Scott blew away some of Fielding's drifting smoke. He sharpened his already dour focus on Fielding. "She said you came by carrying on about her being a commie and screwing me for information. A stupid and incorrect course for you to pursue."

"I expect she exaggerated a little." Fielding sucked smoke from his cigarette, brightening the tip.

"Janet? Not likely!" Scott sneered at Fielding.

Fielding, noting Scott's disgust with his smoke, exhaled a small cloud away from Scott and toward his reflection in the backbar mirror. "She's not special – just one in the sack of suspects."

"Sack full of holes," retorted Scott.

"She was your girl. That makes her a suspect." Fielding looked directly at Scott. "Otherwise, Brock, Harris, and you. Who's your pick, Mr. Detective?"

"Nobody. Alaska killed us all." Scott took a long pull on his Scotch. A slight tinge of ochre, hinting at its original contents, colored the ice that remained in the glass.

Fielding continued sucking his smoke at the same slow pace. "The shots at you..." His words meandered in and out of the smoke. "...they happened before the police came to the train."

"I know the timing. I was there." Scott's sarcasm didn't need Fielding to show itself, but the colonel's presence helped nurture it.

"Irrespective of what you told the police, did you see anything?" Fielding stubbed out his cigarette, adding to the count in the bar ashtray.

"I saw nothing. Nothing for the police, nothing for you, and worse, nothing for me."

"Nonetheless, the two events are connected," declared Fielding.

"*You* should be a detective." Scott twisted back toward Fielding. "So, Phillip Marlowe Fielding, who shot, and why shoot at me?"

Fielding shrugged. He steered his stool to face the back bar and fished out a fresh stick from his pack of Luckies. He tapped one end on the back of his hand before popping the other end into his mouth. The cigarette dangled between his lips as he stared into the mirror.

Following Fielding's lead, Scott swiveled to peer into the backbar mirror. He sighed before addressing the CIA man's reflected image. "The dead Japanese the cops asked me about...was that Hiroshi Ishikawa?"

"Could be." The cigarette bobbed as he spoke. "Haven't seen the body." Fielding flicked his lighter and blazed the end of his Lucky Strike. He drew in and exhaled the fresh smoke before continuing. "All

I learned is that the dead guy was a Japanese diplomat coming from DC to plan MacArthur's baseball tour of a Jap team across America. The FBI and MacArthur's lapdogs are in the know."

"And that diplomat detoured to see me?" questioned Scott.

"Had your address and came to Tulsa, it seems," rationalized Fielding.

"Seems?" Scott shook his head. "Makes sense you're involved though."

"I'm checking all the angles," replied Fielding obliquely.

"Okay. Where does Hiroshi fit in?"

"Shouldn't tell a civilian like you." He blew out another lungful of fumes, obviously preparing to tell what he claimed he should not. "Hiroshi had a line through Jap Intelligence on a spy left over from the war...one that might've been from Alaska."

"Alaska again? Good Lord, Fielding."

"I look into every possibility."

"Every silly one." Scott snickered. "I knew I'd have to find out who shot at me and why on my own. Stupid of me to think otherwise."

"We're looking too." Fielding tapped the ash off his cigarette.

"Who, you and Pierce?"

"Yes." Fielding gestured with his cigarette hand. "Someone from our business might be after you."

"Is that why I ran into Pierce when I found Sleener's body? Have you got him spying on me?"

"I've got him watching over you, yes," admitted Fielding.

"Other than getting shot at, I guess he told you I'm pretty boring."

The spy boss reconnected with his Lucky Strike. He puffed toward the ceiling before turning to Scott. "I'm sure you'll keep looking into this. If you find something or make any connection to a suspect, tell me before you spill it to the FBI."

"FBI?" Scott blurted the initials out across the bar.

Fielding made a quick glance to note if anyone had heard Scott. He took a deep breath of clean air before he explained. "They're falling all over themselves because of the MacArthur angle and this Japanese baseball tour."

"And they don't know Hiroshi came here for you as much as me, do they?" Scott narrowed his eyes and broadened his smirk.

"There's a lot the Hoover boys don't know." Fielding stirred his long-ignored drink but didn't lift the glass. "Do you know who Bruno Pontecorvo is?"

"Italian guy. Physicist who helped drilling outfits with oil recovery. My dad knew about him." Scott posited a quizzical look about the odd conversational excursion.

"He works for the Canadians on reactors now, but he's a commie." Fielding's tone rang soft and out of character for the information he dropped.

"FBI, your CIA intercepts, something tangible, or your gut?" questioned Scott.

"There's an angle on him from Venona; beyond doubt. He's moved on, yet somebody in Tulsa recruited him and ran him here. That's my point. That's my concern." Fielding tapped his smoking hand three times on the bar, emphasizing his objective.

"I still don't get why Tulsa would be any sort of commie hotbed," said Scott.

"Frankly, we don't either, me or the Company. But it's become apparent that something is lurking here."

Sliding through the sea of tables, Charlotte Campion emerged at the bar. Dressed provocatively and elegantly as usual. She looked away from the bartender toward the dim, hazy corner of the bar. While several feet away, anyone could spot the smile she tossed Scott's way.

Fielding jiggled his drink once more and addressed Scott without looking at him. "Scott, I don't care if you carry on with Albert Campion's wife, just don't screw up the business we have with him."

"South American business, I guess." Scott glanced at the spymaster to see what reaction his comment drew. "He flies what; guns, bribe money for your flunkies?"

"You're smart enough to know we use his international air freight, but don't get cute and try figuring out everything we do with him." Fielding cleared his throat and focused a pair of calculating eyes directly on Scott. "Just be discreet if you mingle with his wife."

"Don't worry your scheming little head about that," declared Scott. "I wouldn't go bedsheet camping with Mrs. Campion if she offered me a lifetime supply of Cutty."

"*She* seems interested," remarked Fielding as Mrs. Campion left the bar for her husband's table.

"Men's attention is her hobby. I'm not sold on her amorous intent." Scott watched her in the bar mirror as she navigated among the club's tables. "I think she's slowed that down lately because her brother's murder weighs on her." Scott shifted his attention back to Fielding. "Since you're concerned with Albert Campion and his wife, do you have any CIA angle on her brother, Waldo Sleener?"

"Just that he was murdered, and you and Pierce were there."

"Yeah, I was there, and I didn't kill him. Can't say the same for Pierce."

"He didn't. No reason on our end either. He was there for you." Fielding pushed back from the bar. He stubbed out his short butt and stood. "Let me know anything that comes up about him, who shot at you, or our Japanese friend." He took a single step before adding an afterthought. "Or any sudden revelations about Alaska."

Fielding zigzagged his way through the club. He reached the door without making eye contact with anyone. The mention of Alaska nettled Scott. A few good times, the people, the cold, and death churned and packed into a snowball of conflicting memories. He too wanted revelations about Alaska, just not the one Fielding wanted.

*　*　*

A sunny, warm July day bloomed in Anchorage. Warm being relative, it seemed distinctly so to the trio of SIS diverted to OSS soldiers on leave from their frozen outpost near Nome. Lieutenant Brock fiddled with his camera, while Captains Harris and Scott shared the sunny day with Scott's titular girlfriend and Army Corps nurse, Lieutenant Janet Martindale. Brock waved the other three to fold together as he slid over, placing the sun more precisely at his back and on his subjects' faces.

"No. Left. Close in. Scott, get closer to Janet." Brock kept his eye on the viewfinder while he directed the shot. His left hand alternated between waving the trio around and steadying his camera for the impending photo.

"Just take the picture, Brock. We've only got two-day passes," came Harris with a little sarcasm and a lot of impatience.

The trio shuffled again. Janet broadened her smile, displaying perfect white teeth. Harris mugged with a goofy leer. Scott remained stone-faced. Brock snapped the shutter, rewound, snapped again, rewound, and completed a third shot.

"Okay. One of those should be good." He put the cap over his camera lens. "You looked lovely, Janet. Can't say the same for sourpuss Scott or silly-grin Harris."

The three models separated and ambled across the street. A group of Soviet sailors walked past them. The sailors spoke in hushed Russian, pointing, smirking, tossing their heads, and commenting less than favorably on the U.S. soldiers. They wore short-sleeved shirts which showed their navy tattoos. Two of them laughed. Janet flashed them an all-American sneer. One burly fellow took note of her and her companions. Harris stared their way and slowed his pace. He observed them until Brock worked his way around him to view the Soviet sailors. Brock pulled the cap off his camera and abruptly snapped their picture. The burly Russian glared at him. Scott never slowed as he eyed the Soviet contingent surreptitiously by running his eyes to the corners of their sockets. Harris scrutinized both sides of the event before hustling to catch Scott and pacing stride for stride with him. The other Russians paid no heed, having moved on from their mocking of the American soldiers. The brawny, tough Russian lagged behind his comrades, continuing his scowl at Scott's quartet.

Janet scurried back to Scott's side and took his arm. "Let's get lunch."

Brock caught up with his fellow soldiers in time to answer Janet's request. "As long as they have real burgers and French fries." Joy resounded in his voice as he mentioned the common but tasty traditional American foods.

"You can get that at home. There's all manner of fish, shellfish, exotic Eskimo dishes that you won't have a chance of eating back home," admonished Janet. Her voice showed disappointment that the young man didn't favor the local cuisine.

"We're not going home anytime soon. This is still fucking Alaska even if it's more civilized and warmer than Nome," chided Harris.

"As long as I can get a *real beer* instead of the canned army ration, I'll eat anything." Scott, having added his preference, looked at Janet for some resolution.

Before she could take the initiative, Brock chimed in. "Let's try the one we passed coming to the wharf. The window said burgers, clams, and salmon. Surely, they'll have beer too. That'll give everybody some-thing."

"Come on, guys." Janet tugged on Scott and started trotting. "You guys can tell the waitress what you do in the war." She flashed a grin from ear-to-ear, knowing her sarcastic proposal would be treasonous if truly acted on.

Scott followed her, remaining mute as he did. Brock shook his head at the untenable proposition. Despite the shaking head, his boyish grin betrayed his tangible pleasure at Janet's wisecrack, and he jogged to catch up. For his part, Harris broke into a brisk walk, pulling up beside Janet on the opposite side of Scott.

Just as Brock caught up, Harris replied to Janet's tongue-in-cheek suggestion. "The waitress wouldn't believe us and wouldn't giva' shit if we told her we listened to Russians all day long instead of Japs."

"Yeah, but some army eavesdropper would," admonished Scott. He bent his head and leaned around Janet as he finished his chastisement to Harris's face. "Then you could trade this frozen paradise for a ten-by-twelve in Leavenworth."

"Might be worth it," retorted Harris.

"You goofy boys," shouted Janet. "Forget the damned war for a day!" She broke away into an outright run. "Hurry up. I'll buy the first beer."

Brock bolted straight away. "Now you're talkin'! Last one buys the next round," he shouted as he charged after Janet.

Harris looked at Scott. Neither ran after the gleeful pair. The warm, bright day, jovial companions, and escape from the code-breaking duties did elicit smiles from the pair. They quickened their pace but abjured their friends' sprinting in favor of a trot.

* * *

Winter in Alaska brought flashbulb-length days that barely had time to illuminate the horizon-to-horizon snow and afforded no time to recover from the protracted nights or the bleakness of yellow bare bulbs dangling from ceilings. A Quonset hut with a wooden floor on a cold-poured cement foundation served as the Officers' Club for the ISS and OSS units outside of Nome. Inside the place, spotty heat and drafty doors added to the chill of the long, gloomy nights.

In late February 1945, at a dimly lit corner table, Captain Roger

Harris stared at a drink glass cupped in both hands. Unshaven for days, Wyatt Scott abandoned and ignored his glass, swallowing straight from the Scotch bottle. Outside, the wind whined and created an intermittent whistle when it struck the door just right. The place was cold as usual, emptier than usual, and more depressing than usual. Scott eased the bottle down; his lips wet with alcohol.

"Brock wouldn't kill himself." Scott spoke to the whisky bottle. "He was a happy kid," remarked Scott. When the shy bottle ignored him, he grabbed it up again. He took another long pull, then jolted its bottom on the tabletop. The wallop resounded through the hut. The amber liquid rolled up and down the bottle's sides like an angry sea but did not disturb the ship on the label.

Harris looked up from his glass. "This place could drive anyone to despair," he replied, taking the initiative from the inanimate whisky bottle. "Cold, bleak, boring, just the same intercept, translation, and code tests. The same try and miss. Drive us all crazy." He lifted his drink, still with both hands, and gulped.

As he listened only to his inner dialog, Scott answered himself rather than Harris. "Fielding's covering it up. It wouldn't surprise me if Pierce killed Brock...."

Harris jerked his head up from his funk. "I don't like Pierce, and Fielding is an asshole, but murder is fantastic even for them."

Scott stared back at Harris. "He's hiding something. Fielding won't look into it for whatever reason." He rubbed his chin. "It just doesn't feel right."

"He was a nice guy. Smart too. You and I are just doing our time, waiting out the war in this polar hell." Harris smoothed an eyebrow with his fingers before scratching his chin. "Brock seemed to like the stuff."

"He did. Another reason I don't think he killed himself. He told me he figured out some part of Venona."

"He never told me about it." Harris perked up. "What did he tell you he had?"

"Some code names he believed, and if so, it meant the contacts were spies and not diplomats."

"Spies? For the Japs or the Russians?"

"*Venona*, Harris. We're way past worrying about the Japs."

"I suppose so." Captain Harris tapped the side of his drink glass. "What did Brock say?"

"He didn't have details, just names like Godmother, Quantum, Freezer, Bibi, and locations. Mostly back east, but Freezer was in Alaska." Scott detailed the list as he recalled Brock telling him.

"Huh. Freezer fits Alaska," quipped Harris.

"Cold shithole fits better."

"Russians love cold, though. They could've called it Heaven." Harris grinned a little. He lost it when Scott offered no validation. "If it's in Alaska, I don't know why he didn't warn Fielding too," said Harris.

"You knew him; probably wanted to be sure. He was so thorough in everything. Kid even rolled his socks a certain way." Scott smiled at the thought.

Harris coughed out a small chortle. "Yeah, his socks." Harris grinned at the thought.

Scott grabbed the Scotch and downed two gulps. With the bottle still in his grasp, he spewed out whisky drops with his invective. "Fucking war! Killed a good kid."

"That and this frozen hole. I'm not sure how much longer I can take it."

"Are you going to shoot yourself?"

"Nah, I wouldn't want to give Fielding the satisfaction. I'd take that walk in the snow."

"Like the Bailey guy did last year?" quizzed Scott.

"Yeah."

"They never found Bailey," Scott reminded his fellow officer.

"Nope. I heard there were a few others who did it in forty-two before we got here. This place just drives people nuts."

"It does. It truly does."

"Brock never liked the cold, so that long walk wouldn't do for him. Perhaps he did shoot himself," opined Harris.

"I can't see it." Scott bumped the table with his fist.

Harris swigged the remaining Scotch from his glass. "I hear when you stop walking, you quit feeling cold and just drift off to sleep and don't wake up."

"I heard that too." Scott sucked in a whisky-flavored breath. "That's not you, Harris. You've got a survivor's attitude. You'll stick it out. I might shoot Pierce or Fielding, but not me either. We'll both be here when the crapped-up war ends."

"If it ends," lamented Harris.

"Eventually, all shit things end just like good things."

"Maybe Brock couldn't wait," offered Harris as a last observation.

"Maybe so." Scott continued his effort to empty the whisky bottle.

Harris sneezed. "The damn cold!"

"Drown it in Scotch." Wyatt shoved the bottle toward Harris.

* * *

An enlisted man working as a waiter in the Officers' Club exhaled steam with every breath as he prepped the tables. As expected, at seven AM outside Nome, the sun had yet to rise; the bar was closed, and the liquor remained locked away. The powerful aroma of coffee promised consolation for early soldiers, via a thermal burn on the esophagus instead of an alcoholic one. In the end, that scent carried the only morning hope against the Alaskan bleakness.

Looking surprisingly crisp in his uniform, Captain Scott sipped coffee between intermittent puffs of fog rising from his mug. Hot, black, and strong, his cup of joe served its multiple roles of warming his hands, warming his insides, and awakening his sun and light deprived brain. A blast of cold air caught his unprotected ears. Scott didn't move to witness the new arrival. The waiter offered a strong clue about the entrant's identity when he snapped to attention with a sharp salute.

Colonel Fielding came into Scott's view and hovered over him. He did not mince words. "Harris is missing."

Unlike the enlisted waiter, Scott did not snap to attention. He made no salute. Beyond his usual disregard for military rank, he showed his disdain by remaining seated. "Missing? Hard to lose someone in Ass-freeze, Alaska; nowhere to hide."

"He's not hiding. It looks like he took the walk in the snow." Fielding's countenance verified the seriousness of his statement.

Scott jumped from his chair, disturbing his coffee mug sufficiently to produce a black tide over the lip and a brief flow onto the table. "Shit! You've looked around camp to see if he's just pissed at you and giving you grief?" The question struck closer to a plea than a true interrogative.

"Everywhere. We looked every goddamn place either of you ever dreamed about hiding and a dozen the natives figured." Fielding let loose a sigh large enough to make its own condensation cloud. "I sent Pierce in the tractor and some sled dog teams with Eskimos. But with the new snow, we don't know which direction he went."

"I'll get my gear." Scott made a step for the door.

Fielding grabbed his shoulder. "No, you won't!" Fielding's eyes were adamant, if not maniacal. "If he took the damn walk, I'm down to only you who speaks fluent Russian and no other officers for code analysis. Much as you piss me off, I need you. You go and do your job, captain. If Pierce or the Eskimos don't find him, you wouldn't."

Scott stepped back. Fielding loosened his grasp and dropped his arm. Scott remained dumbstruck. The colonel waited, watching his man.

"He acted gloomy as hell the night we talked about Brock, but I never thought Harris was the type." Scott passed on his impression from their whisky-drinking night.

"Who goddamn knows. This place is a frozen hellhole." Fielding calmed himself. His voice softened. "Go to work. Keep the enlisted men busy. When Pierce gets back, I'll tell you what they found."

CHAPTER 4

THE FBI AND CLEVELAND

The morning after Scott's Tulsa Club meeting with Fielding, he scribbled on a pad as he sat at his desk. Scott had no direction in which to search for his would-be slayer. Cleveland promised to call him if anything substantial came into the Tulsa Police Department. Scott reasoned that his less than savory contacts would not be privy to knowledge of such professional work. Yet, with nothing else to do, Scott wrote names, their dodges, and hangouts on his pad. He stopped in the middle of a list of bootleggers, knowing no matter how desperate he was for leads; they were ridiculous to consider. His cynical thoughts continued to circle back to Fielding and Pierce.

He still blamed Fielding for Brock's death, at least indirectly, and considered it murder covered up as suicide. Scott's most charitable reasoning for the man covering up a murder was the colonel's doggedness to break the Russian code, and murder would upset things more than suicide. Fielding's deviousness fit his espionage work, while making him suspect in all other worldly things. Pierce's thuggish demeanor and sycophantic devotion to Fielding irked Scott. His confrontations with him in Alaska provided a semblance of a motive for him to move against Scott. If either wanted to harm Scott, they had the last few weeks to do so. The timing didn't fit. He considered the pair, dismissed them, reconsidered, dismissed again, and analyzed the event from every tactical position he could imagine. They remained unlikely suspects despite his antipathy for both.

Without an appropriate knock, his office door opened. Scott glanced up to see two suited men enter and shut the door behind them. While not identically garbed, the pair exhibited a dress code akin to a college fraternity. They approached Scott and loomed over him. Their expressions blank, their eyes dull, they stared down at him like bill collectors about to repossess his furniture. First one, then the other, produced badges from their pockets. Each had 'FBI' emblazoned on the metal.

One took the lead and spoke. "I'm Agent Fleming." He nodded to his partner. "This is Agent Phillips. We are from the FBI." Fleming uttered the redundancy that his credential had previously confirmed. He stashed his badge in his coat. Phillips did likewise.

"You Wyatt Scott?" asked Phillips.

"We'd like to ask you some questions," stated Fleming before Scott could reply to Phillips.

"Ask away," answered Scott. He felt as curious to hear their questions as he suspected them of being about his responses. A slightly snarky expression drifted into residence above Scott's chin. His face knew how cagey he could be. The FBI agents would have to ascertain that for themselves.

Phillips reclaimed his spot in the interrogation. "We understand you knew a Japanese national named Hiroshi Ishikawa. Is that right?"

"In nineteen thirty-four, yes." A quizzical look replaced his smirk. The question came from so far out in left field it had to be ten rows up in the stands.

"Have you seen him since you were in Japan before the war?" asked Agent Fleming.

"No."

"Did you correspond?" Phillips tagged in.

"No."

"Not at all?" Phillips followed up.

"No. I didn't know if he survived the war." Scott looked from one to the other. "Then you identified the dead Japanese man killed on the train as Hiroshi?"

"We ask the questions, P.I." Fleming rejoined curtly.

"You speak Japanese, right?" asked Phillips without a pause after Fleming's admonition.

"Yes, but Hiroshi spoke fluent English."

"He wouldn't need you for translation then," said Fleming.

"Any reason he would have your address?" Phillips changed the subject before Wyatt could reply.

"I suppose so. He could look me up when he got here and say hello."

"Did he call you before he came?" Phillips took two tries in a row.

"No."

"So, you don't know why the dead Jap wanted to see you?" Fleming made sure he got another crack at Scott.

"I heard there's to be a Japanese ballplayer tour of America. If that's so, possibly he wanted to ask me about baseball parks or even players. Beyond that, I have no idea unless he wanted to reminisce about the Ruth tour." Scott started to point to his wall of memories but thought the last thing he needed was a dozen supplementary, puerile questions about his past. His right hand hid in his lap to be sure.

"Several Japanese nationals are working on that. Jap players against American teams. They are planning on behalf of General MacArthur himself." Phillips stood a little straighter as he mentioned MacArthur.

"Are you helping on that?" quizzed Fleming.

"No. I just heard about it. That's all."

"Hmmm, heard about it," recapitulated Phillips. The two agents shared a glance.

"That it?" Scott swept his scrutiny from Fleming to Phillips and back. "I told the local police what I've told you. I knew Hiroshi Ishikawa fourteen years ago. Why he would want to visit me is beyond my guess. He never contacted me or made it to see me if that was his intention. Could be as simple as I am one of the few Americans he ever met."

Fleming stepped a little closer. "Locals said you were shot at the same night."

"True. I suppose they also told you they don't know who or why on that either."

"Seems odd that a Japanese, you haven't talked to in years, has your address and gets killed. Then you get shot at." Phillips did not disguise his skepticism.

"It seems more than odd to me. Still, I know nothing about what he wanted or how I could be involved." Exasperation filled Scott's reply. "I'm all ears if you guys have an explanation."

"A connection is apparent." Fleming stated the obvious.

"It's apparent to the shooter. Unless you can tell me something new, the connection is a mystery to me," rebutted Scott.

"So, it seems," added Agent Phillips.

Fleming peered at Phillips. He nodded in reply. Fleming pulled a business card from his coat pocket. "I suppose you will stick around town?"

"I live here. Why wouldn't I?"

Ignoring Scott's reply, he extended the card to him. "If you think of anything further, call me."

Scott took the card. He held it as the two agents quit his office. When they closed the door, he tossed the card in the bottom desk drawer reserved for a bottle of Cutty and a surfeit of unwanted solicitations.

* * *

Joe and Mamie's Diner had slowed from the main lunch crunch where working men grabbed a bite without lingering and an occasional secretary took in a hamburger or a bowl of soup. A few late patrons finished up, while two tables held lady shoppers whose schedules appeared flexible to nonexistent. At a two-top table by the window, Detective Art Cleveland swirled cream into his coffee, while Wyatt Scott sipped on a Coke straight from its classically shaped bottle. Working or not, neither man punched a clock nor worked conventional hours.

"Well, Art, I appreciate you inviting me to buy you lunch. I hope I am not off base about you having some info for me as payment in-kind." Scott sat relaxed and smiled at Cleveland after ribbing him about the occasion of their meeting.

Cleveland remained serious and did not banter back. "I didn't want this to be heard around the station, and since I'm a chump for associating with you anyway, lunch seemed like a good excuse to meet. If I wanted to drain you a little more, I would've gone for chicken-fried steak at Nelson's." He sipped his coffee before sliding it back onto the table and looking Scott square in the eyes. "And believe me, I need an excuse to be seen with you."

"You'd have to wait for Thursday for that chicken-fry, but detectives need free meals the same as beat cops need donuts. Your fellow officers should understand." Scott smiled again.

"Yeah, that's what Morgan will figure," replied Cleveland.

"What Morgan figures will usually be so obvious that it hurts unless it involves flights of his conspiratorial imagination. Either way, don't waste your effort."

"I want him to think it's just lunch; a free lunch you owed me for coming to the station the other night." Cleveland scanned the room for overly interested ears. He bent over his coffee. "You want some *real* news, some wild news?"

"Sure." Scott leaned in a little to abet the surreptitious communication.

"You already know the lab guys ran the slugs, and it was the same gun that shot at you and killed your Jap friend. What I have for you now is another comparison I had the lab guys run." Cleveland's face drew a stark, sober tint.

"A different case, good." Scott's eyes brightened with anticipation. "What did you find?"

Cleveland made another glance left, then right. "What I had checked, and Morgan knows *nothing* about it, and it needs to stay that way, is the slug that killed Sleener. They match!"

Scott straightened in his chair, pulling back from Cleveland. "Damn!" His eyes flashed wide as he processed the news.

"Yeah, at least." Detective Cleveland observed Scott's reaction. He nodded his head in empathy with the reaction.

"This thing is twisting like a two-headed snake." Wyatt shook his head in disbelief.

Cleveland continued with the startling news. "Okay. So, who the hell wants to kill Sleener, you, and your Jap buddy from before the war?"

"Whole mess is FUBAR, Art. I thought I had Sleener's killer pegged, if not proven. Might have held water for killing me too, but Hiroshi won't fit the puzzle."

"I plan to work on this on the down-low." Cleveland glanced around the diner once more, displaying a little paranoia over his furtive plan. "Besides trying to keep your shamus ass alive, I thought this might be an interesting nut to crack."

"And you haven't told Morgan or anyone else at the department?"

"Hell no!" Cleveland quieted his voice after his slight outburst. "I'm not digging up another case Morgan's closed. The lab guys don't know where I got the slug. If anyone asks, I'll claim it came from the shots fired at you."

"Thanks for letting me know. Keeping it quiet makes the best sense for us both, Art."

"Yeah. I figured you needed to know for your safety." Cleveland returned to his coffee. One quick sip and he added another thought: "On top of that, I want somebody who I know will work to solve these cases."

Mamie White swung toward the table with her coffeepot. Cleveland saw her first and covered his mug with his palm. Scott waved her off, figuring the courteous, sweet woman didn't need to be exposed to a clandestine conversation that could do her no good. Reversing course, she glided back to her counter. Wyatt turned his attention back to Cleveland.

"This thing is connecting the dots from two totally different pictures." Scott grimaced. "Not sure which way to point my feet."

"While nobody's paying attention, I'm going to look at the Sleener stuff again," replied Cleveland.

"I suppose I can try to dig into more about Hiroshi. Not sure how to go about that. A pair of FBI guys came by to ask me questions."

"Yeah, Morgan probably sicked them on you. They contacted the department, all in an uproar over that murder."

"They didn't give away much to me, and I couldn't help them either. Did they identify the man as Hiroshi Ishikawa?"

"Didn't tell us the time of day. FBI guys just looked down their noses at the stupid Okie cops." Cleveland's antipathy toward the federal agents registered plainly. "I suppose you can try your CIA pals," he added.

"Fielding already told me he knew nothing about it." Scott paused. A quick, pervasive thought ran through his head. "Of course, Fielding lies with the best of them."

* * *

A modest crowd of chic denizens populated the Tulsa Club. Wyatt Scott entered, and C. A. Sanborn strolled to intercept him. Scott caught sight of him and moved to narrow the gap. His arrival at the Tulsa Club and his greeting with Sanborn were not coincidental but entirely calculated and previously coordinated by phone.

"Wyatt, my boy," came Sanborn's greeting.

"Thanks for the heads-up, C.A. She with her husband?"

"Yes, always."

"Mind if I lurk in the shadows and not at the bar this time?"

"My boy, you may lurk anywhere you like. Should I have a drink sent to your hideout?"

"Sure. Cutty on the rocks."

"You find your roost, and I will have one sent to you." Sanborn patted Scott on the shoulder and moved back into the realm he ruled.

Scott slipped into an obscure section where no one claimed a table. He selected a discreet one, mostly in shadow, which had an oblique angle to the key group of guests who congregated in the main dining area. His visit to the Tulsa Club and his intent was to pry at the Sleener end of the three shootings. Morgan notwithstanding, the FBI had sealed things tight around Hiroshi's murder. The Tulsa police showed little interest in the attempt on his life, which left the thin unfinished line of the murdered blackmailer.

He sat with his back against the wall and his eyes on the Tulsa elite. They drank and swirled about. Chitchat among passing bodies and faux cheek kisses from one gentlewoman to another diverted him.

While unrehearsed, the performance flowed with the balance of a master choreographer, changing little as the clock hands spun on.

Scott had yet to see the figures he wanted emerge from the swanky crowd. He shook the ice at the bottom of his second empty Cutty. A movement at a far table and a fancy dress swirling toward the bar signaled one key player he had waited for. He strolled to John's realm of polished wood where the surreptitious concocting of state-prohibited drinks transpired.

John, the bartender, passed through the door into the back as Scott arrived. He sidled up to Mrs. Folger, who presumably sent poor John from the room to make her a lady's drink. She did not react to Scott moving beside her. The woman being cool enough to freeze water on a hot stove; he didn't know whether or not Folger was aware of his presence.

Discreetly looking away and not directly addressing her, Scott made his overture. "We need to talk."

"To what end, Mr. Scott?" She replied with enough condescension to place her on top of the building, looking down.

"I need Mildred Fuller's blackmail book."

"I told you; I don't have it."

"It's important that I get it. I don't care if you did kill Sleener, which I now think you did not. That book, though, may unlock this enigma."

"So nice of you to exonerate me of a murder I didn't commit. I suggest you find the killer, who may well have the damn book."

"I'm looking in that direction as well." Scott watched her reflection in the back bar, hoping to find a clue, a deception, or perceptible honesty. "Do you know any Japanese men?"

"What? No." Brief surprise reflected from the mirror. "Tulsa has precious few Orientals. Not any at Southern Hills or in the Junior League, where you expect me to abide." Contempt swept away the surprise.

The reflection registered nothing on the scale from mendacity to honesty, leaving Scott where he started. "I keep hoping, but I don't *expect* much from you."

"With your impertinence, you won't get much from anyone. Good luck in your pursuit and leave me out of it." Folger became aware of Scott watching her in the mirror. She narrowed her eyes to let him know she had caught him watching her.

"No matter what I do, you may be involved." He stared back at Folger's reversed image. They contacted eyes. He intensified his glare. "It figures that you might be blackmailed again if a new party has claimed the book."

"Good God, I hope not." She broke the glare duel with a haughty raise of her chin. "No one has tried to contact me," she stated flatly.

"If they do, let me know."

"I'm not altogether certain I will, Mr. Scott." She focused impatiently on the door behind the bar. "All I've gotten for my trouble and money is your accusation and now a rather tepid retraction."

"I asked you once to tell me the reason you were blackmailed." Scott scanned wide around the bar and back toward the tables. He returned his gaze to the bar mirror, secure that no one could eavesdrop. "If I know, I can squelch it and concentrate on the bigger problem."

"And I've told *you*, it's important to me not to disclose it." She stayed locked on the closed door. "Not to a nosy private investigator or anyone else."

"Whatever your indiscretion, I'll keep it hidden." Scott pressed his point. He calculated that all the victims written in Fuller's book might be in danger.

"My *indiscretion*, as you put it, remains none of your business."

"What I'm getting at is this business is beyond your role." Scott labored to warn her off.

"Hopefully, my role is complete, and we can once more be strangers."

The bartender emerged through the swinging back bar door. He carried the familiar green cocktail favored by Mrs. Folger. She watched his quick progress, barely disturbing the fluid. He handed her the glass with a small napkin under its base.

"Thank you, John." She blessed him with her usual patronizing smile.

"Certainly, Mrs. Folger," replied John, decorously as always.

Being careful to spin the opposite way from Scott, Folger took her drink and strutted back toward her husband and their table. John stood by. Scott remained no closer to any answers. It seemed he had frittered away the evening. A third Cutty being all he could salvage for his effort, John obliged him.

CHAPTER 5

A Drive with Fielding

Scott lingered in his LaSalle. With the convertible top stowed and the midday sun bearing down, he wore his hat to shade his face. Parked outside the Philtower Building, he had to plug the hated parking meter twice so he could stay in his favorable spot. Pedestrians strolled north and south, passing him. One even entered the Philtower, a dapper, older fellow that Scott imagined glided into the barbershop in the basement. No one departed the building for quite some time until the personage Scott expected slipped out and headed north. Former Colonel Fielding strolled at the common speed. Scott rolled the LaSalle alongside and kept the walker's slow pace.

"Hop in, Fielding. We need to talk." Scott stopped several feet beyond the spymaster.

Fielding looked up and down the street. The usual trifling of shoppers and businessmen paid no heed to the red convertible or either man. Apparently seeing nothing or no one that concerned him, he opened the passenger door and climbed into the LaSalle. Scott checked his rearview mirror before stomping on the gas and veering back into the thin traffic flow.

"So, Fielding, were you shopping at Miss Jacksons or do you cavort with oilmen like you do Campion?"

"No business at all, Scott. I got a haircut."

"If no business, it figures you ducked in the Philtower to use the tunnels to sneak around Tulsa." Scott kept his focus on the road during his digging at Fielding.

Fielding settled nonchalantly into the convertible's seat as if impromptu rides with Scott happened routinely. "I've heard about those but never tried them. What's on your mind, Wyatt?"

"Heard? I'm sure you and your bunch researched everything." The road clear, Scott turned toward Fielding. "Why did you enlist Hiroshi Ishikawa's help in the first place?"

Undisturbed by the query and cool as usual, Fielding replied. "Because he worked on Russian codes during the war. The Japs were terrified of Russia coming in, so they listened to them way before we did. And because I thought he might have information we never thought about; and because he is a spy like us."

Scott whipped a right down Fourth Street and headed east. "Like *you*, not us." He refused to look at Fielding, but he followed up. "I didn't know Hiroshi was a spy. Makes sense, though the way he acted in thirty-four."

"He was before, during, and now after the war. Today, though, his team is on our side. I've been trying to make deals with them." Fielding detailed his insider vantage point.

The LaSalle passed the bus station, a hotel, and myriad small businesses along Fourth Street. "Okay, but what could he do? The Japanese didn't break the Russian codes, did they?" quizzed Scott.

"Not like we did with Venona, but they had one hell of a long log of naval intercepts that we didn't worry about."

Once beyond Peoria Avenue, Scott pushed the LaSalle harder. They cruised out of the track of enterprises and into housing editions built after the First World War. "What good are nineteen forty-five Russian Pacific battle orders when they barely had a navy?"

"Good, because the few ships they had were for espionage; mostly fake whaling boats, and a few subs." Fielding shifted a little toward Scott. "Uncle Joe spied on the Japs in the Sea of Japan, but everywhere else, he spied on us. He always knew he could whip the Japs. His worry was the U.S. and our industry...and our money."

"Thin, but what good would any of it do you after the war?"

"The Russians had spies in Alaska."

"Not a news bulletin." Scott had negotiated Fourth Street, arriving at Harvard Avenue. He took a right heading south. "We all knew the Russian liaison crews that flew Ladd to Kamchatka spied, so we kept them away from our stuff there and in Nome."

"Not the ALSIB crews that are of interest. The Japanese intel detailed that the Russians had a U.S. spy in S-I-S or O-S-S."

"Oh, your spy." Scott pushed down on the gas, sending the LaSalle through a yellow light at Eleventh Street. "So, who did Hiroshi say it was?"

"He didn't know." A lilt of disappointment crept into Fielding's habitually dispassionate tone.

Scott glanced at Fielding. The former colonel had the type of look reserved for the guy who bragged about his hot date only to find out it was with his pal's sister. "Then what did you want with Hiroshi?"

"I wanted to bootleg some Venona decodes for him to read. I had hoped one of them might jostle his memory regarding their intercepts. My thinking is that might help him dig up a clue I could use running it back through Venona."

Scott diverted from the blacktop to take a quick, surprised glance at his onetime army boss. "Fast and loose for you, Fielding." He refocused on the road.

"If I could get a cross-reference with what he knew of the naval intercepts, I hoped…"

"To make a splash with Hillenkoetter and your other new bosses," interrupted Scott. It was easy for Scott to assign selfish goals to Fielding. He had a history of conceit and ass-kissing the top brass. At least he did in Scott's jaded memory of him.

"I was about to say, to find out if Brock's partial decodes of Venona included any local spy details."

"So, Brock told you!" Surprising news to Scott after three years. "You should've let us dig into it," chastised Scott.

"I looked into it myself. The enlisted men had access to nothing but tiny bits of intercepts. None of them showed any interest in piecing the intercepts together, so they were all clear. Only you three got full messages."

"So, there was more to you and Pierce leering at us than our insubordination," mused Scott.

"All three of you palled around together. You kept company with

Janet when she was a WAC nurse. All of you even went to Anchorage together on leave, where Russian sailors walk around." Fielding stared at the passing farmland as the LaSalle sailed on south past Forty-first Street.

"Gaggle of suspects without clues," offered Scott.

Fielding kept his focus on the countryside. "Yeah, guesses. That's my problem. I hoped Hiroshi had the key." Fielding sighed; another rare leak of emotion from the man.

"A professional assassin murdering him makes it more likely he had something someone feared," surmised Scott.

"Going after Hiroshi and apparently going after you too. But why? And about what? Damn it, I need to know that 'What.'"

"I'm not near what, why, or who, but I am beyond coincidence with him as a victim and me as a miss."

The LaSalle took the pair further out of town along Harvard Avenue. They drove past some pastures, scattered houses, and the small airport that sat north of Sixty-first and west of Yale Avenue. After taking Sixty-first, Scott navigated onto Yale and headed south once more; silence settled in. Thick woods full of scrub oaks lined either side of the two-lane blacktop. Fielding held his hat in his lap as he leaned against the passenger side door.

At the next intersection, Scott slowed. "Sharing with you still worries me, but I have an oddity for you to swirl in your commie conspiracy stew." He figured he needed to share Cleveland's shocking revelation about the commonality of the slugs, even if he didn't trust Fielding. "It turns out that the gun that killed Hiroshi and tried to kill me had a previous fatal run in with Waldo Sleener."

Fielding jerked his head from the scenery to look at Scott. "You know this for a fact?"

"Detective friend ran the slugs on the sly. Floored me too. That connection is apples and ball bats."

Fielding rubbed his cheek. He ran a hand through his hair. "Don't tell the FBI this," he warned.

"Afraid they'll get ahead of you?" jabbed Scott.

"Don't trust them to keep it a secret from the Russians. There's a lot we shield from them. My outfit thinks they have leaks."

"I wouldn't want to get my detective buddy in hot water, so you'll get your way on that."

"Good."

"My brief run in with the FBI didn't impress me." Scott recalled the Tweedledee and Tweedledum visit from Fleming and Phillips. "I wouldn't sing a note in their direction anyway if I came up with something good."

"That's smart. They're not a tight organization." Fielding narrowed his eyes and wrinkled his brow. "Your info is a head scratcher though. A hired gunman, perhaps. A coincidence, and Sleener's killing was independent with no connection to you and Ishikawa?"

"Seems as likely as Sleener having a connection to Hiroshi." Scott watched the street but thought of the shots after he discovered Sleener dead. "Professional shooter by all accords." Recalling Cleveland's disbelief in Tulsa hitmen, Scott pitched a notion in Fielding's sphere. "Soviets hiring out assassinations in the U.S. now? You think that's possible?"

"It doesn't stitch together well. M-G-B and G-R-U don't farm out their killings; leaves loose ends, and the commie bastards are cheap too. They hate to pay out rubbles let alone dollars," explained Fielding.

"But there's no reasonable connection between Sleener and Hiroshi."

"Doesn't seem to be." Fielding leaned further against the car door. He shifted his body to face Scott. "I think I need a detective more than a spy where this circus is going. How about I hire you on the government dime?"

Scott smiled. "You're kidding."

"No, I'll get you a two-week authorization. You tell me if you're making any headway and I'll get you more."

Scott became serious and skeptical. "I'm not sure I want you as a client at any price."

"You'll look into it anyway. I know you. Snoop where you please. All I ask is a big-picture report: short and sweet."

"I'll think about it."

"Do that." Fielding righted himself in his seat. He looked at the passing countryside before turning his head toward Scott. "By the way, where are we headed?"

"Campion's house."

"He's back at the Adams Building."

"I know. I want us to see Mrs. Campion about her brother."

* * *

Still in her robe and nightgown at mid-afternoon, Charlotte Campion paraded into her formal living room. She apparently left her true good looks and charm in a drawer in her boudoir, choosing instead to deploy an excessive coiffure and an eyebrow pencil thick as a paintbrush. Scott, Fielding, and the butler, Maxwell, stood on the plush wall-to-wall carpet among the multitude of South American artifacts in glass cases. Chairs, coaches, tables, lamps, and bric-a-brac festooned the balance of the expansive room. Mrs. Campion glided next to Scott.

"The charming Mr. Scott. How nice." She glanced at Maxwell and nodded. He bowed his understanding of the gesture and departed the room. She acknowledged Fielding. "And you brought a pal."

"More your husband's pal," corrected Scott.

"Yes, Mr. Fielding, right?" Mrs. Campion proffered a perfunctory smile.

Fielding nodded in the affirmative but uttered nothing.

"Please sit, gentlemen." Mrs. Campion spread her palms in either direction, offering an array of seats. Fielding sat in a chair, while Scott secured a spot on one of the couches. Mrs. Campion joined him. "What may I do for you, Wyatt?"

"We came to confer about your late brother," clarified Scott.

Her expression hardened. Her eyes drooped. "Oh, so you figure a couple of weeks is sufficient time after his death to bother me once more." She stood. She glared at Scott before turning to the high-back chair and flying into Fielding. "And Mr. Fielding, why are *you* interested in poor Waldo? He certainly had nothing to do with any business you and my husband have."

"Probably not. Scott has the questions." Fielding repositioned himself in the chair. "I'm more of an interested observer."

Mrs. Campion wiped away the start of a tear and forced a smile.

"Then, Mr. Scott, do you have anything new on the crazy heiress who killed him?"

"She may not have done it," advised Scott.

"My goodness. That is frustrating news." She drew back. Her apparent expectation being far from his answer, she blanched white. Both of her hands sought safety in the pockets of her robe.

"The true importance is that no matter who, the reason someone killed him is deeper than blackmail and broader than your brother's involvement."

"What makes you think that?" Her shock morphed into disgust. "Did Mildred Fuller drag Waldo into something else more reprehensible than blackmail?"

"I have no evidence of her beyond blackmail, while other facts do point away from her. Since his murder, have you thought of anyone who would have a reason to kill him?"

"Other than that nutty girl the police claimed did do it and tacky, dead Mildred, I couldn't guess." Mrs. Campion scrabbled once more for reassurance inside the pockets of her robe.

"He never mentioned any names from his commie conspiracy searches?" chimed in Fielding for the first time.

"You've heard about that?" Mrs. Campion glared at Fielding for interrupting her discourse with Scott. "No, but I probably paid little attention to any of his rants about communists among us."

Fielding didn't let the topic go. "Any reason to think *he* was a pinko?"

"No. Not Waldo. He spent his time looking for communists. It was a hobby, a compulsion even. Second only to making a fast buck, Waldo wanted to expose communist conspiracies."

"Did he find any?" Fielding pulled out his cigarettes.

"Not that I know about. I mean, how many could Tulsa have? Still, he would trot around looking for suspicious characters." Mrs. Campion pulled her hands out of hiding to wave her arms about, adding pantomime to her description. "Do you think some awful commie murdered Waldo?" She moved her attention back to Scott, trading her Fielding-scowl for a hopeful expression. "I seem to recall him blustering about some union guy, a professor, and writers; maybe an actor too being communists."

"These weren't Tulsans, I'm guessing," said Scott.

"Some were...I think. I only half-listened." Campion sat back down beside Scott.

"A last question." Scott glanced at Fielding before staring at Mrs. Campion. "Did Waldo leave any notebook, diary, bankbook, or the like with you or in a room here?"

"No. He didn't trust banks." Charlotte Campion let her eyes wander as she thought. "I never knew him to keep a diary. I would expect something like that, and pretty much anything else would have been in his apartment."

Scott stood. "Thank you, Mrs. Campion."

Fielding followed and stood also. Mrs. Campion glared at him as if he had caused Scott to stand rather than the reverse. Scott stepped away, causing Mrs. Campion to jump up.

"Wyatt, you don't need to rush off." She looked more like she craved comforting than flirting for the first time in Scott's experience. She glared once more at Fielding. "Maxwell can call Mr. Fielding a cab."

Fielding scoffed as he headed toward the door. Scott pondered

Charlotte Campion's emotions about her late brother. Perhaps she wasn't a mindless flirt with no feelings or intensity. Nonetheless, Scott left Mrs. Campion standing alone, as seemed to be his touchstone.

* * *

In the bullpen of Meiji-Jingu Stadium in Tokyo, nineteen-year-old Wyatt Scott had made his bullpen seat close to the fans, who enthusiastically cheered for both teams. For his part, he listened to the Japanese fans in an effort to improve his limited vocabulary and understanding of the language. Wyatt watched the all-stars slug in run after run, while keeping his ears tuned to the voices in the stands. He would catch a glimpse of some fans, but he didn't need to see them to know they loved the game. They stood when Ruth batted, causing the stadium to rumble. He was sure they all smiled, although he never looked to see. In the excitement, Wyatt did not notice his Japanese guide leaning over the rail.

"Scott-san. How are you?"

Wyatt turned to see Hiroshi Ishikawa bow, then smile as he rose. As always, the Japanese chaperon wore a suit perfectly tailored to his slender body. While even Scott realized he was more of a political minder than a guide, he liked Hiroshi. He even felt sorry for the man having to deal with the flamboyant personality of Moe Berg and his meteoric caprices.

"I am fine, Hiroshi-san." Scott bowed in reply before utilizing his lessons from Berg. "O-genki desu ka?"

Hiroshi Ishikawa broadened his smile. "Kommichiha. You are learning well."

"Arigatou," replied Scott. "I really don't know much yet."

"One day, you will speak with me only in Nipponese." He motioned Wyatt over to the guardrail.

Scott stepped beside the short wall and rail separating the bullpen from the seats. "Wyatt-san, why do you wander the city with Berg-san?"

"What do you mean? I have fun with Moe."

"You are young. You are a fine pitcher with the world in front and citizens paying to see you. Berg-san is old." Hiroshi seemed genuinely concerned about Scott's future and Berg's influence.

Scott grinned at his Japanese guardian. "I'm learning about things from Moe. He knows five languages, books, and he understands how to beat hitters with your brain as well as your arm."

"Yes, his language skills are very good, and you are learning well." Ishikawa stood, dropping his grip on the rail. "Berg-san knows many things and contemplates them more than baseball."

"Probably so. Still, he knows baseball inside out. He taught me how to pitch to Foxx and Greenberg."

Hiroshi nodded his approval. "And he teaches you about Beibu Rusu and Gehrig-sama?"

Scott smiled as he replied. "Ruth is easy—just keep it away from him and he will strike out. As for Lou, Moe told me the best way to pitch him is to walk him."

Hiroshi laughed. He coughed and spewed a laugh larger than Scott thought possible for the slight man. "I believe Moe-san is correct." He reined in the laugh, drew his hand across his mouth, and restored his usual stoic veneer. "What I meant, Wyatt-san, is what Moe Berg is doing during your tours."

"We sightsee. He loves to see parts of Japan that are not on the official tour." Wyatt believed what he told Hiroshi.

"I know. I know too that he likes to take pictures that are forbidden." Hiroshi deployed a look that shared equal parts disappointment and displeasure.

"You confiscated those," replied Scott.

"Yes, the ones he wanted me to confiscate. Others he brought to your American embassy."

"Pictures of me?" Scott screwed up his face with incredulity. "Why would the embassy want pictures of me sightseeing?"

Hiroshi cocked his head. "Young Mr. Scott, you were in the pictures, but it's the background that is important."

"Why? There are just buildings or the bay behind me." Scott didn't understand the concern and never thought the photos were anything other than what Berg stated.

"They are *forbidden*." Hiroshi punched a fist into his other palm, showing more fury and emotion than Scott thought he possessed. "Berg-san knows I will not reveal him to our authorities because my superiors would punish Hiroshi. But let him know I am not stupid. I know what he does." He looked toward Berg, who watched the game, unaware and unconcerned about Hiroshi.

"I don't believe he thinks you're stupid, Hiroshi. Moe just doesn't like rules," explained Wyatt.

"It is not rules that he fights, but Nippon."

"I don't see how."

"You are an innocent, young Wyatt-san. Moe Berg is not." Hiroshi grasped his suit lapels, striking an exceptionally formal pose.

"I didn't know we were doing something wrong."

"Yes. You are guileless." Hiroshi leaned on the rail once more. "You will always be a baseball player. And you are a fine pitcher—a shusen-toushu. Remember that word, Wyatt-san. It means best pitcher, number one pitcher." Hiroshi pulled away from the rail. "I hope *you* come back to play our Nipponese team again." Hiroshi smiled and bowed before he funneled into the aisle and flowed through the crowd.

* * *

Back in his chair at the Sophian Plaza with a Cutty in his hand and the moon hanging over the Arkansas, neither the view nor the alcohol solved the quandary that slithered through Scott's brain. The most logical reason someone killed Sleener was to get Mildred Fuller's blackmail book. Since it didn't appear on him or in his apartment, the killer likely had it. Hiroshi Ishikawa's coming to see him appeared to be about baseball. Nobody kills someone over Japan versus America baseball games. Who would be injured by a baseball game in Tulsa and blackmailed by Sleener?

Trying to piece together the impossible triangle of him, Sleener, and Hiroshi Ishikawa kept Scott from doing any work. Fielding left Tulsa for Washington, or so he said. His friend, Johnny, spent the days in court, while his secretary, Evie Hall, made her typewriter plunk overtime. When Wyatt sat scratching notes to make illogical connections become logical, he drifted through memories of Hiroshi and the deaths in Alaska. All of which were nonproductive.

The swirl of crazy options, impossible connections, and three

Scotches pushed Scott out of his chair. He shuffled to his window to look across the Arkansas River. To his right, north by a compass, the clear sky offered bright stars. He tilted his head higher and consulted the moon one last time. While it didn't laugh at his frustration, it offered no advice. Scott opted for bed with a plan to escape to a tranquil spot for unfettered thinking in the morning. Yet, even when events careen out of control and puzzles pile on one another, there is always room for another quandary to slap Wyatt Scott across his mouth or punch him in the gut.

CHAPTER 6

Murder and Baseball

Long after the last pitch was delivered and more than a half-hour after the other players, coaches, and full-time workers had left Texas League Park, Ronnie Edwards showered in the locker room. He ran late because he stayed on the field doing interviews with every newspaper and radio station until the last reporter grew bored and departed. Edwards turned off the water, grabbed his towel hanging on the showerhead, one removed from his shower, and wrapped it around his waist. Leaving a trail of wet footprints, he swaggered to the lockers and benches.

As he opened his locker, a noise caught his attention. Edwards gawked over his shoulder. The barrel of a bat swung into the right temple of his head. A bone-splintering crunch resounded through the dressing room, while streamers of blood flew from his skull. He quivered. His knees buckled. His eyes disappeared into their sockets. A second wallop hurled a new volley of Ronnie Edwards's fluids across the benches and flooring before he crumpled. Third, fourth, and fifth blows slammed against his head while he lay sprawled on the floor. Hair, blood, and scalp caked the concrete and flecked the lockers.

A blood-blotched bat bounced end-over-end, careening across the locker room and against a wall before it rolled into a corner a dozen feet from the crumpled body. The sound and echo of wood faded as the Louisville Slugger came to rest. Lying on his stomach, Edwards's wide-open eyes ceased recording the scene. Crimson tides from the ballplayer's head poured out in all directions. The deed done, his assailant slipped out of the ballpark and retreated into the night. Silence reclaimed the locker room, while the blood of Ronnie Edwards continued its viscous ooze along the bat's barrel toward its knob.

* * *

A Yellow Cab pulled into the Philbrook Museum parking lot, passing the museum entrance to halt at the southernmost end of the lot. Evie Hall scrambled from the taxi before the wheels had fully stopped. At twenty, Miss Hall owned soft, girlish features, smooth dappled skin with a few freckles that defied her makeup, and eyes as round and large as overcoat buttons. She motioned for the cabbie to wait. Restricted by her tight business skirt, she employed short but swift steps, dashing from the lot into the tree-lined grounds.

Wyatt Scott reclined on the bridge, which crossed the clear brook on the museum property. Built for the Phillips family to traverse the creek running through their villa, the bridge, grounds, and gardens served as a bucolic retreat for city dwellers. The spot, rarely visited on weekdays by Tulsans, was Scott's sanctuary and point of contemplation.

Insane combinations of Sleener, Hiroshi, hitmen, Russian spies, and American spies, sifted through Scott's mind with equally improbable motives to kill either man or Wyatt. Fielding or Pierce be damned; he would search out the facts. Eyes closed and again seeking connections among the dead men and himself, the birds chirping, leaves rustling, or distant traffic noise found no entree to his thoughts. Picturing dead Sleener among the baggage at Union Station, Scott focused on the bullet entry details. He blocked almost everything from his senses. All except an unexpected alert that drifted with the breeze and signaled through his olfactory receptors.

"Evie, I don't appreciate Johnny telling you about my private locus." Scott opened his eyes and sat up.

Startled that Scott noticed her, Evie recovered to address her task. "Take it up with him. Bugler's been arrested; he's asking for you."

"Surely, you didn't come all this way to be funny." He looked up at Evie without controlling his skepticism.

"Not funny at all. I'm the messenger. Johnny thought you'd want to know right away."

Realizing it was not a joke, Scott jumped to his feet. "Good God! Where is he?"

"He's in the county can." Evie slid her feet toward the parking lot. "That old cockamamie Bugler's been in there since last night. Sheriff's probably put him through the wringer by now."

"What did he do?"

"I didn't get crib notes. I answered the phone, but Johnny took the call. May have killed someone. Johnny didn't give me any details, only that he's looking into a lawyer and where I could find you. Just go." She pointed towards the parking lot.

"Good Lord!" Scott bolted through the trees, heading for the lot. Evie streaked after him, falling behind even while doing her best to keep up. He burst onto the concrete pad hell-bent for the LaSalle. Scott flew past the taxicab on his way.

With the cab looming in front of her, Evie yelled out to Scott. "Before you run off, gimme' some moolah for the taxi. I don't have a purse."

Scott halted before spinning back to the cab. He pulled out his wallet and waited for Evie to make it. He held a bill out to her. "This enough?"

"Plus, a tip," replied Evie as she took the bill. She panted to catch her breath.

Scott pulled another bill from his wallet. He held it out. She plucked it with her right hand. With her left, she seized his hand. She tugged it and peered up at him.

"How did you know it was me? Your eyes were closed." Evie left the question in her eyes even after it departed her lips.

"Downwind from your perfume," answered Scott, running away as he did.

He raced across the pavement toward his open convertible. Gene Autry with a motorized horse, Scott jumped in his Caddy without opening the door. He fired it up and roared off to help his old friend. Evie watched Wyatt and the LaSalle leave the parking lot. The cabbie watched the meter run.

* * *

Wyatt Scott sprinted into the county courthouse. He scrambled down the hall, heading toward the sheriff's office. Like most private investigators, he often had two or even three cases going at once. Last month, the unstable heiress Ruth Brown interrupted his search for the whore-killer that was the demented radio personality, KTOO Joe. But now, with the sheriff and Tulsa Police unlikely to strain themselves for an addled elderly man, Wyatt knew he had to force his full attention on freeing the helpless old gent. He calculated he would have to stop hunting for Hiroshi's killer and his would-be assassin to spend every waking effort trying to exonerate Bugler.

He made his way through the doors to plunge into a jumble of reporters, clerks, and deputies. A hum of voices swirled through the lobby amidst the nattering confederations. As he craned his neck to find a familiar figure, Deputy Sheriff Sampson Cline emerged from the multitude. Cline was a thin fellow with a friendly disposition and an open mind. Scott had casual and formal meetings with him on cases Johnny Grayhawk handled, more often than not concerning Osage men and liquor violations. Cline wiggled and twisted out of the thicket of humanity toward Scott.

"Hear about old Bugler, I guess," stated Cline with a hint of sadness in his voice.

"I am. What is all this about?" asked Scott.

"He's been arrested for murder. We found him with a bloody baseball bat in the Oiler locker room and Ronnie Edwards beaten to death." Cline delivered the pertinent facts succinctly with no hesitation.

"Ronnie Edwards! Wow!" Personifying the victim made the story more mindboggling to Wyatt.

"Head beat in." Cline swallowed before elaborating. "Beat in good, too. Blood and hair all over. It wouldn't surprise me if some of the goop on the lockers is brain."

The added graphic detail cautioned Scott about the violence of the murder. For him, fathoming the event proved difficult. Imagining that Bugler committed such a heinous act, found no compartment in his brain. "Doesn't make any sense. Bugler isn't violent; never has been."

"You're right. It doesn't make good sense, but here we are," rationalized Cline.

The clamor in and around the sheriff's office continued to grow. A thickening soup of reporters, lawyers, politicians, secretaries, janitors, and citizens with no business other than curiosity simmered in the lobby. Scott drifted closer to Deputy Cline as the tumult grew. Shuffling feet and murmured questions raised the background din markedly enough to prevent lucid conversation.

Cline looked at the crowding, bumping throng around them and shouted to be heard above the furor. "Come on. I'll take you down the hall away from this hubbub."

The deputy began sifting through the characters. Wyatt followed. A reporter seemed to recognize Scott, but the pair slipped past him before he could lay claim to Scott's time and attention. The crowd thinned as they pushed down an intersecting hall. Deputy Cline opened a door and ushered Wyatt in. The modest room held two empty desks and a secretary typing at a third. She halted just long enough to identify the deputy sheriff before her fleet fingers resumed their task. Cline stepped into the corner as far from the secretary as the room's walls allowed.

"Okay. Better to talk here," advised Cline.

"Who called you?" Scott needed facts before he could wade through them and find where Bugler fell in the proceedings.

"Tulsa Police. They phoned in and told us that Bugler had called them. Our jurisdiction on county property, you know. Couple of deputies show up, see the messy scene, and call for the whole megillah. I made it there about the same time as the coroner."

"Bugler called it in, so why think he did it?" quizzed Scott.

"Lots of culprits call it in." Deputy Cline sighed before he began to explain. "He had the bat. He had blood on his hands and his pants. Since then, a couple more damning things come through. We hear he had a row with Edwards."

"He liked the kid, Sam. Bugler bragged on him – thought he was the best player on the team." Scott's incredulity over the report came out with every word.

"We talked to a few players and the coach. They said Bugler and Edwards argued. That's just what we heard, Wyatt." Cline shook his head. "That's not the clincher. We got a witness. Came forward early this morning."

"Who?"

"Not allowed to say yet. Sheriff Blaine wants things tight." The deputy detailed the policy and his position.

"I'd like to talk to this witness."

"Can't help ya', Scott. I can let you see Bugler. That's about it." Cline's eyes expressed sympathy, but his jaw held firm.

"Yeah, I'd better see him."

Deputy Cline signaled Scott to follow. He opened the door, and they passed into the short hall. They made their way to a longer one that bypassed the lobby throng. "I'll get the jailer. Wait here."

Scott stood by while Sam Cline left to fetch the guard. A dramatic murder excited law enforcement and the public. While curiosity and voyeurism drove the public's interest, the voiced outcry for legal action and the furor for justice fell Bugler's way. Yet nothing in the situation fit Scott's experience or understanding of Bugler. The old man was docile. He might complain about a ballplayer's play, but he didn't even cuss. Violence didn't register in him.

A chubby fellow in a khaki uniform, whose jingling keys tattled his approach, ambled from a side hall into the one where Scott waited. He stopped at the junction several feet short of Scott. He tossed his head in the direction whence he came, signaling Scott and avoiding the added steps and wear-and-tear on his U.S. Keds high-top sneakers. Wyatt took the prompt and stepped toward the man. The county guard, having seen Scott's intent, did not await him but ducked back around the corner, where the jingle of his keys and the squeaks of his shoes communicated the path to follow.

Scott caught up to the guard as the guard opened the outer steel bar door to the lockup. They passed an empty jail cell and a vagrant asleep in another. Sitting on the hard bed in the third cell, a downtrodden Bugler ignored the clang of the key in the lock and only looked up at the scrape of the door sliding open. Scott stepped into the unit, and the jailer pulled the door shut with a clang.

"How are you managing?" asked Scott as he sized up the befuddled old man.

"Wyatt, I ain't skeered or what, but I jus' don't know why I'm here. I didn't do nuthin'." Bugler's face played like a film loop of bewilderment.

"Have they treated you okay?" asked Scott.

"Yessir." Bugler fiddled with his whiskers. "Hard ta' sleep. And they ain't no privacy."

"I mean the people, the deputies. How are they treating you?"

"Oh, fine. They's a few of 'em knows me. They played school ball, an' all. This one feller…"

"Deputy Cline said you killed Ronnie Edwards with a baseball bat." Scott cut short Bugler's digression.

"Did no such thing!" Bugler's mouth fell open at the suggestion.

"Some say you were yelling at Edwards."

"I called out at him 'bout his overstridin' at the plate and losin' power." Bugler's feet shifted like a batter in sympathy with the subject.

"Not teaching, yelling at him."

"He's a thick-headed slugger, but he has big-league talent." Bugler looked down sorrowfully and repentant. "He did have, I mean."

"Did you argue with him?"

Taken aback, Bugler blinked, delaying his response. "He argued back all right. I jus' said, he's taken power from hisself." The blank look of perplexity covered Bugler.

"You didn't threaten him or say anything about hurting him?" questioned Scott.

"Naw. Old man an' all, what could I do to a young ballplayer?" Bugler's eyes ranged the cell. Some lucidity seemed to drift off.

Scott understood the flaw in the police's case based on strength, but they seemed bent on ignoring it. "We'll let that go. There's a witness who says he saw you with the bloody bat in your hands."

Bugler rejoined Scott and their conversation. "Don't know on that." He returned his gaze to Wyatt's worried face. "I called the cops after I found Edwards. You know, Wyatt, that bat shouldn't been in the locker room...don't belong there. I picked it up to take back ta' the equipment." Bugler completed his explanation before launching back into the timeline. "The sheriff's boys came ta' the ballpark. Not Tommy Tulsa, he left'em and come back to be with the Oilers. He used to be good. Have ta' see now." Bugler gazed directly at Scott. His meandering thoughts brought him back to his friend. "Tommy Warren weren't no Wyatt Scott, not by a country mile, but he is better'n fair."

"Tell me what happened, Eugene. I don't need to know anything else right now. Just give me the events in order, like they were innings in a ballgame."

"Must be in trouble when ya' call me Eugene." The old man hung his head. His true Christian name taken as a scolding.

"Okay. *Bugler*, tell me everything that happened. Start when you came in and you found Edwards."

Bugler looped his head as if he might start a windup. "I finished cleanin' like I'm supposed to, like I was told by Mr. Snider. Ever'body gone. Jus' me an' mysef'. Then I think I hear some commotion, bangin' like, and well, ain't nobody allowed in the park at that time. So, I go take a look-see in the locker room."

Bugler stood. He reenacted his movements. "I seen a bat on the floor where it don't belong. Ain't the first bat I picked up and put away after a game, so I think nothin' of it. You know how baseball players are. Though it might be Drake's bat; thirty-four inch, probably too heavy for him. He went oh for three; struck out twice and ..."

"I don't need the box score," broke in Scott. "You're in a jam here. Tell me your story step by step. What happened next?"

Bugler licked his lips and wrinkled his brow. "Weren't a normal bat, had blood on it. I guess I got some blood on me when I picked up that bat. A Louisville Slugger, like most, 'cept it had wet blood on it; the bat had blood and that weren't right." He paused, fishing for his thoughts, before looking back at Scott and starting again. "Then, I catch somethin' on the other side by the shower." Bugler stepped around an imaginary object and looked down. "There's a nekked ballplayer on the floor and his head's all bloody." Bugler swayed as he stared down at the cell floor. "I seen it's Edwards, the kid that's sa' good; hits liners and throws hard." Bugler bent down. "I bend over ta' see if he's okay, and he ain't Wyatt... he ain't okay a'tal...." A mist formed in Bugler's eyes. "Not okay. He's starin' at me. He's plumb dead." The tears slid out of the corners of the old man's eyes and dripped through wrinkles, meandering down his gray-stubbled cheeks and chin.

"Take a breath. No rush, Bugler. Just start again," urged Scott softly.

Bugler took the advice. After a heavy exhale, he continued. "Well, I just sat there. I seen dead bodies before. When I rode with Teddy. All shot up fellas and them with the fever, but nothing like this." Bugler scratched his chin. The rough sound of rubbed whiskers diverted his thoughts again. "There was this one guy who ..."

"What about this eyewitness?" Scott broke in, stopping another side trip through Bugler's memories. "Where'd he come from?"

"Honest to Pete! I don't know." Bugler focused on Scott, but nothing seemed to ripple through on the subject. "I call the cops. I never saw no one. Sheriff deputies come talk at me and take the bat. I'm here all night 'for the call ta' find you. Your phone didn't answer, so they called that little girl what works for Johnny."

"Okay, Eugene. You take it easy. I'll sort this out. Johnny's working on a lawyer for you, and we'll see about bailing you out."

"Grumpy Johnny doin' that for me?" More than a little surprise filled Bugler's question.

"He's not always grumpy. Deep down, he might even like you, Eugene. He's really a sensitive guy. He'll help us out."

Bugler sat back down on his cell bed. Scott moved close to him and rested his hand on the old man's shoulder. He smiled at Bugler, but even that kindness could not evoke a grin in reply. Sullen and bewildered, the scatterbrained old gent stared blankly at his pal. Seeing that little more could be accomplished, Scott searched for the guard. Catching his eye, he signaled the end of the interview with a two-finger wave. He returned once again to the befuddled old man. "Keep your chin up, Bugler. I won't let you down."

* * *

Scott entered Johnny Grayhawk's outer office. Without an occupant, Evie's chair and desk appeared forlorn. The room sat empty; no action, no snappy lines from Evie; not even the hum of her oscillating fan as it stood switched off. He noted Johnny's closed office door and wondered whether he sat at his desk or played hooky as well. With the urgency of the situation and little or no formality between the two longtime friends, Wyatt stepped to Johnny's door and swung it open.

Johnny Grayhawk stood as soon as he saw his friend open the door. As Scott entered, Johnny addressed him. "Before you ask, and so I don't have to tell you 'no,' I won't represent Bugler. You know how I feel about him, despite our friendship."

Scott began to speak. Johnny raised a finger and swayed it back and forth to hush him. Grayhawk sucked in a deep breath.

"I have not practiced any serious criminal law in donkey's years, and I was not all that skillful at it. Nathan Benjamin will handle Bugler's defense." Johnny alerted Wyatt to his maneuvering without fanfare or further explanation.

"I thought you despised Benjamin." Wyatt stood flabbergasted by Johnny's pronouncement.

"Oh, I do. He is a shyster of the first water. He is also excellent at getting his clients off," rationalized Johnny.

"Is it that bad for Eugene that you would resort to hiring Benjamin?" worried Scott.

"It's not pretty. I hear the county attorney likes his chances. It's an election year, the Oilers are pretty good, and Tulsa likes its baseball. Kid was a comer and starting to attract the right kind of attention." Johnny laid out the emotional case against Bugler.

"That's all background prejudice against anyone charged. Have you heard of any actual evidence against Bugler?"

"Bugler was there. He held the bat that killed the kid when the deputies showed up." Johnny sighed. "A *Tulsa World* reporter told me his sources claim there's a witness." He gave Scott a sympathetic half-smile and raised eyebrows. "Knowing the old fart, it seems preposterous no matter the evidence."

"Do your reporters, or the sheriff's people, have any other suspects or clues about who the actual killer is?" Scott asked, such that an argument over Bugler's guilt stood moot.

"Nothing from any sources on that. Also, wouldn't think the law would work it too hard." Johnny cleared his expression as he switched subjects. "Anyway, I've sent Evie to the bank to get money for Nate's retainer. He doesn't come cheap," lamented Johnny.

"I think that's for me to do, John." Impressed by his best friend's kindness and efficiency, Wyatt still felt the obligation fell to him. Old Bugler had been his friend, if not his ward, since he came back to Tulsa.

"Maybe, maybe not. I said I would not defend him. I did not say I wouldn't help. Besides, I'll just overcharge some Osage oil baron or some white man looking for influence in tribal affairs, and things will roll along as usual." Johnny smiled at his witty sarcasm.

"Thank you, Johnny. I am grateful. Bugler will be too."

Grayhawk waved his hand in reply before he remembered something. "Wyatt, one more thing. Before I sent her out, Evie told me President Cleveland called and wants you to meet him. I guess she means Detective Cleveland."

"Yes. Her little joke. Thanks again, Johnny. I'll get hold of Cleveland, but I have some more important places to go first."

CHAPTER 7

Texas League Park

Scott walked through the empty passages beneath Texas League Park. The locker room door stood open and unattended. He pressed into the deserted chamber. The chalk outline of Edwards's body remained as a mute testament to the crime of murder. He stepped to the edge of the chalk, where closer scrutiny revealed the dried brown stains of blood spatter on the floor and against the locker doors. Everything else appeared unsoiled and in order. He stooped to look at the outline. After mentally recording the body's position, Scott peered into the showers, which proved to be sparkling clean. He maneuvered around the locker benches to a training table. He sat on the table, then recreated the crime in his thoughts. Edwards's back had to have been to the assailant, making the initial blow a shock. Whether or not it took another blow to drop him to the floor, the death blows surely came with Edwards prone on the locker room floor. The repeated bludgeoning could not be fitted into his view of Bugler committing the crime. A single blow from a seventy-year-old seemed highly unlikely; repeated savage blows, impossible.

When he left his internal visualization, Scott caught himself staring across the Oiler's locker room. It fell far short of the grander locker room at Philadelphia's Shibe Park. Except for one day, Scott loved that old ballpark. The newer training table where he sat had more padding, built-in drawers, and a more modern shape than the one he began to recall. Thirteen years prior in Shibe, no murder took place, but a career died. He could still hear the words 'ulnar ligament' sounding like cancer.

Sitting in the Oilers' locker room and rejoining the present, Scott realized he was holding his right elbow. He had been caressing it like an injured pet. He dropped his arm to his side and scolded himself for drifting from his work at hand. Helping his friend and digging out the truth mattered, not self-pity from a baker's dozen years ago. Footsteps behind him signaled company.

"Wyatt Scott. What are you looking for in my locker room?"

Scott glanced to see Al Vincent, the Oilers' manager. His gray tinged hair and creeping belly correctly detailed his long absence from the physical game. He wore his clean Oilers uniform, complete with a ball cap. He would've looked ready to step onto the field and manage, except for the slippers on his feet rather than baseball cleats.

"Ray Snider said you would probably stop by." Vincent stood with his hands on his hips, further expressing his displeasure. "Can't say I much appreciate it."

"Why's that?" replied Scott as he jumped off the training table.

"Oilers are down a man, and I have a season to finish. The kid might have helped, but that's done. We need to focus on finishing out the Texas League season."

"Al, I'm trying to get answers. I'll find the killer. That should help you get the team's focus back on baseball."

"It's a matter for the police, not a gumshoe," grumbled Vincent.

"You don't want to find out who killed your player?" countered Scott.

"Course I do." Vincent dropped his hands, along with his stern look. A sheepish, apologetic expression popped out. He averted Scott's eyes, looking without purpose around the locker room.

"Then you should be happy that I'm helping the overworked Tulsa County Sheriff on the case that directly affects you." Scott took command of the stern look. He added a squint, his best sneer, and a slightly cocked head for maximum impact.

"I mean, I have a team to take care of," whined Vincent.

"Figures the players on your team want to know all there is about the killing. The *team* might get nervous wondering who's next if there's a crazy guy killing ballplayers."

Vincent straightened his Oilers cap. "Authorities think your buddy Bugler killed him...after an argument. That's what I hear."

"Easy culprit for the cops. Way too easy. Nobody's put any thought into it yet. If they're wrong and another one of your guys gets killed, you can kiss more than the season goodbye."

"I dunno, Scott. Who just kills ballplayers for no reason?"

"Who indeed." Scott began a meandering stroll. He made a small circle, returning to coach Vincent. "An old man that reveres baseball players up and kills one; kills him brutally; a kid over fifty years younger and in great shape. Eventually, even the sheriff's department will see it doesn't fit." Scott stood facing Vincent. He held out his arms in a gesture of goodwill. "Al, you can help your team, help keep them safe by helping me solve this correctly."

Vincent pulled off his ball cap. He ran his fingers through his thinning hair. He fitted it back in place, tugging the back and straightening the bill. "I suppose today's shot, anyway. What is it you want to know?"

"Do you know of anyone who'd want to see Edwards dead?" The detective in Scott reclaimed full attention from the manipulative psychologist who wrangled cooperation from Vincent.

"Damn near anyone who met him. He was a pain in my posterior. Didn't take instruction well, even when it would've helped him. Edwards was undisciplined and, to boot, a walking hard-on. Couldn't stay away from other folks' bedrooms from what I heard." Vincent shook his head, pulled off his cap again and slapped it against his leg. "Hell of a ballplayer. Bad luck that he's gone." Vincent sighed. The gears in his head didn't make noise, but they took time before his next statement. "The kid wasn't as good as he thought he was, not yet, but he had potential equal to his double-deck ego. Focus and a few setbacks would have made a difference; helped his attitude." He pulled his Oilers cap back on and tugged at the bill before dropping his arm and glaring at Scott.

"The sheriff claims Edwards had an argument with Bugler. Do you know what they argued about?" Scott backed away from Vincent, giving him more room.

"God only knows. Bugler never shuts up. Runs his mouth like it's not connected to anything. Likely he saw Edwards do something he thought coulda' been better. Then, called him on it, and the kid took exception. Our older players can handle Bugler; hell, he's even right more times than not. The boy didn't know how things were. Might have taken it personal."

"You don't know any specifics?"

"No." Vincent moved closer to Scott. "Look, Scott, I know you and Ray care about that old man. You two may even be fascinated by his baseball statistics and every old ballplayer that ever got a hit back to eighteen-eighty, but he gets on people's nerves. And what you don't seem to understand is I have to put up with it all season long." The manager's voice slipped into a groan.

"Ray owns the team, so take it up with him, Al."

Vincent shifted from foot to foot like a guy on a diet asking his wife for the last piece of pie in the icebox. "I'm just sayin' Tris Speaker's batting average in nineteen twenty-two is not instructional. I am the goddam coach, not some mule-kicked old man, and I would like folks to remember that!"

"Take it easy, Al. Nobody thinks Bugler will replace you as manager." Scott waited for Vincent to calm down. "Okay?"

He nodded, took a couple of breaths, and nodded again. "What else?" The words mixed with an exasperated sigh.

"Tell me more about this business of Ronnie Edwards being a ladies' man."

"Edwards came up from Shreveport." Evidently tired of standing, Vincent moved to one of the benches and sat down. "He got some girl pregnant. Apparently, her *husband* couldn't. Our GM did a favor with a player swap; thought the kid might settle down in Tulsa. If it worked, it would be the player steal of the decade."

"Any sign that happened?"

"Naw. Kid ruts year-round – distraction to his play too." Vincent pulled at his chin. "Probably bat thirty points higher and hit ten more dingers if he worked on baseball instead of women."

"This sounds like something the county law boys haven't poked into. You have any details about the gals?"

"Word on the field is he just changed his lineup."

"You got any names?"

"Some young gal, but that talk just started; not sure on the particulars. Before that, heard he fished closer to home."

"Home-spun euphemisms aside, you know *who*?" grilled Scott.

"Not swingin' at that one, Scott." He looked away, but the crimson of embarrassment colored his face.

"Vincent, if I decide I need to know, you might get a bean ball not a question over the plate." Scott stared down Vincent, who shuffled his feet. "You know something?"

"No, I don't. Rumors fly around locker rooms twenty to the pack. I can't remember most, and I wouldn't know where to start. Just that the kid loved getting his pecker wet."

Scott paced off some of his frustration. He knew Vincent wasn't exaggerating about locker room rumors, but he hoped to draw out one or two new ones with substance. He decided that pitch wouldn't cross the plate. Wyatt pivoted back toward Vincent and tried another. "The law talked about a witness. Do you know anything about that?"

"Frank Dodge talked to the sheriff," stated Vincent.

"Dodge is this so-called witness?"

"Didn't tell me direct. He talked to them; that's all I know."

"What do you think? Is he the witness?" quizzed Scott.

Vincent shrugged.

"Where were you when it happened?

"Home where I should've been, and with witnesses." Vincent stood up from the bench. "I wish the man no ill will, but from what I can gather, your old buddy, Bugler, is the most likely guy." Vincent meandered towards the chalk outline with his back to Scott. "Now, if he did it, then that's a load off. If he didn't, then there's a killer out there. *And* no one knows if Edwards was the only target."

"Yes. I told you that."

Vincent ambled toward Scott. "Maybe the killer don't like baseball players. Worse, could be another player, a teammate. That makes me nervous, and it makes the players nervous. Frightened players don't win ball games. That puts a lot on my plate. I got plenty on my plate without that."

"Sure, Al, so now you get it. Everyone's nervous."

Vincent looked down at his feet. He kicked his left heel with his right toe. "So, I guess I'd jus' soon ol' Bugler is guilty, and it all goes away."

"Al, it's easier for you, easier for the law, just not likely to be right. You believe Bugler would kill someone—a young ballplayer, no less?"

"Scott, I don't think. I manage a baseball team." Vincent popped a false smile. "So, if you will excuse me, I have a practice looming and a season to finish." He shuffled toward the door.

"Three forty-four," said Scott.

Vincent stopped. "What?" He squinted and wrinkled his nose.

"Tris Speaker's batting average in nineteen twenty-two. He batted three eighty-nine in twenty-five, his best season." Scott spat out the statistics like a stern history professor rattling off dates of ancient battles.

Vincent stared blankly before he shook his head and dashed from the locker room, fearful of more statistics being hurled his way. Scott chuckled. Brains hold massive inventories of facts, some more useful than others. He would gladly trade some of those stored bits for new ones to help Bugler.

* * *

The Tulsa Oilers practiced under the noon sun. Without fans, the routine of baseball practice persisted with a defined pulse. Wyatt Scott watched it unfold as he weaved his way through the stands to the barrier near the dugout. Fly balls were shagged, grounders scooped, throws let fly, fungoes played, and coaches grumbled out commands. Their murdered teammate not yet buried, the movements and chatter of the players seemed unremarkable.

When Scott reached the handrail, he leaned over and yelled toward the concealed players in the dugout. "Tommy Warren. Tommy Warren, come out. It's Wyatt Scott."

The clack of steel cleats assaulting concrete steps presaged a player exiting the dugout. Wearing a clean practice uniform, Tulsa Oiler pitcher Tommy Warren emerged from the third-base end. His ball cap sat well back on his head, revealing a broad smile. His face showed some of the wear from years of playing ball in both the big leagues and the minors.

"Wyatt. Haven't seen you since I came back to the Oilers," declared Warren.

"I just read about it, Tommy. I thought you were still with the Sheriff's office." Scott leaned over the seating rail. He extended a hand to Warren.

Tommie Warren clasped his hand and shook it with gusto. "Nope, I left there to come back," replied Warren. "I missed the game."

"It does take a while to get over." Scott nodded his head in affirmation of their shared feelings about baseball.

"Yeah...it does."

"Tommy, I guess you heard about old Bugler being arrested for Ronnie Edward's murder."

"I did. That old man's a character, but I never thought he'd do such a thing," Warren looked at Wyatt with a wrinkled brow and a pair of sympathetic eyes.

"I don't believe he did. Is there any talk around the team about Edwards's killing?"

"You mean beyond the gossip as to why Bugler went crazy and did it?"

"Yeah, Tommy, anything else beyond that."

"A poor joke or two about Vincent using a bat to knock some sense into Ronnie's head or Dodge going a little extreme to get his spot back," answered Warren. "Ballplayer, locker room crap, you know." Tommy Warren shrugged his shoulders while offering a supportive smile.

"Not much value in that black humor." Wyatt took a fresh approach. "Did you know the Edwards kid well?"

"Retread vets and young up-and-comers don't have much social exchange. I never talked to the Edwards kid outside of the field."

"I understand." Scott shifted his fedora to better shade his face from the afternoon sun. "Even so, what did you think of him, Tommy?"

"A few games ain't much time to form a strong opinion."

"Sure. Just the same, you saw some games before coming back, and you can size up a ballplayer pretty quick in a locker room."

Warren nodded. "My impression, he liked the game; played hard and had natural talent, real talent." Warren glanced around and took a step closer to Scott. "Upstairs, Ronnie Edwards was not the sharpest tack." Warren did not whisper, but he lowered his volume to reach only Scott's ears.

"How about the other players? Locker rooms are full of yammer and gossip. What did you hear about him?"

"Nothing unusual from the guys. He blabbed a lot. I've only been back about two weeks, and I already heard farm boy stories about his childhood, some homer in high school that got lost in a hayfield, and how he stole home during a game in 'A' ball." Tommy Warren smirked, "In general, he bragged more than most."

"Besides being full of himself, was he in any trouble? Gambling. Shady friends. Dangerous company or bad girls?"

"No trouble I know of." Warren rubbed his chin. "Now that you mention it, he did like girls, pros and amateurs, from what I heard tell. I haven't been back with the Oilers long enough for him to give me his bedroom stories directly."

"Have you heard any girls' names by chance?" asked Scott.

"No names," replied Warren. "Heard he visited the May Rooms more than a little."

"Heard from whom?"

"Guys gabbing, like I said."

"No jealous husbands came around, or rumors of that?"

"None that I heard about." Tommy Warren shrugged. "With that kid, the whole mess could of' been a snow job about what a peachy lover he was. If he had a girl, you could bet he liked himself more than her, anyway."

"One more thing, you can help me with: a young gal, maybe more recent than the rest?"

"Sorry, Wyatt, I don't know anything that would wander in that direction."

"Okay, Tommy." Scott looked past Warren at the players on the field. "Say, is Dodge around? I can't see him out there."

"Coach said he wouldn't be around until later. Had some business that he couldn't put off." Warren pulled at his cap. "Vincent didn't say, but I don't think he or any of us cares whether Dodge makes practice. He never was that good, and now he's slower than a snail."

"You're likely right about that." Scott loosened his grip on the rail and dropped his hands to his sides. "Thanks a lot, Tommy." Wyatt paused before smiling at the comeback ballplayer. "When are you pitching next?"

"Doubt much chance until the road trip to Wichita; need to get back in the game a little more. Should be full of vinegar by then." Warren brandished a big grin.

Scott stepped back from the rail. "Good luck then. I'll try to catch your Tulsa start during the next home stand."

Warren nodded. "Nice seeing you, Wyatt. Why don't you stick around and tell us what you think of the team? It's always good to get a veteran's view of things."

Scott continued climbing the stadium steps. "I'll take my time and watch from the bleachers."

Warren waved his cap at Scott and ran to the dugout. Scott took a seat and stared at the field and the practice routine. He had seen that routine a thousand times. Wyatt recalled it. He missed it. He missed the camaraderie of his fellow players. A guy learned things in practice that didn't cost his team a loss. The game had taught Wyatt a lot, and his time with Moe Berg helped him absorb lessons beyond baseball.

* * *

Wyatt Scott wound up, pivoted, drew his right arm back, and whipped it forward, releasing the two-seam fastball before the follow-through carried his arm across his body. The pitch flew fast with just the right amount of wiggle. It rose a bit and drifted in on Jimmy Foxx. Scott's teammate on the Athletics, old Double-X (just one of his nicknames), ripped at the pitch, but his bat swept nothing but air. The great hitter smiled at Scott before he offered a dare. "Okay, Rookie. You throw that one out over the plate and see what happens."

Scott shook his head at the offer. Moe Berg tossed the ball back to him. Morning batting practice was the only time Wyatt got to pitch in Japan. Connie Mack had told him to bear down and make the all-stars have to work to hit. They had won the first five games, but there were nine more to be played. He didn't want them to get lazy on the tour. Connie Mack, for his part, was adamant about winning, hence using his star rookie pitcher for high-intensity batting practice.

Berg didn't signal any pitches since it was batting practice and not a game. Scott had to make his own calls. He worked the ball in his glove, twisting it until it set right. He dug his index fingernail into the hide next to a seam. The inside of his middle finger nestled against the adjacent seam. He wound up and spun the ball so that it departed his hand between his thumb and forefinger. His arm made the delivery overhand and high. It sailed toward the plate, spinning hard against the air before diving down and away. Scott thought he had it: a curve, the perfect follow on to his inside fastball.

Double-X thought differently. Jimmy Foxx swung the barrel of the bat down to the pitch, his muscular arms generating remarkable bat speed. The exploding sound of horsehide and lumber cracked against Scott's ears. He whirled toward left field to see the ball arc majestically high and far out of the park. Surprised more than downtrodden, he looked back at home plate where both Foxx and Moe Berg stood grinning at him.

"Out-gamed you on that one, kid," howled Foxx.

"He knew you'd never throw the fastball again; certainly not over the plate," explained Berg. "You might as well have yelled out that you were coming with a curveball."

"It's just B P, Moe. They're supposed to hit them," rationalized Scott.

"Don't fool yourself. We all know you're trying to strike the guys out. We understand Connie wants to keep us on our toes, and it's your way of trying to prove yourself. That's the game. The Beast baited you into throwing that pitch. Learn the lesson, Wyatt. Think it through. Sometimes the *other fellow* is a step ahead of you."

CHAPTER 8

ANSWERING QUESTIONS, ASKING QUESTIONS

Standing by his kitchen counter, Wyatt fixed his after-breakfast agenda on Dodge and Ray Snider. He stared at a plate holding a piece of dry toast. Void of eggs, bacon, and practically everything else, his refrigerator held a pair of colas that kept a jar of pickles company. He could forgive its barrenness since that was his fault, but the damn thing didn't warn him it housed no butter. He picked up the toast, deciding his strong coffee would have to soften the toast once inside his mouth. He took a sip. He took a bite. The door buzzer took a turn. Hoping for good news; fearing bad luck, Scott headed for the obstinate notification.

Scott opened his door to find the two FBI agents, Fleming and Phillips. The pair presented an interruption and annoyance flawlessly timed to irritate the last nerve Wyatt possessed for government workers. Each man reflexively slipped a hand inside his coat, retrieving his credentials. The actions displayed near choreographed precision as two badges flashed their initials.

With the men swinging their badges, Phillips announced them. "Wyatt Scott? We're with the FBI. We have some questions."

"I remember you both. Why have you come to my residence?" Scott stood with his fingers gripping the doorknob, and his body blocking the way.

"We came to ask questions, like he said." Fleming forced the redundant reply with his misunderstanding of Scott's intent.

Wyatt calculated the fastest way through the narrow-focus fixations of the Hoover brood was to bring them in and offer gratuitous answers to their pointless questions. "Then I think you gentlemen should come in." Scott swung the door wide as he stepped back and to the side.

Fleming trudged in, staring straight ahead. Phillips swung his head left and right, taking in Scott's apartment while gliding in his partner's path. Wyatt eased his front door closed. He held back to see if the two agents would light somewhere or flit around his place. Fleming stopped and turned toward him. Phillips drifted toward the picture window beside and behind the sofa. He peered through the narrow gap in the curtains.

"Anymore Japanese make contact with you?" asked Fleming.

"No. None ever made contact. Hiroshi Ishikawa was killed before he got to me, remember?"

"Okay. We're not asking about him. Have any new Japanese friends called or sent you a telegram?"

Scott stared at the two Feds. "I don't know any; never became friends with any." Aside from being a nuisance for him, he saw little reason the FBI men could hope to get meaningful information from their simple questions. He braced for more dissembling conversation before they made it to their actual point.

Phillips gave up peeking and tugged the drapes open wide. He gazed west across the river. "Nice view. Not much water in that river, though."

"Best the poor Arkansas can do in July and August." Scott focused on Phillips.

"Nice apartment, too," Phillips turned from the window and swept his eyes across the living room. "Must be expensive for a shamus working for an Indian lawyer."

"I manage. I have other clients besides Grayhawk Law."

Fleming circled the coffee table to drop on the sofa. "We know you do."

"We do our homework," chimed in Phillips. "That's why we want to ask more questions."

"You're here. Ask away." Scott raised both arms more from frustration than surrender.

Phillips sat in the armchair. Fleming removed his hat and dropped it beside him on the sofa cushion. They looked at one another playing eyeball-high-card to see who went next.

"Have you gotten anywhere on who shot at you?" Fleming won the draw.

"No. I'm ready to hear anything you have."

"We're still working. We have a source that might come through." Fleming smiled at Phillips.

Phillips flipped a knowing nod back. "Shame you don't have any leads. Have you tried to find out more about Ishikawa?"

"I couldn't guess where to start. You guys have a line to MacArthur and the baseball group. The best I could do is phone the Japanese consulate office."

"No other pals from your baseball days that know him?" asked Fleming.

"That I wouldn't know. I haven't seen a major league player since I went to college in thirty-six."

"How about you shot Ishikawa mistaking him for the Jap you were supposed to shoot?" Phillips tapped on the coffee table to emphasize his conjecture.

"It's been fourteen years, but I would recognize Hiroshi. How did I get on the train, and why would I want to kill any Japanese?"

"The killer took everything other than the Jap's watch and the slip of paper with your name and address." Phillips sat back in his chair. "We hear you're slick like that."

Scott laughed. "Oh, so you talked to Morgan."

"You do seem to ruffle his feathers," broke in Fleming.

"Morgan's personality aside, what are you guys trying to get from me? I'm willing to share anything. The killer tried to shoot me too."

"We need to be sure you have had no contact with Ishikawa," said Phillips.

Fleming glared at him, then jumped to Scott. "The paper on him and your past require complete vetting. You were with OSS; spy work isn't far removed."

"During the war. Just a P.I. since I got home. I know you fellas ran FBI checks on me."

"We check on everything, all right," affirmed Phillips.

"And everyone," added Fleming.

Phillips leaned forward in the chair. "Does that worry you?"

The full Wyatt Scott sardonic grin rippled forth. "The shooter having more success the next time worries me. I'm eager for any good information you get. I'm also prepared for any ignorant notions you have, or stupid moves you boys make."

Phillips came out of the chair. Wyatt stood his ground. Fleming just laughed.

"We're making a nice file on you, Scott." Phillips pointed his finger at Wyatt.

Fleming stood, calmly retrieved his hat, and walked the long way around the table, coming alongside Phillips. He patted his partner's shoulder. "I told you, he's a nobody. If I'm wrong, we can figure out what we need from the bullets they take out of him."

Phillips snorted. "Sure. Playing dumb probably comes natural to him."

"He did a pile of college and that war decoding. I think he's more a civilian bystander than a dullard. Either way, I think we have determined he's a waste of time. Let's go; unless you want to see if his bedroom meets *Good Housekeeping* standards."

Fleming grinned at his partner. Phillips gave Fleming the finger. Scott felt like giving both something worse.

* * *

In an apartment building halfway between downtown Tulsa and Texas League Park, Scott came to a second-floor hall filled with identical entrances. The lack of piquant aromas or those from spilled alcohol spoke of working-class Oklahoma families rather than single men living behind the hallway doors. Scott worked his way down the corridor. Below each doorbell button, a tiny name tag differentiated the generic entries. When he found it, Scott rang the bell marked 'Dodge.' He removed his hat and considered the man as he waited for him to open the door.

Other than being older and holding on by his fingernails to a roster spot in double-A ball, Scott knew little about Frank Dodge. Bugler's analysis of his paltry talents aside, Dodge rarely showed up in the box score, and more rarely showed up with a hit or an RBI. A minor leaguer older than Wyatt seemed destined for the baseball scrapheap and, if lucky, a menial job that kept him fed after his last failure in the profession. Scott had seen him around the ballpark but had never bothered striking up a conversation with the man. The door opened not with Dodge, but a woman.

"Mrs. Dodge?" asked Scott with a lilt of surprise and uncertainty.

"Yes, I'm Helen Dodge."

"Is your husband home?" Scott sized her up. She looked close to Dodge's age. Her face bore rouge and lipstick applied with care. Her hair displayed the detail of a professional perm, while her facial features were neither dissatisfying nor appealing. She wore a light green summer dress that barely peeked from behind the door as she squeezed the opening down under a foot.

"No. Why do you want him?" Perplexity in her voice mingled with skepticism in her eyes.

"I understand he saw something last night at the ballpark."

"He told the police about that already...or the sheriff's office; I think they're involved." She narrowed her eyes and inspected Scott from his felt hat to his wingtips. "Who are you, anyway?" Her question seemed to be more commentary on her annoyance than genuine interest in an answer.

"Wyatt Scott. A friend of mine is accused of Ronnie Edwards's murder. It might help if I could talk with Frank about what he saw."

"Still not sure if it's any of your business, but like I said, Frank ain't here." She clung to the door, using it as a shield. "He might be back at the sheriff's office, or maybe he's made it to the ballpark now."

"Did he say anything to you about what he saw?"

"No." She further narrowed the door's opening. "You should speak with the sheriff's office and leave me alone."

"He saw a murdered boy, and he said nothing about it?" A little surprise and a double helping of incredulity topped Scott's question.

"I don't know what he saw. He told me some kid got killed. Frank said he needed to talk to the police."

"So, the event didn't bother him."

"I told you, I don't know. I didn't see anything. I don't know anything. He told them what he saw and what he knew. He didn't go into it with me."

"Did it bother you?"

"You bother me. Why would I care about some ballplayer?"

"I guess you wouldn't." Scott tendered a half-smile, nodded, and put on his hat. He sauntered down the hallway, drawing out his departure to gauge the visit's impact on her ill-mannered personality. The door slam echoed down the corridor.

The encounter brought him no specifics beyond her frosty disposition and Helen Dodge's perfume, which smelled as if the Oklahoma Tire and Supply Company had designed and blended it. He would need to continue his sojourn elsewhere in seeking answers for Bugler's release. He reckoned on trying the other end of the baseball spectrum.

* * *

As the sun set, the LaSalle cooled down in the long, sweeping driveway of the ritzy home of Ray Snider, owner of the Tulsa Oilers and multiple other enterprises. The three-story gray stone mansion loomed over its detailed gardens and perfectly shorn lawns. On its porch, Wyatt Scott pushed the doorbell and heard the multiple tones chime and echo through the home's expanse. When the door swung open, Amanda Snider, Ray Snider's only child, stood in the entry, surprising Scott by her presence. Amanda, seventeen, comely, and dressed like the high school senior-to-be that she was, did not greet Scott but immediately retreated toward the inner rooms of the dwelling.

"Dad, there's a man at the door," yelled young Miss Snider as she disappeared through an archway.

Scott took the liberty of stepping into the abandoned foyer. He removed his hat and held it with both hands in front of his belt. He had visited the Snider's home before. While not the largest mansion in the Forest Hills area, it rated close enough to be considered a dominant dwelling. The home contained more modern furnishing than customary for the wealthy in Tulsa. English manor-house furniture or Louis-the-Fourteenth elaborations found elsewhere failed in finding a station within the Snider domicile. Without a perfect recollection of the décor on his last visit, Scott could not pinpoint all the changes, but its transformation was clear from the last time he set foot in the house. No doubt Snider's wife had once more become bored and procured new furnishings and appointments.

Following her summons, Ray Snider responded to his daughter's call by strolling into the foyer. His crisp, light blue suit fit him as perfectly as his pricey tailor could manage. A little over fifty, his hint of gray seemed recent to Wyatt. Snider's eyes widened, and he broke into a smile when he spotted Scott. He quickened his stride and extended his arm as he arrived at Wyatt's side.

"Wyatt Scott. I'll be doggoned. Come in. Been a long time. How are you doing now days?"

Scott held out his hand. "Ray."

The two shook hands before Snider dropped his grasp in favor of clasping Scott's right bicep. "How's the arm?"

"Threw some balls with Johnny. Two had some zip, the rest were pitchin' like an old lady without Geritol."

Changing his expression as quickly as he changed the subject, Snider asked; "Have you seen Bugler yet?"

"I just came from there. It's hard on him, Ray."

Snider looked away before he gazed again at Scott. "Wyatt, you and I know Eugene couldn't kill anyone." He stared down at the floor like a kid not wanting to confess that he had broken the window. Summoning about the same courage as a kid, Snider looked back up and continued. "But I just got off the phone with George Blaine, and things don't look good for our boy. They're telling me they have an open and shut case. Sheriff Blaine says the County Attorney thinks it's a gift, waiting for the jury to put a bow on." He hung his head after delivering further negative news.

"I know you and Sheriff Blaine go way back. I get this isn't just scare talk." Scott cut his statement short. He scrutinized Snider. Both remained quiet.

Unlike Scott, the silence unsettled Snider. "Yes," he swallowed to lubricate his further words. "That and Dewey being a law-and-order candidate, all the sheriffs are getting on the bandwagon. Perhaps not here in Democrat Oklahoma, but Dewey's gonna' win nationally. Tulsa being a little bit more Republican than the rest of the state, Blaine wants to be out front of it."

The politics of the day should not shape the law, but Scott knew it would. "All the more reason we have to hurry." Scott, the detective, took over. "What can you tell me about Ronnie Edwards?"

"Full of himself, undisciplined." Getting on with business eased Snider. He relaxed his posture as he continued offering more. "His play is short of his ego, but his potential is good – *was* good, I guess. Lots of speed, a powerful arm. Good outfielder for a kid that young. Fine hitter but swung at too many pitches out of the zone. Lacked self-control with the bat." Snider's musings brought him back to Bugler. "Coach Vincent told me Bugler got on him about it, swinging at bad pitches. Vincent hates the help, but he agreed with the assessment."

"I talked to Vincent. He said, you warned him I'd come by."

"Not a warning. I thought you'd drop by and check things around the ball club. Calling Vincent was to smooth things along because I expected that you'd ask him questions. I told him he should help you out."

Scott gave Snider a sideways glance. "Must've been a poor phone connection when you told him that." He straightened his head and glared at Snider. "I'll ask you, Ray; was there anything to the kid being randy with married skirts?"

"I guess that could be, but I don't pay heed to ballplayer morals, only their batting averages." A flutter of eyelids did not confirm the veracity of the statement.

"I heard the kid's a mattress-tester and not too discreet. I'd guess you check into your guys to stay ahead of trouble, so you're sure you have heard no stories?" Scott scrutinized the wealthy businessman for his answer.

"No. Like I said, I don't care about their days off." Snider paused. "If any of them get mixed up with gamblers or get in trouble with the law, that's different. Any real trouble, and I'd trade them off or cut them outright."

"Edwards mingle with that sort?" asked Scott.

"I hope to God not. I have no reports of that, not even a rumor. That doesn't fit Edwards. He wanted the big leagues from all I heard." Snider crossed his arms. "Any hint of that would destroy his chances of moving up to the majors."

"I plan on keeping an open mind, but there's not much money in fixing minor league games," said Scott.

"I thought Al could help you. Managers need to know what's going on to keep the team focused on baseball."

"Vincent didn't give me much," Scott sighed. "I need more leads to help Eugene. Do you think your GM would be familiar with any of the kid's personal habits or at least his history?"

"I don't know if Paul knows anything beyond how we got him and his stats from 'A' ball, but you're welcome to talk to him." Snider peered around. "Did Al mention his lady problem in Shreveport?"

"That Vincent did tell me. Edwards knocking up some woman fits with what I hear about him catting around."

"Shush about that!" Approaching footsteps triggered nervous shuffling in the local tycoon's feet. He tossed Scott two short, frenetic headshakes.

Amanda Snider swung around her father toward the front door. Ray Snider stepped away from Scott, truncating the conversation. He grimaced slightly as his eyes scanned her clothing choice.

"Amanda. I thought you were packing for your trip." While the statement was passive, an undertone of fatherly displeasure snuck out.

"I'm mostly finished," explained young Miss Snider as she slowed her progress toward the door before halting.

"As long as you're ready for the train in the morning." Snider shifted his gaze to Scott. "Amanda's traveling to meet her mother in New York for a few days, then they are going to visit Bryn Mawr together. I still prefer Stephens because Missouri is closer." The wealthy, doting father addressed Scott but made his thoughts clear to his daughter.

Scott acknowledged Snider before addressing his daughter, "I'm sure you'll enjoy yourself, Miss Snider." Unsure what subjects he should tackle with a teenager, Scott commented on the college, "And Bryn Mawr is a fine school."

Becoming aware of the etiquette of the situation, Ray Snider made the introductions that he had initially skipped. "Oh, sorry." He addressed his daughter. "Amanda, this is Mr. Wyatt Scott. Best ballplayer to come from Tulsa. Now, he is a private investigator working out of the Pythian Building."

Upon hearing Scott's profession, Amada wrenched from smiling at Scott to shooting BBs through her eyes at her father. "You hired a private eye?!"

"What?" Flustered by the unfounded recrimination, Snider explained Scott's presence to his daughter. "No. He's here about his old friend who's mixed up in that ballplayer killing."

"Ronnie Edwards." The name seemed to slip out. "Somebody killed him last night." Her voice trailed off.

"Yes," replied Snider rather matter-of-factly. "A shame. Such a young man." He shifted his view and made his ultimate statement to Scott. "And he had promise."

Amanda hurried out of the foyer, her heels clicking on the hard floor. Her head down and singularly focused, she sped out of the door, leaving it wide open. She rushed down the sidewalk toward the garage and out of sight.

Snider yelled at her back after she scampered away. "Be home before ten." As Snider reengaged with Scott, frustration challenged embarrassment for supremacy on his face. "Girls seem to get harder to raise every year."

Tired of the family drama, Scott came to the most important point of his visit. "Ray, I hear there's a witness – someone who claimed they saw Eugene with Edwards after the murder. I'm trying to find out who that is."

"Vincent would be the one to ask. His ears are usually open in the locker room. You didn't ask him about it when you saw him?" questioned Snider.

"I did. As I told you, he wasn't very forthcoming." Scott sighed out his frustration. "Reading between the lines, Al hinted it was Frank Dodge."

"Dodge." Snider paused a moment. "Edwards replaced him in the lineup. You don't suppose he had it in for Edwards over that?"

"A guy losing his position would be a sad excuse for murder; for Dodge more than most. At his age, he's never going up, and he must have lost out to young kids a dozen times before this."

A head bob showed Snider's concurrence with Scott's view. "He's a journeyman all right. I couldn't tell you much about him other than he can play right or left and fill in at first base in a pinch." After his assessment, Snider smirked. "And he fills a roster spot cheaply."

"I just want to talk to him about what he told the sheriff about Bugler," explained Scott.

"If that's what you need, Wyatt, I'll call the ballpark and tell them to make Dodge wait for you." Snider appeared pleased about finding an opportunity to finally assist.

"Thanks, Ray, I appreciate the help."

Scott moved to leave, but Snider grabbed his shoulder. "Wyatt, Bugler is a pain in the ass, but he doesn't deserve this. Do I need to hire a lawyer for him?"

"Johnny Grayhawk has one set up."

Snider nodded. "You need me to hire more investigators to help you get to the bottom of this mess?"

"No, Ray." Scott headed to the door. Without further elucidation, he replied, "I'll take care of it myself."

CHAPTER 9

CARL AND JANINE

The sun had been up an hour and a half; Wyatt Scott just the half. He steered the LaSalle off the road. Its tires spun and spit gravel from the driveway of a converted frame house. The gravel broadened into a parking lot where once a lawn had flourished. Above the door in bright red lettering, a wooden sign announced the spot as 'Wilton's Café.' Located on the north side of Tulsa, the café catered primarily to the black patrons who lived in that segregated section of town. One of the few Caucasian customers, Wyatt Scott enjoyed Wilton's food even though his visit today involved meeting another of its denizens.

He parked his car and made his way to the screen door. Before he pulled it open, his nose sampled the fragrance of Wilton's breakfast. The unmistakable aroma of bacon, ham, eggs, and strong coffee reminded him of the fine fare the local spot offered. Short on décor, but long on flavor, Scott reckoned he should try to stop by Wilton's a little more often, even at the expense of a visit or two to Joe and Mamie's.

Inside, the wooden floor supported a few tables and chairs, booths on the left and right, and a countertop with stools. Wilton's framed favorites of Ethel Waters, Ella Fitzgerald, Lena Horne, and Mina Mae McKinney smiled down on the new entrant as he traversed the floor toward the grill. Two ceiling fans whirred away, already serving notice of the mounting summer heat to come. Carl Jefferson, the all-purpose helper and factotum for Queena Capps of the May Rooms, sat alone at the counter. With only a cup of coffee on the counter before him, it appeared he had not yet been served his breakfast. Scott threaded his way to a stool next to Mr. Jefferson.

Behind that counter, a skinny black man in a well-worn butcher's apron cleaned the counter and his hands with a bar towel. The gentleman being the owner and namesake of the establishment, Marvin Wilton. He had a bright, shiny grin, which spoke of his oral hygiene or his lucky heredity, since nary a filling, capped tooth, or blemish could be detected in his smile. That smile elongated beyond his canines as he noted Scott.

"Hey Mr. Scott. My victuals bring you here on the poor side a' town?" Wilton stopped wiping and threw the towel over his shoulder. "What can I get ya?"

"A cup of your famous coffee, Marvin." Scott leaned on the counter. "This morning, I came looking for Carl here. I need to pick his brain about something."

"Won't get much, Mr. Scott. Seeing how he ain't et' yet." Wilton grinned at Carl, who glanced back indifferently. Still grinning, Wilton swung his gaze toward Scott.

"In that case, bring him whatever he wants for breakfast on my wallet." Scott eased onto the stool next to Carl.

"You must need them pickin's pretty bad." Wilton grinned and rocked his head. He turned to Carl. "Carl, whata' you have this morning?"

"Thank you, Mr. Wyatt. Appreciate it." Carl squinted at the chalkboard rendition of the day's menu. "Wilton, I'm thinkin' scrambled eggs with lots of bacon." Carl pursed his lips in further contemplation of breakfast. "Add some biscuits and gravy, too." The big man smiled but dropped it quickly in favor of clarifying his order. "Best scramble half dozen when I say scrambled eggs."

"That's an order then," confirmed Wilton.

Carl snickered, "Oh, for ya' run off Wilton, gimme' a refill a' that *famous* coffee."

Wilton gave Carl a joking version of the evil-eye before grabbing his coffee pot. As he poured Carl Jefferson's refill, he pulled a clean mug from under the counter. He slid it in front of Scott and filled it up. "How about you, Mr. Wyatt? Best have some breakfast too."

"Don't think I could keep up with Carl." Scott sighed and grinned. "I do like the notion of biscuits and gravy. Give me that with a couple of eggs over easy."

"No bacon?" questioned Wilton.

"No. Maybe Carl will offer a stick of his." Scott grinned at both of them.

Wilton laughed. "You, Mr. Wyatt, are some optimist." He cackled all the way to his refrigerator.

Scott began to sip his coffee when Carl interrupted him. "Okay with you if we take a booth? More private there, and some things don't need ears overhearin'."

Scott finished his sip and nodded his agreement. "Sure, Carl."

Carl picked up his coffee mug. "Wilton," he called out.

Straying from his cooking duties, the genial owner sidled over to the two patrons. "What ya' need, Carl?"

Carl stood. "Takin' a booth 'stead a' the counter."

"Sure thing. I'll bring your eats when I finish'em up."

The pair left their stools. Scott let Carl lead the way. He chose the booth in the far corner. Scott followed Carl's choice and slid in first. Carl lingered, scanning right then left, combing the empty room before sitting across from Scott.

The big man stared at him with solemn intent. "Mr. Scott, if this is about that radio feller; that's done. Talkin' 'bout it won't change things none." Carl jumped in on the subject he seemed to expect Scott to broach. His face expressed sober reflection; his eyes absolute finality.

"I can't say it's none of my business, but I have no intention of asking about that." He didn't dodge Carl's eyes as he replied. "If Queena was careful, I'm pretty sure no trouble will come your way." Wyatt leaned toward Jefferson. "I have other concerns, urgent concerns. That's why I'm here. I need your help, Carl."

After a moment of surprise, Mr. Jefferson resumed his familiar, stoic expression. "What help ya' lookin' for?"

Scott reached into his coat pocket and withdrew a newspaper clipping. As he unfolded it, the printed likeness of a ballplayer wearing a Tulsa Oilers cap could be seen. He spun the clipping to angle it for Carl's view. He tapped the player's picture. "Carl, have you ever noticed this kid at Queena's?"

Carl took his time letting the topic settle in. Only after he seemed to trust Scott on the previous subject did he consider the picture. He squinted at the image, scratching his ear as he scrutinized it. He deliberated for several seconds before slow-rolling his answer. "Edwards boy; Oiler ballplayer that got killed."

"That's right," affirmed Scott.

"Far as the May Rooms, he come by a few times." Carl slid his sizeable hand across the paper as he cataloged his thoughts. "Sorta' new this season ta' the Oiler ball team; definitely new at the May Rooms." Whether the memory just flowed back, or he identified it all along, Carl pressed it out. "He talked at me a little while one time. Real stuck on himself." He looked back up at Scott. "Said to me he's gonna' be the next Joe DiMaggio. I didn't laugh in his face, but by my way a thinkin' he's just another Joe." He peered back down, giving the picture further study.

"Did he ever make any trouble for you and Queena?"

"He got into it once with Jeanine. Thought it might come to something, some violence or force, anyhow." Carl glanced up from the picture. "Never did."

"What was it about with Jeanine?"

"Hear her tell it, he smarted off about her lack of love makin' skill, and she told him that for a baseball player he needed a bigger bat." Carl smirked. "Jeanine always had a smart mouth on her. I put him on notice that if he expected to come back, he'd best behave. He made like he wasn't afraid of me."

Scott laughed out loud at the notion.

Carl grinned his confirmation of Scott's non-verbal comment. "You know how dem' peckerwoods be. I told him it'd take him a long time to get to first base with my boot up his ass."

Still smiling, Scott asked; "He ever come back?"

"Cain't say. I don't think he needed the service. Jeanine said that he yelled at her that he wouldn't be back. She said the boy told her he didn't need no stinkin' whore. Went on about having a married woman that was better than her and didn't cost him nothin'." Carl shook his head. "Braggin' and actin' like cheatin's a good thing."

"Married woman, huh?"

"Claimed so." Carl regarded the picture, bending the paper up for a closer look. "Young boy...to be dead."

"Awful young, Carl."

Carl twisted his coffee mug in a circle. He peered back up at Scott. "Your old buddy they arrested is a strange one, but he ain't no killer, Mr. Wyatt," opined Carl Jefferson.

"No, he isn't," agreed Scott.

"I suppose you askin' questions ta' get him out a' county jail." Carl abandoned his mug, looking toward Wilton carrying food, and drew his hands back to his lap.

"That's right, Carl." Scott glanced down at the inverted image of Ronnie Edwards. "Bugler's not a murderer, but I'm short on suspects."

Wilton arrived at the booth with two plates of biscuits and gravy. Steam drifted up, testifying to their hot freshness. He held one plate with a rag, while the other balanced on the sleeve of his arm. His other hand clasped Carl's plate of bacon. Scott pulled the newspaper clipping back across the booth. He folded the page and stuffed it in his pocket.

Wilton slid the bacon plate in front of Carl before he set each man's biscuit plate before him. He smiled his usual toothy grin. "Back with you fellas' hen fruit platters fast as Jackie Robinson."

Scott watched Wilton race away, giving a suitable imitation of the Dodgers' rookie star. Indifferent to Marvin Wilton, Carl attended his breakfast. He scraped his knife across a gravy doused biscuit, cutting a chunk free. He speared it with his fork and took it in. Scott sprinkled some pepper over his gravy while he continued to worry about Bugler.

"Carl, if you hear anything else around the May Rooms about Ronnie Edwards, please let me know."

"You know I will." Carl pushed the plate of bacon toward Scott. "Take that stick a' bacon you're needing."

* * *

Scott knocked on the door of Janine's room. No rustling of covers, no scurrying for clothes, and most importantly, no cussing about being interrupted came in reply to his rapping. He engaged the knob and entered, finding what he expected – a partially clad Janine alone in her room.

"Come in," replied Janine without looking up and without realizing Scott had already done as she asked.

A petite, peroxide blond, Janine lay propped in her bed wearing yellow baby-doll pajamas. She puffed away on a cigarette held in a long ivory holder. In line with her profession but paradoxical to reason, she looked like a child pretending to be a glamor queen. She smiled with an innocence belying her situation. She wiggled herself against the headboard to sit up straight. In so doing, the movement allowed a breast to bounce out of her pajama top, revealing a portion of brown areola the size of a silver dollar.

"Hello there, Wyatt Scott." She broke a huge smile without sensing her exposed breast. "Sure wasn't expecting you." Her round eyes took him in while her smile deepened her dimples. "Taking a break from Paulette? I mean, I don't mind, but I'd hate to make her sore."

"It won't." Scott stepped to the bed. "She won't know. I asked Queena if I could talk to you; just talk. I want you to tell me everything you know about the baseball player, Ronnie Edwards."

A quizzical look drew across her face. "Why?"

"You had a row with him recently."

"Nothing different than a lot of johns. Why do you care?"

Scott paused, sizing up her expression and anticipating her reaction. "Someone murdered him. My friend has been accused of it, but I know he's not the guilty party."

Janine recoiled slightly. "Somebody killed that boy, huh?" She refocused. "You think I did it? I was mad at that dumb creep, sure. In this business, ya' get'em; creeps, jerks, assholes, even perverts."

"No, Janine. No, I don't think you killed him. You had him as a customer, and I need help to figure out who else ran in his world."

"He was just a john. Younger than most, dumber than most, but not mean or nasty." She raised her chin high, forcing her eyes to peer down to see Scott. "He wore cologne and kept himself clean."

"I see." Scott stepped away from Janine and her bed to grab the simple wooden chair against the wall. He dragged it back to her bedside and eased into it. "So, tell me about him. Everything you know."

Janine shifted, which made her exposed breast swing a little. She became aware that it had escaped confinement. Her jovial expression vanished, replaced by coquettishness. She tucked the rogue puppy back beneath her pajama top as nonchalantly as she might toss her hair back. Not a dust mite of embarrassment clung to her face, but her impish expression missed the mark with Wyatt.

"Janine, I need to know what he said and how he acted on your dates." Scott withheld any expression or comment, while his face articulated congeniality and politeness.

"I had a few appointments with the kid, is all." A circumspect stare acted as a postscript to her further elucidation.

"Appointments?" Scott drew the word out, emphasizing his sarcasm.

"Hey, bub. I don't make fun a' your *cases,* do I?" She clasped her arms across her chest before noting her cigarette holder. She rearranged her arms to slide it into her mouth for a long draw.

"Fair enough." Scott smiled and offered conciliatory eyes for a truce. "So, what went on between you and Ronnie Edwards?"

Blowing a long blast of smoke and pulling the holder to her side, Janine apparently accepted the truce. She scooched further up the headboard to get a better view of Scott. "First time was okay, but he talked on-and-on-and-on about baseball. Well, baseball and how great he played it." She took another draw through her long holder. As she wafted the smoke out, she relaxed her posture and dropped her free arm from her chest to the bed. "When it comes to our time, he rushes through like he's stealing' second. I barely had time to fake a groan. He pays, and I tell him he done great in the sack. Instead of rushing out and trotting down the stairs, he stays and tells me again how great a ballplayer he is. Again, he goes on, Joe DiMaggio this, Lou Gehrig that, Babe Ruth, and all. I have to walk him to the door, practically shove him out. I pat him on the head and say, sure, kid, you'll be great."

Scott grinned at the odd details of the young man's first visit. "When did this initial visit take place?" Scott reached inside his jacket for his notebook, thought better of it, and dropped his hands in his lap.

"May. I figure he's a one-timer. You know, most of us girls can tell." She peeked at Scott for confirmation.

Scott nodded to reassure Janine. "Not him, though. He was an exception. When did you play game two with him?"

"More than a week." Janine stared off. Apparently reconsidering her estimate, she amended the timing. "Ten days, maybe. Ball team might've been out of town." She looked back at Scott. "Queena said he asked for me. So, I work for a living, and I take him on again." She raised her hands. "I mean, done in six minutes, clean, grateful – just easy money."

"Sounds like you made a good impression."

Janine dropped her arms and shrugged. "Johns are fickle."

"And the next visit?" Scott left his question simple and open-ended.

"And...about the same. He enjoys himself a little longer. Not that I even got warmed up." Janine tilted her head down but lifted her eyes up, still looking at Scott. "You know..." She didn't quite blush, but she flickered in that direction.

"From what I've heard, he was no virgin."

Janine straightened and smirked. "He made a good impersonation of one."

Scott nodded. A brief grin slipped out as he considered her commentary on the subject. "Go on."

"He makes it in a little more often, then comes a break." Janine took a quick puff and exhaled toward the ceiling. "He visits a few more times, then he comes in all happy; giddy, even. He still talked about baseball. Talkin' how great a ballplayer he'd be, better than Guy Todd or Babe Ruth, or some other fellas."

Scott laughed out loud over Janine's misunderstanding of Edwards's reference to Ty Cobb, and her creative insertion of the watercolor painter, Guy Todd.

She giggled back, thinking the big joke was on Edwards.

"Yeah. I bet he thought he was as good as those guys." Driving back to his resolute task, he lost his grin and renewed his questioning. "After that, what went on with Ronnie Edwards?"

"Later in June, he strolled in arrogant and all like he owned me. I seen he was actin' different." She paused to tap her tobacco ash into her bedside ashtray. "I know he's doll dizzy, most payin' guys are, but somethin' ain't square this time." She watched Scott, gauging his interest in her story, or perhaps searching his face for gratitude. Either way, she sucked on her holder once more before exhaling the smoke and continuing. "Instead of wanting to get his weasel warmed, he tries to order off the *speci-al-ity* menu; says he knows about mature sex things now."

"I got it. He's not wanting the normal." Scott noted her discomfort and worked to ease Janine's concerns about the details.

"Yeah, Queena says we don't have to do funny stuff; just some gals do." She looked at Scott to make sure he understood. A subtle nod from Scott cleared the way. "I tell the kid... I tell'em, no dice. So, the little peckerwood ups and says, he don't need no whore." She cleared her throat before spinning on. "Tells me he has a real woman. I don't care, and I don't believe the kid. I figure any sharecropper wants to give it out free, why's he here askin' to pay for it?" Janine revealed a quizzical look, appealing for confirmation of her assessment.

"Did he say he learned the off-menu things from this woman?"

"Never said directly, but saying he knows more now has to be from some gal teaching him. With me, he barely knew what to do with the thing after it stood up."

"He give you any details about the woman? How old she was or what part of town she lived in?"

"Nothing like that. Not specific, not details or age, but I figure by his talk, she's older, and not just a year or two."

"Okay. Go on then. Just tell me what happened and what he said to you."

"The stupid kid tosses out his cockeyed story about havin' it regular now. Pretty sure he told me he got it regular from this married bimbo. I might've laughed a little; maybe more than a little." Janine smiled. As her memory rolled on, the smile dropped. "Then the little creep gets personal, sayin' I was *practice*, and this gal was a real woman. I told him, a *real woman* would know he needed a lot more practice." She interrupted her story to get out of bed and stand up. "You see, I'm a real woman, don't you?" She dared Scott more than she asked him.

"Surely I do, Janine."

"Yeah, you do." Her cigarette had burned perilously near the holder. She wet her thumb and index finger before plucking the stub out. "You're full grown, a man. You understand." She reached back and ditched it in the ashtray. "And another thing, true or not, I don't care for that term 'whore,' you know?"

Scott nodded. "He said it to your face?"

"He did! The bastard shit!" She paced around the room, purging her temper. Cooled off a little, she began again. "So maybe by now I'm screamin' at him a little. Half-dressed, the little turd starts to run off, not that he got any attention to his pecker, but he took up my time. A working girl only has so much time to sell, so anyway, I yell louder about paying up. He grabs his shoes and starts to leave in his socks, but when he opens the door, Carl is standing there." She cracked a little smile, evoking the scene.

"I've talked with Carl Jefferson. He painted the same scene and told me he didn't touch Ronnie Edwards because the kid didn't try him."

"No. For a second, I thought he might try Carl, but I guess he wasn't that dumb," related Janine.

"A wise decision by the kid regarding Carl." Scott stood. "That it?"

"He gave me ten dollars and slid by Carl. Since he paid, that was it."

"Thanks, Janine." Scott took a ten-dollar bill out of his wallet and placed it on her dresser.

"You don't have to do that. We didn't have no business." She smiled and dropped her head demurely. "Could, though, if you like."

"What would we tell Paulette? Besides, we conducted some business. You helped with my investigation." Scott winked at Janine and left.

CHAPTER 10

BALLPLAYERS AFTER LUNCH

Nineteen years after Nelson Rogers opened his buffeteria, Tulsans stood in lines stretching onto the sidewalk outside; on Thursdays, ordering his chicken-fried steak and gravy became a ritual. Inside Nelson's Buffeteria, beguiling scents of chicken and steak, ham and roast, pies and cakes, vegetables, rolls, and gravy hovered, allowing noses to tease tongues. The buffet service supported the tasty food variety with speed, aiding those with limited lunchtime. City workers, housewives with kids, bankers, lawyers, engineers, and dignitaries frequented Nelson's restaurant. This noontime, a P.I. and a police detective shared a two-man table.

Cleveland popped the last cut of breaded steak into his mouth before clearing his palate with a swig of coffee. "Okay, Scott, thanks for the meal." He regripped his cup with both hands. "First off, I have nothing on your old friend's murder charge. The whole shebang is county. They don't much like dealing with the Tulsa department and certainly not with the new detective from New York." Cleveland slouched a little, relaxing his posture and stretching his legs. "If by accident or luck, I hear anything on that front, I'll pass it on."

"You're welcome for lunch." For his part, Scott abandoned his last bite of fried steak and gravy. "I'll be grateful for any information you can give me, Art."

"Save your gratitude. I probably won't get a thing." Cleveland put down his cup and wriggled back, righting his sitting posture. "You know, I haven't been in Tulsa all that long, and I have more dead bodies and unsolved murder files on my desk than at any time during my New York City days." He lowered his eyes and stared at Scott. "The funny thing is, you are connected to all of them."

Scott started to speak, but Cleveland held up his hand to stop him. "First there's the crazy young gal you escorted at the charity ball who tried to throw herself off the roof. You get me to tag along without the details, but fine, I go. Then, it seems she killed two people for some Oklahoma Indian reason I don't quite understand. Then there are the two dead whores whose killer is yet to be apprehended; and there's their madam that you are protecting about something. I'm not sleeping well because of all that." Cleveland placed both hands behind his head. "And then there's good ol' Waldo Sleener – another mystery. His case brings me to the business part of this lunch and my show-and-tell."

Scott perked up. "And what did you find? I trust that it's worth the price I'm paying for this once-a-week special lunch."

"It was tasty, but you got a bargain. There are new things of interest." Cleveland pushed the dishes to the side before he grabbed a mystery paper bag he had carried to the lunch summit. He dropped the sack onto the table, opened it, and pulled some papers out. He handed

Scott a Rexall Drug calendar and some pamphlets. Pencil marks accented the calendar. Color print handouts, overstimulated with red ink, declared the value of workers and unabashedly displayed the hammer and sickle insignia of the Soviet Union.

"What do you make of that?" quizzed Cleveland.

Scott perused the pamphlets. Determined workers displayed their joyous exaltation in support of their party and red flag. A wrinkled brow betrayed his thoughts. "Sleener was a commie?"

"Looks like it. Why else would he have them?" Cleveland took the moment for a return to his coffee cup. He slurped the cooled, creamed coffee residue left.

"I wouldn't know a good reason." Scott transformed from serious to jocular. "Well, it expands your hunt for his killer to Mother Russia. Shouldn't take long to narrow it down."

Cleveland swept his mouth with his tongue. "No reason for a fellow traveler to do him in."

Scott abandoned the papers for the calendar. "This calendar has several days marked. Looks random. Mostly Thursdays, starting in March."

"Look ahead." Cleveland pointed out clear dates on the calendar. "Everything else is marked with just 'X's." He tapped it. "Nothing between July first and September thirtieth except that one date. Whatever it was, he won't be there for it." He sifted through the pamphlets as Scott discarded them.

"Yes. That odd date has a question mark scribbled on it." Scott flipped the piece over and over in his hands. "Mind if I talk with his sister about this?" He waved the calendar.

"Probably couldn't stop you. Keep me posted. I dealt with some pinkos in the city. They are as crafty as they are serious."

"Of course." Scott rolled the calendar and put it in his pocket. "It'll be some while before I do." He stood. "I have to clear Bugler of this ludicrous murder charge."

"Not yet," commanded Cleveland. "I know you want to help your friend, but I have a couple more things on my mind that you're going to hear."

Scott sat back down.

Detective Cleveland leveled a stony stare at Scott before he began. "In addition to all the murders swirling around you, I now have a prominent, popular radio personality missing. Would you know anything about that?"

Scott returned the stare. He paused for a moment as if thinking. "Unless it's some sports figure, I wouldn't know."

Cleveland pulled back. "You do not know?"

"No. So, who's missing?" asked Scott.

"Radio Joe from KTOO," stated Cleveland with a lilt, accenting the rhyme like the station promo for the show.

"Well, I'll be," declared Scott.

"You know the guy?" quizzed Cleveland with a note of anticipation in his voice.

"Heard his radio show. The music is okay, not top of my list."

"Ever meet him?"

"Can't say I have." Scott's poker face held firm.

"All right. Morgan was looking into you about him." Cleveland sighed. "Makes no sense. He's also looking into mobsters, bootleggers, jealous husbands, and if the guy skipped town with stolen money." Morgan's notions apparently not clicking with Cleveland, he threw his hands up.

"Well, I never could follow Morgan's logic," said Scott.

"He's not happy with your answers on things."

"He'll have to live with those answers. If he wants different ones, he'll need to look elsewhere for solutions."

Cleveland shrugged. "I don't know why Morgan has it in for you. Truth is, he'll try throwing anything and everything at you, hoping something will cause you pain."

Scott laced his fingers together. "Morgan being Morgan causes me pain."

"No matter. Just try to avoid people who might get murdered and perchance cooperate with us once in a while." Cleveland's pitch rose at the end, signaling a slight positive tone.

Scott stood. "I'll see what I can do." He glanced at the pamphlets still on the table and touched his pocket with the calendar. "Thanks for the Sleener info."

As Scott stepped away, Cleveland grabbed his arm. "And remember this: I don't owe you."

"Sure, Art. I got it."

* * *

The May Rooms played to thin afternoon crowds, the more so during the intense heat of summer. Scott's visit came in search of the names of the ballplayer companions who introduced the rookie to the brothel. The warning bell announcing his entrance greeted him. No girls occupied the main parlor. The oscillating fans distributed warm air across the room, and the white noise from them suppressed the echo of his steps on the wooden floor before the carpet eliminated the sound.

Scott paused on the carpet when he heard distinct high-heel footsteps. Queena Capps strolled into view in her blue pumps and a dressing robe that screamed faux kimono. She made her way toward him, surprisingly without a cigarette in hand. She glanced around the empty parlor. Scott couldn't tell if she was unhappy that no girls kept watch or preferred the lack of prying eyes and eavesdroppers.

"Odd time to work out your love muscle," said Queena.

Scott tossed her a quizzical look. "Love muscle?"

She narrowed her eyes and sharpened a stare. "Just trying to be a little classy, poetic even. I suppose it's wasted on you. Dip your prick fit you better, Scott?"

"No matter the euphemism, I'm looking for more information on the Edwards kid, not a quick lay."

"Hell, not even a paying customer." Queena shook her head. "Well, ask me, so you don't bother any of my girls."

Her tone rang harsher than usual. It surprised Scott. She had always been sarcastic, but never hostile toward him. Given their shared secret, with far worse repercussions possible for her, he wondered about her irritation, but he had more urgent business. "Okay. I'd like to know who brought the Edwards kid here the first time."

Miss Capps' sour expression did not waver. "Couple of other ballplayer nitwits. Tony Todd, who I call Toad because to me he looks like one, and Pat MacPherson are the culprits." She fished around in her dressing robe pocket but withdrew an empty hand. "Shit!" Her annoyance rose another level. "Sit your ass down somewhere. I need to get a new pack of butts." She spun and dashed to her office.

Scott ambled to a waiting area with a couch, a chair, and a coffee table. He chose the couch, knowing Queena's preference for a throne over shared seating. Wyatt met MacPherson for a minute last season. He was an outfielder who came to the Oilers in a trade the year before. His play was fair-to-middling but not up to Ronnie Edwards. His only knowledge of Todd stemmed from watching from the stands and some so-so reports on his play by Bugler. He calculated the best approach to two guys he didn't know would be finding more about them. Which gave him more reason to seek direction from Queena.

Queena's fresh pack of cigarettes and her Zippo lighter clacked when she dropped them on the coffee table. A coffin nail gripped between her lips and glowing from a fresh puff, the madam swayed more gracefully, and her face appeared more serine than on her departure. She took either a long, calming draw or a histrionic one and blew the smoke in Scott's direction. As he predicted, Queena took her place in the wingback chair.

"So, the toad guy jabbered like a kid in line to see Santa Claus. He stayed in that Edwards kid's ear during that first visit. A few girls mixed with those two and the MacPherson fellow. I think that's how Edwards started with Janine. Todd bounced around between girls, not sticking with one and not impressing any." A well-earned smoke signaled the completion of her testimony.

"Could you tell if Edwards was close enough to either to confide in them?"

"I wouldn't know. Janine was probably your best bet."

"She helped some, and I appreciated it."

"I heard you paid her." Another smoke and a cocked-head glare completed Queena's comment.

"I did. She deserved it, and you get your cut." Scott sized up the madam. "Why don't you tell me about the burr under your saddle?"

A stare straight out of the Los Alamos testing grounds burned into Scott. After a long moment, the madam curbed her radioactive glower to speak. "Paulette. You should stand up and tell her she's a whore and not your future bride." Straight to her point, Queena spat out the words with a coat of vitriol.

"I've never..."

"Not *about* you, Scott. The silly girl created a fantasy. Still, it's up to you to set her straight and let her get on with her life." Queena scolded Scott by shaking her cigarette hand at him.

The admonition struck him like a hammer on his bad elbow. Scott knew Polly had a crush on him. He just assumed working girls had them off and on with their regular johns. He didn't want to hurt her, but if she truly had notions of love, she needed those corrected.

"Is that why you're being so surly?" asked Scott.

"Surly, is it? You, of all people, know I take care of my girls. It is partly your fault. You act too nice. Whores aren't used to nice. Best that most can hope for is courteous and clean."

"You know I haven't been regular. Except to talk to Janine, I haven't been here or talked to you since we met in that alley."

"Don't know what alley you're talking about, Scott." She took solace in her cigarette.

"Okay, if you say so."

After her puff, she coughed, which engendered some hacking and rattling. When she settled down her lungs, Queena leaned forward and pierced Scott with both eyes. "Now, I'm going to finish explaining our world to you. Occasionally, a sad sack john falls for a girl, but the smart ones know he's too desperate to be any good in the long run. Less often, a working girl dreams up the guy she's been wanting. Down to earth gals like Janine know the score. But Polly thinks she's Cinderella and you're the prince. You need to show her you're just another frog with pleasant manners." Her lecture ended; Queena relaxed her face.

"I didn't realize her sentiments drifted that far. As soon as I get Bugler free, I'll tend to Polly." Scott stood up. "Look. You give me a little better rundown on these two guys, and I'll leave you and your girls alone."

Queena remained in her chair. "I understand you want to help your old buddy. It's not like I keep a book on the customers, especially the ten-buck ballplayers. Neither is married, so there's bupkis there. When Edwards got regular with Janine, he came alone. My honest opinion is you should fish at the ballpark, not the May Rooms."

"Guess I will. I'll visit the two ringleaders at the ballpark." Scott left the couch and walked toward the door. He halted with one foot on the hard floor and the other on the carpet. He gazed back at Queena. "Thanks." She nodded and smoked. He left.

* * *

Texas League Park baked like the rest of Tulsa. The grass kept somewhat green from the water poured on it, yet its color paled. The three outfield spots patrolled most regularly tended toward light brown and thin. A scattering of players caught fly balls hit by an assistant coach with a fungo bat. Wyatt Scott slipped unnoticed out of the empty stands along third base and swung into the dugout. He cornered Al Vincent at the end of the bench before the manager could make a run for his clubhouse office.

"Al, I need to talk to a few of the guys." Scott crowded the Oiler manager while smiling and adding as much ball club congeniality as he could muster,

"Scott! What the hell?" Vincent drew back until the wall stopped him. "Get out of my dugout."

"Calm down, Al. You know, if I have to, I'll call Ray and he'll tell you to let me see them. Let's make it easy, and you can keep control of your clubhouse." Scott backed up a step, allowing the manager to shift around and consider the suggestion.

"Scott, you're cleating my ankles!" Vincent composed himself. "Who the hell do you want to talk to this time?"

"I just need a few minutes with Todd and MacPherson."

"That's an odd pair to draw to." Vincent pulled his cap and scratched his noggin. "Why not? If it gets you off my diamond, sure." He worked his way to the edge of the dugout. He pointed to the outfield. "MacPherson is shagging flies. If you can wait a few minutes, he'll come in." Scanning foul line to foul line, Vincent squinted. "Todd must be in the clubhouse; most of the infielders are still in there."

"Thanks, Al." Scott patted Vincent on the back. "I'll duck into the clubhouse for Todd so as not to interrupt MacPherson in the outfield." He smiled and bolted through the dugout door to the clubhouse before Al Vincent moved a muscle.

The place looked normal despite the murder just days prior. Having never been close to Todd, Scott didn't know if he'd recognize him. His single Oiler friend, Tommy Warren, remained on the field, jogging with the pitchers. A trainer picking up pieces of tape and dirty towels caught Scott's attention.

"Say, can you point me toward Tony Todd?"

The man stopped, with a string of used tape dangling from one hand. "He's around the lockers." He pointed. "Some of the infielders are playing cards on a training table."

Scott nodded. He meandered through the benches and around one row and another set of lockers to enter a training area. Six men in Oiler uniforms stood encircling a long table meant for working on an injured ballplayer. Two seemed disinterested, while the other four studied playing cards arrayed for five-card stud.

"Tony Todd!" shouted Scott.

All six men looked his way. After a short pause, an Oiler player with a quizzical look and too much grease in his hair spoke up. "That's me."

"Can you step over here for a minute? I need to talk to you," said Scott.

"We're in the middle of a poker game." Todd pointed at his poker hand. "I got fifty cents in the hand, and live cards."

"I'll give you a dollar and you fold," offered Scott.

"It's a pretty good hand."

"Not so good since you told me out loud for the other guys to hear.

Besides, if you don't talk to me, I'll have to get Vincent and break up your game."

Todd glared at Scott. He swung his attention back to the card game. The others strayed from Scott to focus on Todd. After scanning their expressions, he mucked his cards. "I fold. Be back in a sec."

The card-playing infielder clomped toward Scott with his spikes grinding on the cement floor. Scott directed him toward the lockers by removing his hat and waving it in that direction. He needed to isolate Todd to keep the conversation private and uninhibited. Taciturn or a blabber, Wyatt needed to dig out what he knew about Edwards, including what he didn't know he knew.

Around the lockers and out of sight, Scott sat on a bench. "Tell me about Ronnie Edwards."

Todd stood looking down at Scott. His blank face suggested his thinking gears ground slowly. "So, who are you barging in the club-house?"

"Wyatt Scott."

"Okay. The old ballplayer who hangs around with the owner and the crazy old man in the stands."

"That's right. I know Ray Snider well enough that he allows me to come here and ask questions. So, tell me about Edwards."

"Besides, that the poor guy got murdered?" He shifted his weight from foot to foot. "What do you want?"

"You and Pat MacPherson took him to the May Rooms. I hear he moved on to a girlfriend rather than a pro. You better tell me what you know about that and who the girl is."

"May Rooms tattling on customers now?" Tony Todd glared at Scott.

"Not so's you'd have to worry. No one there cares about you, Todd. Just get back to what I asked."

"We started him there cause the kid complained about needin' sex so much that we just wanted to shut him up. Never seen a fella' so doll dizzy. We only took him twice. After that, he started seein' one whore regular."

"Janine, I've heard that part. What happened after he stopped going to the May Rooms?"

"I know nothing as a fact. The mouthy kid talked all the time about all kinds a' stuff. That also included more than we needed to hear about his love life."

"What did he say about his lovers? Did he mention any names?"

"No names. Hell, most of it was like we were ignorant, and he was educating us on sex and what you could do besides screw."

"If no names, any clues about who the lady is?"

"First sharecropper, right after he stopped going to the May Rooms, was older. He talked about that broad teaching him how to be a lover." Todd rolled his eyes. "Bragged about French kissing and nastier stuff like we never knew about women."

Unsure what to make of this revelation, Scott plowed ahead. "Other than older, any clues?"

"Hmmm." Todd pulled on his ear, then scratched it. "I think he claimed he loved on her better than her husband, so she must've been married."

"Let's try a new at bat." Scott twisted his head around before focusing back on Todd. "I heard he dumped the older woman for a younger one. What have you heard on that score?"

"He may have bragged about that too, but I tuned him out. I wasn't really his buddy. He talked more with the other outfielders. Ask MacPherson; he might know."

Scott realized this episode had played out. "Okay. Thanks, Todd." He reached into his pocket and pulled out a dollar bill. "Go back and win some money." He extended the bill.

The infielder grabbed the dollar and clacked his way returning to the other players. Scott stood to return to the dugout and the field. Before he made the door, Vincent trotted in. He looked at Scott but continued back toward the training table. A new batch of players shuffled in. Among them, Scott saw Pat MacPherson.

"Pat! Pat MacPherson." Scott waved his arm for the ballplayer to join him. "How have you been?" asked Scott as MacPherson veered from the gaggle of outfielders to approach him.

"Happy as a pig in mud. What are y'all up to, Wyatt Scott?" The young man offered his hand.

"Hello, Pat." Scott extended his hand, and they shook. MacPherson hailed from rural Georgia, and it took Wyatt more than a meeting or two with run-throughs to crack the man's homegrown code. "I'm asking around about Ronnie Edwards's killing."

"Oh." MacPherson's pleased veneer melted. "Nasty, bad business." He sighed and played with his ball glove. "Why are you poking around that patch? The law jailed your old, slow-minded pal." Signs of cognition swept across his face. "Oh, I see. You're lookin' to help the old geezer."

"I am." Scott sized up MacPherson concerning his possible prejudice against Bugler and how best to approach him for information. "My search is trying to learn more about Ronnie Edwards. I know you and

Todd brought him round to the May Rooms when he first got to town. I also know he graduated from frequenting Janine to an older, married woman. But what I really want to hear is the woman's name."

MacPherson drew back a little. Scott deduced that something clearly hit home. The young outfielder shifted and shuffled his feet. Scott waited, hoping the awkward silence might engender some sudden revelation of news.

"Yeah, we brung'em along to the May Rooms." A dollop of skepticism swirled in MacPherson's uneasiness. "I can't feature how that or who he dropped his drawers with has slop dash to do with his murder."

"It may not, but until I connect all the threads of his actions, I can't be sure what matters." Scott proffered an avuncular smile and spread his arm to a bench. "Just sit a minute and tell me what you know."

Having loosely held his glove in his left hand, MacPherson tossed it onto the bench. "I suppose I might could." He sat next to the glove.

Scott eased down on the bench, leaving ample room between himself and the ball glove, which added a further buffer. The card-playing infielders emerged from the back and paraded past, mumbling, grumbling, and chatting as they headed to the dugout. Coach Vincent followed, herding them like the bleating sheep he likely thought them to be.

"Umm...Edwards didn't tell me much." After the marching infielders cleared the clubhouse, MacPherson opened up. "He did jabber on a lot." MacPherson reached for his glove and toyed with the stitching. "He didn't spill his guts to me. I don't think he did to any of us. He spent too much time bragging and refining his stories. The kid was too big for his britches to make any friends."

"That tracks with what I've heard. What about the girls?"

The apparent comfort of his glove drew the young outfielder's other hand. His index finger outlined one of the three fingers. "I never heard the name. Rumor on Dodge's wife, but just rumor. Edwards bragged on his older skirt for some decent spell. He wore me slap out on it. Even got kinda' nasty talkin' about her quim." MacPherson sucked air through his teeth. He looked up to Scott. "I mean, who wants a recital of details on that!"

"Yeah. I heard Edwards was more brag than anything. Sounds like he didn't have much filter on his mouth either."

"You heard right on that score."

"I also heard Edwards threw over the older woman for a young girl. Pat, can you help me out with who that young dish might be?"

The outfielder dropped his gaze to his mitt once more. "I don't recall exactly when, not too awful far back, the fling with the older belle went cattywampus. He started running off about meeting up with a young cookie. I figured he met her at a diner, some waitress."

"He give her name or say the diner?" Scott jumped in, his impatience with ballplayers mounting.

"She wasn't a waitress." MacPherson eyed Scott. "I just figured that's where he might meet some dish. He was still pretty new to Tulsa, and he didn't spend that much time outside the ballpark. I know better now." He wet his lips and took a breath. "I didn't get her name. From his bragging, she's ginchy, rich, and she's no shy southern virgin."

"Okay." Scott mulled over the combination. "You think she might be a college girl at Tulsa University?"

"Got me on that. I couldn't guess where the hell he'd meet a college peach. Even if he met one all full of steam, why would that beauty spend time on a broke, dumb ballplayer when she could take up with a smart college boy?"

"A valid point, Pat." Scott cleared his throat. He almost spat the pesky phlegm but choked it down to keep up his questioning. "Anything else you recall Edwards bragged to you about this good-looking, younger skirt?"

"I never saw her, so it's all his say." MacPherson paused. "You know, I don't know where he went with her. He didn't mention movies or dancing."

"Sneaky again. Was this young skirt married?"

"Naw. Mayhap her folks didn't know about them. He was slippery about all of it."

"Any mention of parents or whereabouts she lived?"

The Oilers outfielder shook his head. "Not a snort in the wind."

Al Vincent clunked back into the clubhouse. He glared at Scott and MacPherson before continuing to the training room. "Infield looked like shit!" he yelled loud enough to be heard clear back at the lockers. "Get your dumbasses out for batting practice!"

The shouting manager disrupted the conversing pair. MacPherson peered past Scott to a gap in the lockers from where Al's voice emanated. From his position, Scott had to spin almost halfway around. The sound of Vincent's grinding cleats stopped as Scott completed his view of the manager wearing them.

Grumbling under his breath, he noted Scott's parley again. "B P for you too, MacPherson. You need it!"

MacPherson jumped up after the admonition. He slipped his glove on and punched the pocket. Scott nodded his acquiescence to the discussion's end. The outfielder blended into the flowing mass of his teammates. He halted and dished out a last nugget of information to Scott.

"Edwards told me he got all gussied up to go to Bishop's. That might be the date with the young babe." He caught the tail of the player stream and disappeared out of the locker room.

CHAPTER II

Bugler and the Dodges

Long afternoon shadows fell across downtown Tulsa, but none covered the sheriff's office or the Tulsa County jail. Inside, the comings and goings persisted at an average pace while the ceiling fans scattered the heat more than dissipated it. Wyatt Scott strode briskly through its halls and down the stairs to the jail cells. Recognized by the deputies, the door opened for Scott before he could ask. The guard led him to Bugler's cell, unlocked it, and slid open the door. Bugler sat on his lockup bed with his head buried in his palms. Even the sound of the door sliding did not rouse him from his despair.

"Bugler!" half-shouted Wyatt.

The old fellow jerked his hands down and grinned at the sight of his pal. "Wyatt, ya' come ta' get me outa' here?"

"Gonna' be a bit more time, I'm afraid." Scott stepped into the cell. The jailer slid the door shut. Scott stiffened at the sound. The deputy waved a hand as he sauntered away. Bugler watched the jailer's slow gait before refocusing on his pal. "Are they still treating you well, Eugene?" asked Scott.

"Yeah. Couple a' nice ones can talk baseball. Said they might be able to twist up the radio sounds so's I can hear it, but they ain't done that yet."

"I'll see what I can do about that."

"Wyatt..." Bugler interlocked his fingers in his lap. "...this place is awful at night. Fellas yell and screech. It ain't like my room."

"I know, Bugler. I'm working to get you out," assured Scott.

"Yer my pal. I figured ya' was." He pulled his earlobe. "Just not a good place stayin' in the pokey."

"Just hang on. You had it rougher in the army. Tents and mosquitoes in Cuba had to be worse than the Tulsa County lockup."

"That's a fact!" Bugler started a head nod rhythm that cycled through several bobs. "Skeeters were bad." The old man stared, presumably into the past rather than at the iron bars.

With the hope that he had eased some of Bugler's fears, Wyatt recommenced measuring Bugler's recollections of Ronnie Edwards. "I need to know some things, Eugene...um, Bugler. What was it you and Ronnie Edwards got into it about?"

"Shoulda' been nuttin' to it, Wyatt." Bugler broke his distant stare. "I was in the corner behind third base. Ball come his way. He caught it and threw to the pitcher." Bugler reenacted bits of the catch and throw. "I yelled at him to watch where he put his feet. He was throwin' flatfooted; plumb flatfooted, Wyatt. Any runner could move up 'cuz he plays off balance and cain't put no mustard on those long throws. His arm is danged good, one a' the best, but a throw needs that foot shovin' off to get speed."

"What did he say back to you?"

Bugler peered down. "He trotted over close to the seats an' tol' me he'd put a goldarn foot up my be-hind." A bit sheepishly, he looked up at Scott. "Only he gets vulgar and common with his words." Antediluvian sincerity emanated from every wrinkle and stubbly hair on the old man's face. "I tol' him cussin' old men won't improve his throwin' none, and he best learn how ta' throw the ball proper if ever he hopes ta' make it to the bigs."

"Where was Coach Vincent during all this?"

"Vincent? He's over in the dugout, I guess. Anyway, Edwards didn't care so much 'bout ball no more from his braggin' an' spoutin' off. As of lately, he kept claimin' he had a rich gal. He strutted more than usual. He went to given out orders like bein' a coach. Got on mouthing more an' more that besides being a great player he just might own a team to boot. None a' the players believed'em, far as I hear tell."

"Was Edwards serious when he went on about a rich gal?"

"Seemed like it. Had his nose in the air, but for his short time on the Oilers, he was more yarn than true life." Bugler scratched his chin. "Like I said, none of the fellas believed it. That boy was as big a' tall tale talker as the old fishermen when I was a young pup," Bugler sat up straight on the cell bunk. His face stiffened with conviction. "Not that I believed any a' his stories, but I tol' him just the same that he oughta' practice his long throws and keep away from all womens, gals, and their perfumes."

"Good advice for any player." Scott struggled with it before succeeding in keeping his grin inside.

"I try to give 'em my best, but they don't pay no never-mind to me,"

Bugler shook his head. "Now, that coach, he listens sometimes." A smile broke out. "Once that feller behind the plate, he kept callin' fer' all the wrong pitches and I says to him ..."

"I know this story, Bugler. I need to know more about the ruckus between you and Ronnie Edwards." Scott avoided being harsh, but he had to steer the conversation back to the business at hand and away from Bugler's twisting, snaking trail of memories.

"Yeah, Ronnie Edwards. *Jackass* Edwards is more like it. I just remembered. You figure what he had the gall to ask?" Bugler's eyes narrowed and his tongue pressed against the inside of his cheeks. "He asked me if I ever had a woman. And I told him it wern't none of his gol' darned business. That's what I told him. Then he said I probably tried one of them mules, an' that's why I got kicked in the head. Wyatt, you know I don't go in for that kinda' foul talk. An' I wouldn't ever do nuthin' what would embarrass my mother." Another distracted look presaged the coming of a story. "Some people's pretty disgraceful though. There was this fella in Cuba..."

"I heard that story too, Eugene."

"Sure ya' have; I forget who I told." Bugler nodded and found his way back to the current, proper story. "Well, anyway, Edwards uses some more awful language and says to me, he's gonna' see Ray and his daughter and get me throwed off the field. And I said, go right ahead, big man. Wyatt, I ain't ever been so cotton pickin' mad in my life."

"I don't doubt it, Eugene. Sounds like that kid had a small mind with a big mouth. Have you ever seen him with Ray's daughter?"

"Never seen no daughter. Ol' Ray only comes on special days or special games. Good owner as those kind go. Not sure I'd keep Vincent on if I was owner, but they's worse, I suppose. Ray's been nice ta' me though. Let's me sweep up and make a quarter after a game. He's a crackerjack of a fella. Even says, hi, Bugler, and all."

"Ray's all right for a rich man." Scott considered the millionaire for a moment before continuing with present matters. "Now you sit tight." Scott patted Bugler on the shoulder. "I have a couple more people to see. Then we'll get you out of here." He waved toward the jailer, who wasn't paying attention.

"Be real good ifn' you could get me out by game time." Bugler smiled, then wrinkled his brow. "Or get a radio brung in."

Scott chuckled at the request. "I'll do my best." He tapped the bars and addressed the deputy. "Jailer! Ready to go here."

The man responded like a tortoise on vacation. Scott watched patiently as the fellow executed his slow saunter toward the cell and clicked the lock with his key. He slid open the door, grunting like it weighed ten-thousand pounds. Scott tossed Bugler a final smile. He almost tossed a middle finger at the jailer but thought better for Bugler's sake.

* * *

Wyatt avoided the lobby, which continued accommodating reporters even as the larger crowd no longer congregated to share in the drama. He slipped through a side entrance; most often used for bringing prisoners to their cells. Before his eyes could adjust to the sunlight, Scott came face-to-face with Lieutenant Morgan. The Tulsa detective had his standard frown fixed for Scott.

"What are you doing at county, gumshoe?" Morgan took a step back, folded his arms across his chest, and upped his scowl a notch.

"Could ask you the same, Morgan." Wyatt stood his ground, questioning the detective with his expression.

"Difference is, I don't answer to you." Morgan dropped his arms to his sides. "You need to come clean about that dead Jap guy. I know you're not telling me everything, even if the damn FBI boys think you don't matter."

"I told them what I told you; I met Hiroshi Ishikawa in nineteen thirty-four and haven't heard from him since."

"Sure, you did." Morgan raised an arm and pointed his finger at Scott's face. "You lie with the best of them. I still think you know more about those dead whores, and I'm positive you know more about Queena Capps." He dropped the pointing finger but kept his scowl. "You better keep your Indian lawyer handy cause you'll need'em when I get the goods on you."

"Are you really mad at me, Morgan; or did those FBI suits piss you off stealing your case with their federal badges?"

"Damn FBI will go away. One more dead Jap, more or less, doesn't bother me. You being involved in every murder in Tulsa starches my shorts."

"You manufacture connections that don't exist. Ask Cleveland, he's checked into me too."

"You've only got him half-fooled. He's got questions same as me." Morgan hacked up a slug from his sinuses and spat it into a bush. "First chance I get, you'll be in a hard chair under a hot lamp."

Frustrated by the waste of time, Wyatt took an aggressive step toward Morgan. "I'm working. Whether you are too or just wasting taxpayer money, I am moving on."

"I heard about your old, loopy pal killing that kid baseball player. I suppose that's your work. Sounds like a waste of time from all accounts."

"You're so sure, tell me the details you've heard," countered Scott.

"It's county. I don't care. I know the call came into us. We turned it over to the sheriff. Word gets passed along the crazy old ballpark rat beat the kid's head in. City police have other problems. Me, I have a Wyatt Scott problem," Morgan snorted as emphasis to his last sentence.

"As usual, no help from Tulsa cops." Scott stepped past the petulant detective. "I'll solve it myself."

Morgan spun to claim the last word at Scott's back. "You do that. Check with that Indian lawyer before you run along to the May Rooms and see what old Queena wants you to do."

* * *

Late in the afternoon in an otherwise deserted locker room, Wyatt Scott lurked behind a set of lockers. The entrance sat oblique to his position. Squeaky hinges alerted him to an entrant. Frank Dodge ambled in, wearing a loose flowered shirt and khaki pants. Scott darted around the lockers and grabbed Dodge by his shirt, ruffling more than flowers. He jammed Dodge against the wall. With his nostrils flaring, eyes flaming, and fists forming, Scott squared Dodge up eye-to-eye.

"What is this horseshit you're shoveling about Bugler killing Ronnie Edwards?"

Dodge wiggled, but it seemed closer to a fidget than a struggle for freedom. "He was in here." The journeyman ballplayer avoided Scott's galvanic gaze. "Cops found him here too," added Dodge, seeking some combination of words that might secure his release.

"Sheriff's deputies didn't find you here." Scott's grasp harvested several printed flowers and stretched the shirt taut. "Why did you leave and then tell them you saw Bugler?" Scott held his grip and maintained his anger.

"Hell, Scott, I didn't know what to do. Never seen a dead guy before. When I heard they arrested Bugler, I thought I should tell what I saw." His eyes pleaded at Scott with drooping lids and fearful side glances.

"Okay. What did you see?" Scott eased his hold marginally. It remained firm and imposing. "No speculation. No, *what-it-seemed*. No, *anything* but exactly what you damn well saw!"

Dodge coughed. Pinned against the lockers with Scott in full control, he answered with downcast eyes and a timbre of dread, "Bugler holding a bat and looking down at Edwards."

Scott loosened his fingers. He dropped his hands and stepped back. Dodge exhaled his relief. He cleared his throat and straightened his collar. Perspiration watered the creased and wrinkled flowers on his shirt.

Continuing his glare at Dodge, Scott interrogated him further. "I want the facts. Did you witness Bugler hit Edwards?"

"No. I told the deputies that too." His expression pleaded for belief. "I told them I didn't actually see Bugler hit Edwards. What else they brought into it didn't come from anything to do with me." Dodge scrutinized the locker room, presumably for help. It remained empty. "I gave them what I saw – Bugler with the bat and Edwards beaten dead."

"You inferred it though, didn't you?" Scott's hard glare reemerged.

"No. Just said what I saw and left. The questions they asked, I answered, but mostly I said; 'I didn't see' and 'I don't know.'" He looked away from Scott, perhaps hoping for someone to intercede, or perhaps weary of Wyatt's censorious eyes.

"Not sure I buy that, but there's more to this. What were *you* doing back in the locker room that late?"

"I came to see Edwards. He took my starting spot." Dodge glanced around. "I wanted him to know I was okay with it. I'm drifting down the minors. He was headed for the bigs. Thought I might give him a couple of veteran pointers."

"Drifting? Dodge you're *falling* down the minors. And that big brother story doesn't hold water." Scott left Dodge like he would a bum with body odor and strolled toward the far lockers. "Hard to keep secrets around a ball team. You want to tell me the real reason you came to see Edwards?"

"I told you. I didn't have any hard feelings about being benched, and I wanted him to know I would help."

"That story is worse than your hitting." Scott strolled aggressively back to Dodge. "Locker rooms have eyes and ears. If *I* have heard about Helen and Ronnie Edwards, it's a down-the-middle cinch the entire team knows it... and so do you." Scott put the facts and rumors he'd collected into a gambit to trap Dodge. His stare defied the veteran to contradict his accusation.

"What are you saying?" Dodge stammered out his cowed reaction.

"Dodge, you came after Edwards because he took over more than your place in the Oiler lineup. He took over your place in Helen's bed. That's what I am saying!" Scott raised his voice one tick below an outright yell.

"You think my wife was having an affair with Ronnie Edwards?"

"No. I think you killed Ronnie Edwards because of the affair I *know* your wife and Edwards were having." His-volume lower, but his tone sharper, Scott made the indictment with the clear intent of unnerving Frank Dodge.

Dodge retreated at the accusation. "Look... old Bugler may or may not have killed Edwards. You dragging my wife through the mud won't help him."

Not continuing his denial about his wife's infidelity cemented its veracity to Scott. It also gave him license to press on. "She made the mud herself. I don't care what she did with Edwards. I do care that you're trying to pin the killing on Bugler. You have a motive; he doesn't. You were in the locker room just as much as he was."

"I didn't kill the kid!" Dodge shifted and panted like a hound in August.

"I think you did. Can't blame you if he was making time with your wife." Scott employed a calm tone, clear as a courtroom summation. "I blame you for allowing your vengeance to be answerable by an innocent old man."

"I'm telling you, man-to-man, ballplayer-to-ballplayer, I didn't kill the kid," implored Dodge.

"Well then, Mr. Ballplayer...," Scott moved back, leaned against a row of lockers, and relaxed his tense face before continuing. "...tell me what you were really going to say to Edwards - and not the crap in that alibi fantasy of yours."

"Okay! I planned to tell him to drop Helen." Frank Dodge hung his head and looked away from Scott. "If he dropped her, I thought she might finally give up trying to be a locker-room-Sally. He wasn't the first. Eventually, the young guys get shipped out, or I do. It's not like her flings end well."

"You say you never talked to him about it?" Scott folded his arms and projected as much skepticism as he had launched since he confronted Fielding about Brock's staged suicide.

"No." Dodge swallowed hard. "I swear I just saw Bugler there." He raised his arm with an open palm. "For all I know, some other player had a beef with Edwards. I wouldn't think anybody would kill him, but he was a stuck-up little prick."

"You didn't know he had already broken it off with Helen? Or that he was about to because he had a new girl — a young girl?"

"No." Puzzlement fell down his face. "How do you know that?"

"I know because that's my job." Scott sized up Dodge's apparent puzzlement. "Your wife didn't tell you he broke it off?"

"You think my wife tells me about her boyfriends?" Consternation crossed with bafflement in Dodge's reply.

"Since it seems to be her hobby, I thought perhaps she shared it with you."

Dodge glared; for the first time showing more anger than fear. "Maybe if you had a woman, Scott, you might understand. She acts like it doesn't happen, and I pretend I don't know. Sad choices for us both."

"Your choices are your own, but I think you know a lot. You had better go back to county and tell the sheriff the truth about Edwards. If you don't, I will elaborate on your wife's cheating and give them a story about how you're the jealous husband and likely killer."

"Okay, Scott. I'll talk to Helen when she gets back from shopping. I'll figure out something to tell the sheriff that leaves her out of it."

"Not so sure you can leave her out of it. Where's she shopping?"

"Seidenbachs, I think. She wanted a purse or something."

Scott stepped next to Dodge. "You two better come up with some suspects or her name will be in it, and you'll be the one in jail." One last glare of disdain, and Scott marched out of the locker room.

* * *

Wyatt Scott leaned on a no-armed bandit, as he called the city's nickel and dime collectors for parking, outside the Seidenbachs front entrance. Seidenbachs department store remained a Tulsa essential. It survived the shortages of the war and transformed itself to become a wealth of options for clothing and home goods. On the occasions when Wyatt opted for a clothing store, it did not make his list. They catered to lady shoppers, and he tended toward tailored suits when he had the cash or smaller men's stores rather than the broad-spectrum retailers.

Catching his attention, a burst of shoppers emerged from the store. He pushed off the parking meter to inspect the faces in the throng. Helen Dodge did not appear among them. Scott's memory of her appearance might've been cursory, but it proved to be fresh enough to eliminate those in this first flood. He reposed once more with an arm propped on the city's meter. A few minutes passed with businessmen, moms with children, lady pairs, and individuals filing down the sidewalk with no one entering or leaving Seidenbachs. Just after a pregnant woman walked through the glass doors, a pair of dawdling gray-haired ladies coasted out, followed by a single, hastening woman that he confirmed to be the one he sought.

"Helen Dodge!" yelled Scott as he abandoned his leaning post to confront the other member of the odd marriage.

Mrs. Dodge responded to the voice that had called her name. "What are you after this time?" She hauled the Seidenbachs store bag from her side to hold it in front of her chest and glared over its top at Scott.

"Some truthful answers," declared Scott.

"You are annoying. That is the truth." Smugness poured from her lips like water from an open fire hydrant.

"So's the fact that you were bed-buddies with Ronnie Edwards."

"I'm a married woman!" rebutted Mrs. Dodge.

"That stopped you where? Not in Mobile or Shreveport." Scott sharpened his already piercing stare. "You can move to a new town, but your reputation gets shipped along just the same as your furniture."

She dropped the bag back to waist level. "You know nothing about me or Frank. We do just fine."

"That is a laugh. I don't believe that now or ever."

Her eyes narrowed, and she took an aggressive step toward him. "What the hell are you up to?"

"I want some answers that are true and complete." Scott took his own step, narrowing their separation. "Did Frank find out you were bedroom wrestling with Ronnie Edwards?"

"I shouldn't dignify that with an answer. Crawl back in the sewer where all you investigator shitheads belong!"

"I'll ask again—Did Frank confront you about Ronnie Edwards?"

"Frank has never said anything about Ronnie Edwards or anyone else." Helen Dodge glared, leaned forward, and sniffed like a she-wolf sizing up her adversary.

"He didn't catch you or hear it from Edwards?" grilled Scott.

Mrs. Dodge surveyed the street to see who might stroll from either direction. She glared at Scott before pivoting to take in the Seidenbachs' doors. No one came out, and the pedestrians on the sidewalk seemed far out of earshot. "Frank has never wanted to know *things*."

"So, you admit you were having a go with Ronnie Edwards." Scott jumped on her oblique confession.

"What I do is nobody's business, least of all a nosy fool like you."

"Other than Frank, it wasn't much of a secret around the team." Scott pushed harder to make Helen Dodge flinch. "Maybe you got sloppy about being discreet. Or perhaps you wanted to get caught and show off your young lover."

"Maybe you're a jackass poking 'round in folks' private lives." She showed no sign of backing down. Her sharp features matched her choice of words. "Scum chasing and window peeping is a nasty way to make a living, but it suits your filthy mind, I guess."

"I just want to find the kid's killer. Don't you want that?" Far too much sarcasm drifted out with Scott's question, but too late to retrieve the words or the tone, he owned them.

"It's that brain addled old man, according to the papers and what the cops told Frank." The intensity of her glare waned even as her sneer deepened.

"You got that backwards, lady. Frank told the cops it was Bugler. Said he saw him there at the ballpark late."

"He did, huh?"

"I suppose Frank didn't mention any of that to you?"

"Frank being at the ballpark early or late is not news. He doesn't tell me every time he's there."

"That makes it easier for you to hop around, but that's not the point." Scott shifted his feet and squared up to stare down at her. "You don't think possibly Frank killed your lover boy?"

"Frank's not the jealous type. He just wants to play ball, not that he's any good now days, but he'll plug along till no team will take him." Mrs. Dodge remained cool, bottom of the lake cool. Except for the slight pull of her package, nothing seemed to bear on her.

Not breaking her at all, Scott dropped his cards on Helen Dodge. "Jealous type or not, I think Frank killed the kid. It's the only way it plays out."

"Look, you for-hire flatfoot, you better face it; that crazy old coot beat Ronnie down then pounded him to death." She glanced down the street and back at Scott. "Now, I'm going. You're staying. End of story."

Helen Dodge stormed off down the sidewalk, obliging others to veer lest she collide into them. Scott watched a moment as she barreled between two elderly women, forcing them apart. He flicked the sweat from his forehead more from frustration than heat. Getting Bugler out of jail didn't seem any closer. The more he learned about Ronnie Edwards, the wider the playing field grew. The kid's batting average and fielding percentage were the only verifiable facts.

CHAPTER 12

MIKE AT THE LAKE, EVIE AT THE OFFICE

The early morning sun tormented Scott's eyes as he drove straight for it. The LaSalle clipped along State Highway Twenty after leaving Sixty-six at Claremore. Scott was meeting former Tulsa police detective Mike Barton at a marina near Disney. Wyatt agreed to fish with him while they discussed Bugler's problem and the murder of Ronnie Edwards. Mike and his wife, Maddie, had been close friendships with Scott's parents, and Wyatt held both in high esteem. He thought the retired detective to be the sharpest cop he knew, so he seized the chance to pick his brain, even bobbing in a boat.

His path along the two-lane highway had a farm truck heading west and oncoming in the opposite lane from his Caddy, but otherwise clear to the next hill. A glance in the rearview mirror showed a dark sedan at a distance behind. From the mirror, Wyatt checked his gas; the gage threatened to peg left on empty. Having passed Spavinaw, he'd need to catch a filling station before Disney.

At the junction east to Jay or north to Disney, a road sign claimed gas two miles. Wyatt took the detour east toward Jay to fill up. While the pump jockey ran ethyl into his tank, Scott noticed the sedan had pulled over just beyond the station. He couldn't make out the tag, but its color declared out-of-state.

His gas tank filled, Scott paid and pulled up to the highway. He waited, watching a car pass going east. The parked sedan started and pulled onto the road. Wyatt whipped a left, heading west back to the junction to complete his journey to the marina in Disney. The sun in his mirror almost washed out the pickup truck that came from the east, and behind it, the sedan making a U-turn.

* * *

Wyatt sat in the small boat as it drifted around a dead tree poking above the water, where Mike Barton claimed a lunker bass hid from him. The former Tulsa police lieutenant had insisted Wyatt fish with him while they ruminated about Bugler and the Ronnie Edwards murder. Barton stared at the decoy bait like a failed colleague as he dragged its empty hooks to the boat; the phantom bass having eluded his enticement once more.

"I know that S-O-B is around here," claimed the frustrated angler.

He swung his empty line above the boat and grabbed the leader that held the silver spoon with its veiled hooks. Scott watched Mike fix the lure on one of the guides and slide his pole along the inside of the boat. Taking the action as a signal, Wyatt slowly reeled in his empty line and secured his fishing pole.

"Thanks for letting me ponder things in my odd way. Casting and reeling grounds my body while I think." Mike Barton began his judgment by scratching his ear. "The rage of the murder gives a distinct clue. The best motive points to that Dodge fellow you told me about. Jealous, cuckold husband makes for a good suspect—obvious motive."

"I just didn't see it in his eyes, Mike. You're a much better detective than I am; tell me what I'm missing."

"Wyatt, a good detective builds a case with his brain. Still, he never ignores his gut. How did this guy act when you talked to him?"

"He squirmed, but it didn't seem like fear or guilt. I just figured it was a lot to tell another man that his wife cheats and has for years, but he still stands by her."

"Mmm hmmm." Mike unlatched the steel straps that secured his ice chest; a plume of carbon dioxide formed a tiny cloud that drifted out of the boat and skirted the lake surface.

"Dry ice like my dad used," remarked Wyatt.

"Sure." Barton pulled out a bottle. "We both hated that water mess from ice." Barton popped the cap with the bottle end of a church key and stretched the beer to Wyatt. "Like a Falstaff?"

"Thanks." Scott took the bottle and swigged.

"What did you make of the cheat wife?" Barton pulled another beer out of the chest.

"Pretty nasty dame, that one. After a short minute of denial, she painted Dodge to be a longtime cuckold who let her affairs slide. Hard to figure why they stay together."

Mike opened the beer but didn't drink. "Doesn't get you any further. This affair could've been his breaking point." He took a long pull on his beer. "You know Ray Snider; did you ask him about this?"

"Yes. Claimed he didn't care what the ballplayers did off the field."

"Bet he would if the thing ran deeper." Barton sipped his beer and studied the placid lake. "You mentioned the kid might have moved on to a younger girl. Some promise in that. No name, I suppose."

"Details on the young girl are vague. I'm still searching on that rumor."

"Might be a younger player's girlfriend. Could be a local Tulsa gal with a jealous boyfriend." Barton tipped the bottle high and chugged. He finished with a new thought. "Husbands and boyfriends make the best suspects, but a dad blowing his top over a guy using his daughter fits too. If I had a little girl, who got used by some baseball Casanova, I'd be near the head of the line to let him have it."

"I'll keep going after the young girl." Scott took a swallow of the sudsy, normal beer that remained illegal in Oklahoma. "Awful brutal murder; took a lot of rage."

"It did," agreed Barton. "Logic says Frank Dodge. More than a case or two in my time where logic was wrong, though." Barton opened his cooler, tossed the empty in, and grabbed a fresh bottle. "I had a few murders where the wife killed the husband: a couple from jealousy." He grabbed the church key and pried off the cap. "Young girl killer is unlikely, but anything is possible with human beings."

"I plan to push harder at the players checking for her identity, but I'd be looking at boyfriends more than her."

"You know the ballpark gang much better than me. Keep an open mind; not just for new suspects but about Dodge." Sweat dripped down Mike's face even though the morning sun remained over two hours short of its noon peak. "Despite your gut, he's still the most likely."

Scott wiped his own brow, finding a thin coat on his forehead. "I could talk to Vincent again to see if he's shading me about other players." He tapped a finger on his bottle. "Beyond that, I guess you've convinced me to make one more run at Frank Dodge. If for no other reason than to give him a chance to bungle retelling his story."

"You've got a good head on your shoulders. Annoy as many suspects as you can. Somebody will trip up. They always do." Barton opened his cooler once more.

"I appreciate your thoughts, Mike. It helps to run it all by someone else." Scott sighed and smiled at his old family friend. "And I guess I needed a little encouragement too. I worry that I'll fail Bugler."

"You'll get it. No need for encouragement, you're a pro now; a smart one to boot."

"A frustrated one, but thanks, Mike. I'll nag the whole ball team till I get what I need."

"Check that chippy wife too. She knew the kid as well as anyone if they had that much bedtime." Barton reached into his cooler and pulled out two sandwiches. He flung one at Scott. "No sense waiting for noon. We'll eat a ham sandwich and head back."

* * *

Evie Hall leaned against the outer doorway of the Grayhawk law office. Alone as Johnny pled a case in court and Wyatt Scott trailed off to Grand Lake trying to get ideas on how to exonerate Bugler, Evie perused the second-floor landing. She imagined the cornucopia of visitors she had processed in her eighteen months on the job. She had seen dozens of humdrum nobodies, but the crazy young heiress and the sharp-witted whorehouse madam etched her memory deep. The dull emptiness of the building gave way to an intruder disrupting her reminiscence. Evie sized up the young woman as she scaled the steps to the second-floor landing. She noted the girl's fashionable, expensive outfit, the likes of which she hadn't seen when window-wishing even in Miss Jackson's pricey display.

"Can I help you, miss?" inquired Evie.

As the girl ascended the last step to the Pythian Building's mezzanine, her baby-faced features reached Evie. The teenage interloper glanced toward Evie and dismissed her before trying Wyatt Scott's closed door. She jiggled the knob; finding the door locked, the girl spun back to Evie. "Is Mr. Scott in? I really need to see him."

"No, he's not, and I don't know when he'll be back," replied Evie with more than a cupful of snark in her tone.

"Oh, damn it!" The girl's features offered a meek apology before she withdrew it. "I mean, I saw him with Daddy yesterday at our house and thought..." She cut her sentence off, then began pacing in front of Scott's office door. She eyeballed Evie while continuing her pacing. The girl retried the knob; it remained locked. She dropped her hands in frustration while staring down at the intransigent apparatus. She peeked over her shoulder at Evie. Her eyes, if not her lips, petitioned for help.

"Okay, kid, what's wrong?" asked Evie, dropping her critical tone for a soothing, sisterly one.

She turned around and took three hesitant steps toward Evie, then blurted out, "I think my father killed my boyfriend."

"Wowzer." Evie pulled a double take any comic would've been proud to offer. "What's your situation, little sister?"

The teen replied, "My name is Amanda. I go to Holland Hall. I'm going to be a senior."

"Tell you what, Amanda, let's me and you go to Mr. Scott's office and sort this out. You know, woman to woman." Evie ducked back into her office and grabbed Scott's office key from her desk drawer. She picked up her pad and a sharp pencil as well.

Evie Hall unlocked Scott's door and escorted Amanda in. Unsure of her next move, Evie focused on Scott's chair. She paused, considering the implications before judging herself fit for the role. Evie sat in Wyatt's chair and scooted it close against the desk. She placed her pad and pencil at the ready, then signaled Amanda to sit opposite in the guest chair. The young woman sat as directed, but with charm school correctness hitherto unseen in Scott's office.

"My name is Evie Hall. Among other things, I'm Mr. Scott's assistant." Evie straightened some papers from force of habit and moved them to the side. "I help him with his cases. Talking to me is just like talking to him, and I will communicate everything to him; everything you want me to, that is." Evie conveyed an understanding smile. "Is that okay with you?"

The young woman nodded, fidgeted, shifted around in the chair, and nodded again.

"So, Amanda, what's your last name?" Evie took her pencil in hand.

"Snider. Amanda Snider." She squirmed once more. "My dad is a businessman," she added.

"Snider, as in the awfully rich Snider outfit?" Evie squirmed a little this time.

"I guess so. My dad owns lots of things, lots of businesses." She took a breath. "And I suppose we have oodles of money."

Evie whistled and shook her head. "Okay. So, Daddy is ol' man Snider. That is something."

A quick reddening of her complexion signaled Miss Snider's embarrassment over her wealthy lineage. It continued as she dropped her head before answering. "He is, yes. He is my dad."

Evie snapped back from her surprise to conduct what she calculated a professional interview to be. "What about this boyfriend, and why would your pop kill him?"

"Well, he was killed at the ballpark." Amanda looked back up. "You know my dad owns the Oilers baseball team."

Evie nodded. "Yes. I wouldn't know all the things he owns, but that one I do." She smirked and added a further explanation. "Baseball talk fills these offices."

"Okay, good. Well, my boyfriend, Ronnie played for the Tulsa Oilers baseball team..."

"Ronnie Edwards!?" Stunned by the name, Evie broke her pencil lead.

"Yes."

"Dang! This is more than a nickel's worth." Evie tapped the desk as she thought. "Besides the kid being a ballplayer, and your pop the owner, what makes you think it was him that killed Ronnie Edwards?"

"Ronnie and I had been seeing each other." Miss Snider dropped her head and stared into her lap.

"Okay. So, you met a young ballplayer at the ballpark. It happens."

"I met him shopping downtown. He was in the ladies' department at Renberg's. He asked me, what a grownup woman might like."

"Shoppin' for his mom then."

"No. He didn't say who, but we were in lingerie—nobody buys lingerie for his mom." Miss Snider peeked at Evie for confirmation.

"Natch, they wouldn't." Evie scratched her head. "You think this booger was on active duty or just doll dizzy?"

"What?" Amanda Snider gave Evie a dirty look. "He never bought anything, and I don't know who he was seeing before me."

"All right. Keep going."

"Well..." Amanda took a breath. "... anyway, I liked him right off. He looked kinda' cute and had nice muscles. I told him to meet me at Bishop's for lunch." She grinned at the thought. "He said he couldn't afford it. I told him I could."

"Got the background." Evie crossed her arms, pencil still in hand. "So, you take up with the baseball hunk and see him on the sly while ol' Pops doesn't know."

"Yes. Daddy would blow his top about me and a ballplayer."

Evie dropped her hands back onto the desk. "So, Daddy is some hairy fuddy-duddy." Evie continued trading slang with her generational cohort. "Daddy doesn't want you seeing someone outside your social standing; that the story?"

"Yes, and more too. He has people that work for him." Amanda rubbed her hands. "At first, I thought he hired Mr. Scott to spy on me."

"That's why you came here to see if Wyatt was a private peeper for your dad?" Evie bit the eraser end of her pencil as she processed the situation.

"No. I know he isn't. When he came to our house, he said he was looking into Ronnie's death. After that, I thought I needed to tell him I was worried about my dad being involved."

"So, did dad spy on you with another detective, find you're smooching the dreamboat ballplayer, and flip his wig?"

"I'm not sure. He could've. I worry he found out about Ronnie and me. He just knows stuff and could be wise."

"So, his spy tells him you date a ballplayer on the sly. He doesn't like it, but what's to make him dust off the kid?" asked Evie.

"You know." Amanda looked down. She wiggled her feet. Her shyness faded, being replaced with teenage aplomb. She peered back up at Evie. "You know, we were *together*."

Evie sat up straight in her chair and cocked her head. "You did the actual deed?" Shock leaked out of both sides of her mouth and through her nose with a tiny snort. She placed her pencil on the desk. She peered back at Amanda. "All four bases – a little loose for a high school kid."

Opting to take offense, Miss Snider reacted with a head jerk and squinting eyes. "Not every gal is a cold-fish secretary."

Evie met the squinty stare with a glare from her own squinting eyes. "And Khaki-wacky will get you in trouble. So, tell me; are you PG?"

"No!" Amanda's hot stare cooled. "He wore a thing."

"So, he was prepared." Evie glanced away to think before recasting her eyes on her high school client. "Then he didn't force you or coerce you into giving it up?"

Amanda laughed. "I've been to college parties. I've been to Europe. A baby is the last thing I want. I had the thing in my purse." Any embarrassment or hesitation had left Amanda. She waited matter-of-factly for Evie to reply.

Evie opened her eyes wide and tried to scribble a note with the stubby point of her broken pencil. "You're a very modern girl." Evie looked back up. "Except when it comes to Daddy."

"He wouldn't understand. He is old-fashioned about me."

"And howdy, I guess. You think he found out about you and Ronnie Edwards playing house and killed him over it, right?" Newly minted detective Evie Hall worked her theory.

"He has a temper... and he thinks I'm ten," groused Amanda.

"Seventeen, ya' got the goods, all right, if not the brains to protect them." Evie leaned back in Scott's chair. "So, where was your father when Ronnie Edwards got killed?"

"He left me at the house with a few of my girlfriends. Said he was going out with friends, but how could I know if he did or not." Worry replaced the bravado she had been wearing.

"What time was that?" quizzed Evie.

"About six-fifteen. Way before dark."

Evie gave up on her broken pencil and ran her hand through Scott's middle drawer for a writing implement. She fished out a mechanical pencil that had its lead showing. She tested it on her pad. Satisfied with the graphite scratches, she wrote a quick note and looked back at Amanda. "Had he been home all day?"

"Aaaalll day." Amanda rolled her eyes at the memory. "He drives me whacky sometimes. It's why I invited Becky and Diane over. Somebody besides him to talk to. As if I care about baseball or some business thing in Texas."

"Men seem to love baseball," mused Evie.

"I suppose. But sometimes it would be nice if he and I could go to a movie or the zoo instead of Texas League Park." Miss Snider twisted her head, looking all about the office. She landed back on Evie. "He wouldn't be caught dead at the Coney Islander, but he has me eat nasty hotdogs with him at the ballpark. That's dippy."

"You have a different playground than most of us, so I can't figure." Evie twirled the mechanical pencil. "Where's mom in all this?"

"She goes shopping in places you have to fly to. She doesn't stay home much. If she's in town, she's at Southern Hills Country Club or lunch at Bishop's."

"Does she know you're on active duty?"

"She doesn't ask...probably only care if I show up PG."

"Poor little rich girl," opined Evie.

"What do you mean by that?" jabbed Amanda more than asked.

"Don't get your skirt twisted. Your daddy didn't kill anybody, at least not Ron Edwards. He was home with you. You can alibi each other," explained Evie.

"But I just said..."

"I know what you *said*." Her best impersonation of Scott, the cynic, blended with her resentment of rich girls. "Honey, when it comes to cops, comes to lawyers, it'll get worked out even if he did do it or if you did it."

"I didn't want Ronnie to get hurt, let alone killed. If my daddy...." Amanda's lips quivered. Her eyes filled. She flickered her eyelids; one tear slipped out and ran down her cheek.

Unsure how to react to the emotion, Evie reiterated her assurance. "I told you, even if he did it, he'll get out of it." Evie stood. "Kid, you and your father will be fine."

"You think so?" With the single tear streak and pursed lips, Amanda Snider looked less worldly and more like the teenager she was.

"Sure. Think about it. No matter how bleeped-off he got, rich, grown men don't beat young guys to death. They have better options."

Evie stepped from behind the desk. She reached Amanda and draped an arm around her shoulder. Amanda pushed herself up from the chair. She smeared her tiny tear with her index finger and offered Evie a half-smile. The meeting concluded; Amanda moved toward the door. Evie followed.

"I'll tell Mr. Scott about your fears."

Amanda opened the door, halted, and peered at Evie with wide, suppliant eyes. "Okay. Thanks."

"You can trust him. The guy is really smart, not like cops." Evie held her gaze on Amanda. "Mr. Scott knows your dad too. Once he gets going, he'll dig out the truth on the whole thing."

"Don't let him tell my dad anything," pleaded Amanda as she held tight in the doorway.

"Wyatt Scott is a professional. He'll be as discreet as this mess will allow." Evie reached to stroke Amanda's shoulder but retrieved her hand before it made contact. "You just don't let that worry you."

"If you say so." Miss Snider offered one more worried frown before she veered away and sidled toward the stairs.

"I do. I do say so," reassured Evie. "It will be fine." Evie stood tall in the doorway as she continued. "You have it made in the shade, kid."

Amanda halted two steps down. "What?" She looked back with a quizzical look. "How can you be so sure?"

"Kiddo, you have cash fallin' out of trees. You'll be going off to a fancy girls' school; meet new rich kids." Evie smiled and shook her head. "Then marry rich. Raise a house full of rich kids. Likely die rich." Evie paused. Amanda kept her puzzled expression and made no comment. "I like nice things, but not sure if I want to be rich," opined Evie as she peered down at Amanda.

With her face still registering blank and nothing further to say, Amanda turned and trod down the steps. She paused for a moment at the bottom of the stairs. Without further comment, Amanda Snider pushed on through the first-floor lobby and out of the Pythian Building.

"Sorry, little rich girl, my money says your daddy did do it." Evie shook her head. "Yeah, not sure I want to be rich," she mumbled. "And then, I don't have your *experience* either."

CHAPTER 13

SCREWBALLS AND WILD PITCHES

The Dodges' apartment building stood five stories high with two interior stairways. Having visited before and knowing the layout, Scott took the west one, which ran closest to their second-floor apartment. He pushed the bell, hearing its muted response through the door. Unsure whether he would confront Frank Dodge or his bitchy mate, Scott pondered his approach to each. If she answered, asking her for Frank's whereabouts would get him nowhere. He figured he would just ask her to pass his visit on to Frank and leave brandishing the best false smile he could manage.

He engaged the bell a second time with a quick jab of his thumb. If Frank showed, he decided on taking a milder, understanding approach hoping he might respond. Wyatt worried Dodge might be telling the truth and didn't know anything other than stumbling on Bugler. In that case, he had to hope a new angle would emerge where Dodge confided information he didn't previously recall. Or perhaps Dodge would bring forth something he thought unimportant but would be helpful after all.

As his index finger reached for the button and a third ring, the doorknob rattled. It gyrated. The door swung open. Frank Dodge stood for a moment. He slumped his shoulders before retreating into his living room. Scott followed through the entryway.

"What the hell do you want now, Scott?" Dodge complained and shook his head with his back remaining toward Scott.

"Frank, I just want to talk." Scott closed the door. He stopped a few feet short of Dodge and continued addressing his back. "If you could give me more details of that night or tell me anything about locker room talk, I might make sense of it. Bugler is just too simple to murder someone."

Dodge rotated toward Scott. "I've told you all that I saw and all that I will. Now, get the hell out of my apartment!"

"I get you're sore. But a man's life is at stake. Seeing Bugler with the bat just means he picked it up." Scott calmed himself. "Please, just think. Did you see anything else when you came back to the club-house?"

"The place was empty except for Bugler and blood all over." Dodge's head sank. "And dead Edwards."

"Anyone outside? Any new cars that didn't belong?"

Dodge stumbled a little, then stepped deeper into his apartment. He glanced around. His eyes drifted everywhere except toward Scott. He coughed. "No." He stared down at his feet, then cleared his throat and coughed again. Melancholy blanched his face, while something more happened behind his eyes.

Scott shuffled his feet, following Dodge. "How about locker room gossip? Was there talk about Ronnie Edwards with any girlfriends or women other than Helen?"

"I didn't bother to listen. Besides, I was the gossip." Dodge stood next to his couch. His knees bent, ready to sit, but they straightened. "The only people that had words with Edwards were Bugler and Ray Snider. The Oiler guys thought he was a bragging windbag, but nobody had it in for him."

With some success and a nugget out of Dodge, Scott followed on. "What words did Ray Snider have with the Edwards kid?" Scott crossed his arms. He squinted at Dodge as he waited.

The journeyman ballplayer began pacing. He glanced at Scott. "I can't say exactly. I didn't hear the main conversation, just Snider cussing the kid about something."

"What did you actually hear?"

"He said: 'Damn it, Edwards, you can't do that!'" Dodge held up a hand. "I didn't hear enough to know what Mr. Snider meant. He was plenty sore, though."

"Okay, Frank. Thanks for that. I will check on it." Scott nodded his affirmation as he spoke.

Scott strolled as he thought. The pair now paced at odds, like two stray dogs sizing up each other's intentions. Scott halted. He watched Dodge wear out the carpet near the sofa. He couldn't figure where Dodge's thoughts were, but Scott knew he had to dig there.

"I still need to understand Helen with Edwards and what you were doing."

Dodge stiffened. He bared gritting incisors. "You think I'm happy with all this?" He shuffled to the couch and fell onto it like a Raggedy Andy doll.

Scott edged close to an armchair. He surveyed Dodge's drained face. Scott saw frustration, sadness, and worry, but not the guilt of murder.

Dodge stared across the room. He blinked several times before he swiveled to view Scott. "I don't know nuthin' but baseball." He sucked air through his front teeth. "I gave up trying to figure Helen out years ago. Seems worse now." He exhaled. "She tried to redo her life by latching onto young ballplayers. It hasn't worked for her any better than me bumming around the minors has gotten me up to the majors."

Scott sat on the arm of the chair. "It sounds like neither of you is happy."

"I know." Dodge looked away. He peered into the bedroom. "I don't want another woman, even if Helen is awful."

The unexpected comment took Scott by surprise. "Your life." He watched Dodge shift his view back toward him.

"Yeah, ain't it though." Dodge snickered. "Don't believe for a second that I like what Helen has done." He sighed. "Then, what else can I do."

"You could get a divorce," offered Scott. "Take some time and start fresh. More fish in the sea, they say."

Weariness seemed to overwhelm Frank Dodge. He hung his head. "Yeah. Feels like I'm too old to fish."

Scott left the chair's arm and stood looking down on Frank Dodge. "Anything else at all you remember about Ray Snider yelling at Edwards?"

"Naw, I don't think Ray had anything to do with Ronnie's death."

"All right." Despite the man's sorrowful life, Wyatt needed all the information he could scrape up. He hoped there might be a fragment hidden in Dodge's conscience. "I know you're not telling me the whole story. Tell me you did it Frank; or tell me what's eating at you."

Dodge stood, the weight still pulling on his mind. "Just leave me alone, will ya'? I'm all played out."

Scott drifted to the door. He wanted more information, but it seemed unlikely that Frank Dodge could provide it. "If you think of anything, I'm in the book."

"Nothing to add." Dodge ambled toward Scott and opened the door. "Just leave."

Scott did just that. In the parking lot, he fired up the Caddy and pulled out. He'd roll on to the Pythian Building and see where Johnny stood with the slick lawyer for Bugler. Perplexed as he was about Frank Dodge, Wyatt worried if he could solve things or if a talented attorney would be all poor old Eugene had left.

* * *

Scott made it to the Pythian Building. He never saw Johnny because he met Evie first. She detailed her conversation with Amanda Snider, complete with reference notes and commentary. The daughter's admissions and fears, paired with Frank Dodge's mention of Ray yelling at Edwards, sent Scott trotting across downtown to Snider's office.

With the millionaire ball club owner as a new suspect, Wyatt Scott burst into Ray Snider's office. Surprise and confusion painted Snider's face. He rose from his desk chair.

"Wyatt, I'm surprised to see you so soon. More bad news about Bugler?"

Scott stopped just short of Snider's desk. "No." He leveled his eyes at the tycoon. "Your daughter came to see me this morning."

Disbelief twisted Snider's face. "My Amanda?"

"Yeah. I wasn't there, so she missed me. But she had a long heart-to-heart with Evie Hall, Johnny's secretary."

"About what?"

"Well, Ray, she seems to think that you're the murderer of Ronnie Edwards."

Snider threw up his hand. "Oh, good God! That's just like her. On Mondays I'm a capitalist swine, on Tuesdays I'm Tojo, now I'm a killer."

Unruffled and unconvinced by Snider's histrionics, Scott forged ahead. "She was seeing Edwards. Were you aware of that?"

A rational calm swept over the businessman and ball team owner. "Yes. There isn't a whole lot that goes on with my family that slips past me." He sat down again. Rather than look at Scott, he shuffled the papers sitting on his desk.

"You didn't mention any of this when we talked before." Scott's glower did not abate.

"I didn't think it germane." Snider finally met Scott's eyes. "None of your business either."

"Did you approve?" questioned Scott.

Snider jerked his head back. "Certainly not!" He stared his own set of daggers at Scott, then took a deep breath. He let his eyes circle the room and cool before alighting on Wyatt. "Edwards was a good ballplayer, but not the *matrimonial* material I would choose for my daughter." He sighed and folded his hands together on his desk. "And before you dig at me for snobbery, let me tell you this. His lothario reputation and his ignorance disqualify him as a suitor for Amanda every bit as much as his station in life."

Keeping a skeptical eye on the millionaire, Scott continued to press him. "Where were you, Ray, when Edwards got killed?"

"You can't seriously believe I had something to do with that," scoffed Snider.

"I'd like to think not." Scott leaned on Snider's desk within a foot of the man's face. "Frank Dodge said you argued with Edwards, shouted at him."

"Did he tell you what I said?" Snider held his ground, eye-to-eye with Scott.

"Said he didn't hear all the words—just your anger."

"Let me fill you in." The millionaire leaned back. "It had nothing to do with Amanda. The little asshole got caught with liquor. The cops let him go but called me." He sat back up. "He's been in plenty of trouble before. I told him he was screwing up his career and my investment. Not sure I really would, but I told him I would cut him from the ball club if he screwed up again."

"Known you a long time, but your story doesn't answer the question. Where were you when Edwards got killed?"

"Scott, I didn't kill Ron Edwards." He took a deep breath, then exhaled. "Stop and think about it. Edwards would eventually be a marquee player, good for business, good for baseball. My killing Edwards would be bad for the business, the team, the fans, my family, and my daughter. To get rid of him, all I had to do was send him back down."

"But you didn't."

Snider bit his lip, then sighed. "I figured she'd get tired of him, and that would be the end of it." He paused for a moment before concluding. "Hell's bells, Scott, I could trade him, sell his contract, ship him to Seattle. Shit, I have enough power in this league to send him to hell."

"Nice speech. And you make a good point. But Ray, you still haven't answered my question. Where were you?"

"God damn you!" He pulled his arms down and pounded his desk. "I was on my way to or at the Petroleum Club. I had dinner with Representative Schwabe and his wife during the time of poor Ronnie's murder. Either way, I don't answer to you!"

Ignoring the slight, Scott redirected his inquiry to the daughter. "Where was Amanda?"

"You'd have to ask her!" Ray Snider composed himself. "I left her at home with a couple of her girlfriends. She was there when I got home about ten." He intertwined his fingers and rubbed his thumbs together. "Just so you know, I am well aware of my daughter's behavior. She doesn't miss an opportunity to throw it in my face. She hates me, or at least my money, yet like her mom, she spends as much of it as she can. I'll give you the full box score; her boyfriends don't last long. Edwards wouldn't have either. I'm not sending her to Bryn Mawr to get her away from boys." Befitting his bank account, Snider tossed out a million-dollar smirk. "I'm sending her there so that the ones she meets will be from Harvard University in Cambridge and not Harvard Avenue in Tulsa."

Scott nodded his understanding and his satisfaction. "I'm sorry, Ray. I have to look at everything to get Bugler free." For the first time, Scott softened his tone. "You and Amanda were a surprising curve in the road."

"I appreciate your loyalty and your doggedness. But your desperation impeded your good sense on this." Snider stood and moved to his window. He peered out, then motioned for Scott to come look out as well. "You see that tree way over there, south of Eighth?" He turned back to look Scott in the eye. "Go bark up that tree, because I am the wrong one." He moved back behind his desk. "My commitment to Eugene stands. But Scott, I don't want to see you again. Take a hike now and restrict your fanny to the cheap seats at Texas League Park!"

Scott nodded. He took Snider's directive and hiked out of his office. He knew a lot more than he cared to know about the Snider family. None of the tawdry details got him one second closer to freeing Bugler. He needed to get off second base.

* * *

The late afternoon sun and the eastern exposure of Scott's office window made the room's central globe the primary illumination for Evie Hall. She stared at Scott's wall of memories until she tired of viewing old baseball players and soldiers in Alaska. Her scrutiny of Wyatt's past fell away in favor of pacing up and down with the photos watching her. She went from Scott's Babe Ruth tour of Japan to his Alaska pals' wartime photos, then another trip to the baseball pictures. She would reach the end of one set, twirl, and stride to the end of the other set. The squeak of the door opening broke her pacing. She spun around to catch Scott entering.

"The rich guy do it?" Evie jumped right to the point.

"No. Not a likely suspect. His kid wouldn't have done it either." Scott flopped into his chair. He placed both hands on his desk, where frustration drained from both palms into the wooden surface.

Evie shuffled to the client-chair and dragged it to the front of the desk before wilting into it. "No, she didn't kill him. She liked him. Though there's plenty of mischief she's been up to."

"Rich girls have more leeway," remarked Scott without looking up or wandering into the insinuation that Evie dropped.

"Don't I know it." Evie rolled her eyes and cocked her head, but her histrionics went for naught as Scott never glanced up from his stare into the woodgrain top of his desk. "So, where do you go to get Bugler out of jail?" quizzed Evie, apparently so eager for a reaction that she went with a sure-bet subject.

"Million-dollar question isn't it" Scott gazed at Evie as he fell back into his chair. "Motive, timing, and evidence pointed all along to Dodge, but it doesn't fit him; his personality, his history, his demeanor when I confronted him. The whole situation tallies for him, but he doesn't fit. I can't make the man's nature or his reactions jibe with the crime."

"I know it wasn't that Snider kid. Fast as she is, she hasn't got up to killer." Evie sighed. "You say it ain't her old man, and that was where my money was."

"It doesn't fit Ray Snider. He's too smart, too rich, and he already knew his daughter was a fast dolly. It all fits for Dodge, except I didn't see it in his face. All my instincts tell me it's not him, but all the logic says it is."

"Maybe the Edwards kid gave the old slut the cold shoulder, and she did'em in."

"From what I've heard, she's played bedroom ball with a dugout full of young players. Have to figure she'd just move on to a new guy in the on-deck circle. Mike Barton thought it possible for a young woman or the wife, but his money was on a dad or a boyfriend."

"No reason it's not logical. Maybe the chippy wife didn't like being dropped like an old shoe for a young dolly." Evie eased back in her chair after she reemphasized her point.

"Beating a guy to death with a ball bat is not a lady's method," rebutted Scott.

Evie Hall forced out an enormous sigh. "Bout all I got. But there are no *ladies* in this."

Scott looked at Evie and smiled. "You took good cuts, Evie. You can't get a hit every time." He stared through the back wall, searching for an answer. He raised his pitching hand, doubled it into a fist, and banged it on the desk. "Damn!" he yelled. Evie jumped back, reacting to the unexpected fury.

"Johnny went to see that lawyer," said Evie, shifting the subject. "I gave him money from the bank. It was four hundred smackers." Evie peered at Scott.

Wyatt glanced at Evie. "That's darn nice of Johnny. I know going to Nathan Benjamin galls him." Scott winced. "I need to do a better job on my end."

"We know it can't be Bugler, so the real guy has to show up eventually." Evie smiled encouragement Wyatt's way.

He sat too far inside his thoughts to notice. Condemning himself for not putting the puzzle together volleyed with spinning suppositions to fit unlikely suspects into the crime. Dodge looked weary, sad, ready to be done, but offered no confession. Wyatt regained the moment to see Evie holding a smile despite his inattentiveness. "Go finish up for Johnny. I'm going to grab a bite and see if any of the sustenance finds my brain."

CHAPTER 14

Paranoia and Resolution

The sun had set, darkness held sway, yet the air sizzled. Flying along Riverside Drive, the evening breeze and wind off the river mitigated the heat enough to evaporate the sweat from Scott's face, but not enough to touch the wetness on his neck. The swirl of suspects swam in circles through the murky waters of Ronnie Edwards's murder. Wyatt knew he needed to find something in that pond to make a case.

The LaSalle motored past Fifty-first Street, fast approaching the end of Riverside Drive and the transition into Peoria Avenue. The lights of a Model A Ford, in the oncoming lane, breezed past him heading north toward the city. Interrupting his consideration of suspects, Scott mused whether the old car's driver came from Bixby or Broken Arrow. The route from either little town could use Riverside as the track to Tulsa.

Wyatt felt his collar soaked with sweat. He could hit August with a throw from his ruined arm, and that month promised to be more brutal than July. He shifted to his right and glanced in the rearview mirror to see droplets on his brow line. Rather than the old Ford diminishing in the distance beside his reflection, the mirror reported a shadowy sedan behind him.

Its outline and headlight design proclaimed postwar; it followed more than a block back. A citizen heading to one of those small towns probably drove the car, or a rich guy with a home like Campion's, far south of the city. Scott slowed. He monitored the mirror. The sedan gained, then leveled off. The end of Riverside Drive loomed, and the cars made the curve onto Sixty-first Street. Both vehicles would have to make a choice at Peoria and pick their direction from there.

Scott and the Caddy made the intersection. Peoria Avenue at Sixty-first had a stop sign. Left meant north and back to the city; right wound south another mile until the rounded changeover at Seventy-first Street and no choice but east until Lewis or Harvard. A rolling stop allowed the sedan to narrow the gap before Wyatt made the right onto an empty Peoria Avenue.

The spectral sedan followed without stopping. Unlikely as it was for the car to be tailing him, having been shot at not that long ago heightened his sensitivity. He depressed the accelerator, leaving his alleged pursuer further behind. He flashed his headlights to make sure the road ahead lay clear. Advancing headlights glistened in Scott's mirror. The sedan was keeping pace. Short of a confrontation, the next move had to come after the conversion to Seventy-first. Eyes glued to the rearview, Bugler's case dropped from Scott's thoughts.

The lonely outlying roads presented a perfect setting. A smart killer could run him off the road and into a tree. No witnesses on the two lanes south of Fifty-first Street. A quick check showed the sedan lagged a little – his headlights smaller in the mirror. The road design left no choice. Scott swung left onto Seventy-first. The sedan would have to follow.

Just south, to his right, the screen of the Riverside Drive-in, where Wyatt met the haughty Catherine Folger, flickered a severely acute angle version of Daffy Duck. In his mirror, the sedan's lights splashed from south to east with the turn. Followed or not, the drive-in theater provided a safety zone. The sedan joining him at the movies would also confirm his fear.

At the last moment, he swerved down the gravel road toward the drive-in. He made a second quick right down the entrance drive toward the ticket booth, where the building and fence obscured the LaSalle. Scott cut his lights as the posted sign demanded. Watching over his right shoulder, he witnessed the dark sedan roll down Seventy-first. It ran slowly, but the curve required that. The car lights drifted east, picking up speed. The share of illuminated street diminished, and the red taillights grew tiny before being overtaken entirely by the darkness.

After the night swallowed the sedan, Wyatt saw the young man in the ticket booth waving his arms to pull up. He did so reflexively. With the suspicious car driving away without incident, he saw no reason to enter. He stopped short. The young man leaned out of the booth.

"Come on. Pull up if you're coming in."

"What's the show?" called out Scott as he calculated his withdrawal.

"Says right there." The young ticket taker pointed across from his booth. "Double feature," he yelled louder than needed for someone in a convertible. "*Check Your Guns* and *Overland Trails*." He followed up with the obvious: "They're Westerns."

Scott looked where the finger pointed. A thin glass case held posters proclaiming the two cowboy films. "Darn!" exclaimed Scott. "I've seen them."

"Both?" asked the attendant.

"I'll try back next week." Scott backed the LaSalle a few feet, circled hard to his left, and switched on his headlights.

Scott made it back to Riverside Drive and conjured narratives about the dark sedan. Just a coincidence; a car leaving town. Or perhaps the killer followed him from Tulsa. He knew Scott liked to drive along the river. He waited for this opportunity.

As Scott motored closer to town, he chided his temperament for worrying about the trailing sedan. Caution is fine. Paranoia helped nothing. Forcing his thoughts back to Bugler, he pushed the LaSalle beyond the speed limit, hoping his thinking might keep pace.

Scott considered Ray Snider. Claiming dinner with a congressman would be overkill for a mendacious alibi. Ray was too smart and too successful to commit such a stupid and violent murder. Wyatt shook his head, shaking the asinine idea out of his mind. Neither Snider fit the picture. Amanda lacked the power to commit the crime, and from what Evie said, too little emotional investment in Edwards to care.

The LaSalle cleared the Forty-first Street tee intersecting Riverside Drive. The air had cooled. He still felt hot, but the open car and river breeze evaporated his sweat. Unless the killer sprang out of the unknown wash of characters beyond the world of Oilers baseball, Wyatt was stuck with the Dodges in one manifestation or another.

Glancing at the speedometer, he'd kicked it up to forty-four. Twisty Riverside wouldn't allow much more. He had zoomed past Thirty-first without notice. Like a living creature, the LaSalle headed for home. He'd make Denver shortly, take Sixteenth north and make the Sophian in three minutes.

* * *

Scott rose with the sun. He parked in his usual alley spot, then walked the four and a half blocks to Joe and Mamie's. He swigged a cup of joe and two refills. Tulsans were off and moving by the time he walked back to the Pythian Building. Scott arrived at his office and almost to his desk before Evie Hall dashed in and flopped in his guest chair. She wore a clean, new outfit paired with yesterday's concerned face.

Without morning greetings or a preamble, Evie jumped in. "Okay, so it's not the kid. We agree. You won't go for the rich dad even though he could pay for it ten times."

Wyatt peered down at Evie. He figured he'd have to point out the error in her logic. Having that much money meant Ray Snider wouldn't do it.

Before he could correct her, Evie grasped the logic, "The rich guy is just too rich. You're right. He wouldn't do it." Evie leaned her head back, matching his stare. "He has too many other good options."

Scott grinned at Miss Hall's new insightfulness. "You got there. Good for you, Evie."

She glowed from the praise. "Did *you* make any progress last night?"

"No fresh evidence." Wyatt finally sat down. He pushed his scribble pad and its two dozen poor thoughts to the side. "Thought about out-of-towners. The kid left some infidelity in Shreveport."

"Are you going to drive there? I can't see an out-of-town killer in this."

"No. I said I thought about an out-of-towner; I didn't say it was a good thought."

"Well, I think you should rough up the Dodge guy; give him the third degree." Evie leaned forward, then backhand slapped the air, demonstrating her point of physical intimidation. "You could force it out of him."

"Did you see a detective movie last night?"

"I've seen plenty. And I know the real cops do that stuff." Evie defended her notion with a cocked head and squinty eyes.

"Cops who do that don't get genuine answers; just what the guy thinks they want to hear. Better plan is circling around the subject to see if the culprit slips up on his story."

"Well, circle him. Get the story so you can get Bugler out." Her strident tone seemed to dawn on her. Evie sat back and relaxed her expression.

"I've been all over and around him. He's hiding something; it weighs on him. I recognized it the last time I saw him."

"And you don't think the nasty cheat wife liked Ronnie Edwards enough to be jealous over him?"

"She's cold and capable of murder." Scott tapped his forefinger on the desk. "I told you this murder was brutal. Not a lady's crime to beat a guy's brains in."

"Who says she's a lady?" parried Evie. "A cheatin' floozy dropped for a younger issue might go daffy with a ball bat." After Evie completed her thesis, she moved forward with the challenge. "Have you met this worn-out sharecropper?"

Scott nodded. "Yes. Talked to her twice."

"Your gut tells you it's not him. What do those *guts* say about her?"

Scott drew a deep breath. He pictured Helen Dodge. "She's detached; bitter. Instead of a chip on her shoulder, she has an iceberg."

"Cold, huh?" Evie rubbed her hands together. She squinted at Scott across the desk.

Wyatt stared back. He sat motionless for several seconds before momentum built in his left leg. It grew into his right leg and then his pitching arm. All three pushed him to his feet. The suddenness of his vault caught Evie off guard. She shifted in the chair before bouncing to her feet.

"I'll go see the Dodges again. She's playing too cagey. And he's hiding something," declared Scott.

Evie watched Wyatt stride purposefully toward the door.

"I thought he was ready to confess and give me the story, but he held back. I'll put it to both of them." Scott grabbed the knob and jerked the door open. "Frank will break or she'll give it away." He sailed into the hallway and made the stairs while Evie followed and closed the door behind her.

* * *

The Dodges lived in an apartment on east Fifteenth Street. The short drive from the Pythian Building gave Scott enough time to work out the accusations with which he figured to bomb the Dodges. He rehearsed, accusing her of covering up for Frank. Then Scott turned the formulation around and accused Frank of covering up for her. He beat Edwards to a pulp because of the humiliation. She killed Edwards because he jilted her for a younger girl after she taught the bumpkin about women. To touch all the bases, Scott worked out a conspiratorial murder whereby Helen hit Edwards first out of jealous rage, then Frank beat him down to point the blame away from a woman.

He arrived at their door primed. Having run through so many scenarios, he knew he could snap off a response to any mendacity or prevarication. He judged the doorbell insufficiently urgent for his anxious disposition, so he didn't bother punching it. Instead, he pounded on the door with a fist formed by his pitching hand. The sound rang out urgently and sonorously.

Before Scott could batter the door a second time, Frank Dodge opened it wide. He slouched, half supporting himself with his fingers on the knob. Without a word and before Scott could speak, he sauntered back into the apartment, leaving the door wide open for Wyatt to follow. He trailed behind, observing Dodge's feet barely lift from the floor.

"Frank, I need to talk to your wife." Scott was brusque, but figured he needed to be to set the tone.

Dodge stopped. He shuffled around to view Scott. "She killed the kid, you know. Helen killed Ronnie Edwards."

Scott stopped cold. He stood momentarily stunned by the suddenness of Dodge's pronouncement of his wife's guilt. "Did she confess?" asked Scott, as he regained his equilibrium.

"Yeah, but I saw her car leave the ballpark. So, it figured to be her—hoped not, but I thought so. Not a surprise when she admitted doing it." A puffy-eyed resignation confirmed the desolate man's chronicle.

"She bitched about you. Helen figured she'd got around the sheriff's office with no trouble. She worried about you, though."

"Then I need both of you to come to the sheriff's office with me."

Dodge made no response. He didn't seem to hear Scott. "I've got a letter here about what I saw and her confessing the killing. I signed it." He leaned down and tapped the envelope lying on his coffee table. "Bugler did nothing except be dumb old Bugler." Frank Dodge straightened up from the table. He walked a meandering circle from his coffee table to the door and back. He stared beyond Scott. "She killed the kid because he got a girlfriend. I never thought she cared that much for any of them. Married woman jealous of a young guy finding a young gal. Kinda' crazy. Sad all around, isn't it?"

"You know the girl was Amanda Snider?" Scott tossed the name into the fetid stew of the Dodge family drama.

"God, no!" exclaimed a shocked Dodge. His mouth fell open, and he stared. "I doubt Helen knew who it was either. Still, it didn't matter who." He composed his face and paced once more. "He told Helen he wouldn't see her anymore; that he was going to marry some young girl."

"I doubt Ray would've gone for that." Scott had gotten over the shock of the confessional session. His tone shifted to calm and steady.

"No, he surely would not," reasoned Dodge. Considering what he had said and the implications, he remained composed, resigned, invoking little emotion.

Scott's eyes sized up Dodge even as his question formed. "You've been covering up for Helen. How come the change now?"

"I lived with a lot of cheating. After you came by, I knew it was

Helen, and I even thought about living with murder." Dodge peered down at his feet. He slid the left one an inch forward. His right foot slipped back a little more than the left moved forward. As if waiting for some signal from his feet, he watched them for several seconds. He lifted his gaze back to Scott. "I decided I couldn't do that. Couldn't take it."

"I understand, Frank." Sympathy slipped onto Scott's face as the two men minded one another. "Can I talk to her?"

Dodge looked toward the closed bedroom door. "She's in there." He ambled to the door and entered the bedroom. He left the door open as he walked through it toward the bed. Scott followed two paces behind.

On the bed, covered by a blood-soaked sheet, Helen Dodge lay face up, staring at the ceiling as only the dead stare. Her expression showed neither horror nor agony, falling between surprise and annoyance. Drawn up to her neck and folded neatly below her chin, the bedsheet belied the violence beneath it. Her recent perm faintly flattened but intact contrasted against the pillowcase. A revolver rested on the corner of the bed. It formed a clear image of Dodge's breakpoint.

"What is this?" Wyatt stared at Dodge for an explanation.

"End of the game," replied Dodge with a wistful tone and a hint of sadness. He moved to the bed and picked up the gun. He let it hang at his side. "She killed the kid, like I said. I couldn't keep her after that, and I couldn't let her go." He gazed at his dead wife.

"What's up with the bedsheet?" Scott's shock asked the question without his rational consent.

"She's in her slip. I thought she deserved her modesty." Dodge kept his stare on his wife's body.

"Thoughtful of you, Frank." The crazy scene forced irony to wait outside. "I have to call the cops." Scott glanced at the gun Dodge held at his side.

He shifted his gaze from his wife's body to Scott. "I know." He stood silent, transfixed for a moment, before continuing. "You think they'll give me the chair?"

"Cheating wife, murderer. I figure prison. Cops, the County Attorney, or a jury won't have much sympathy for Helen. Life, maybe just fifteen or twenty years." Scott imparted his estimate of the situation. After further thought, he added; "There are lots of good lawyers. Some might do better."

With desolate eyes, Dodge's drooping lips finished his forlorn expression. "No good outcomes, but I made the choice and I stick by it."

"I'm going to call the police now." Scott looked for a reaction from Frank Dodge; none came. "I'll ask for Cleveland. He's a square guy, and he's the most professional."

Dodge nodded his acceptance of the situation and Scott's declaration. Scott walked out of the bedroom. He scanned the residence, trying to locate the phone. It sat in a wall alcove where the hall met the living room. Wyatt glanced at Dodge's envelope exonerating Bugler before he made his way to the phone.

From the bedroom, Dodge called out; "Scott, you were a hell of a pitcher back when. I wish I could've batted against you."

Scott dialed the requisite numbers. After a beat, the station's switchboard operator answered. "Detective Cleveland. It's urgent!" exclaimed Scott.

A slight stirring and a click came from the bedroom. Before Scott judged it further, the sound of a gunshot exploded through the bedroom door, blasting his uncovered left ear, while the phone's receiver protected his right. He reflexively lurched away from the sound. In his right ear, the familiar voice of Art Cleveland affirmed his title and name.

"Art." Scott paused a moment before continuing into the receiver. "I've got two bodies for you and a letter exonerating Bugler."

"What?!" Cleveland shrieked through the phone. "More damn bodies?"

"People do strange things, Art. You might call the sheriff for me. He needs to see this letter to free Bugler." Scott sucked in a deep breath. "You come, and I'll explain the bodies."

CHAPTER 15

THE LaSALLE TAKES A BULLET

A breeze swept along the walking bridge, where Scott drew his own counsel. Pensive, brooding, distant, he stared across the manicured perfection of the museum's lawns. Wyatt had not lounged in his private spot on the Philbrook grounds since Evie brought news of Bugler's arrest. That matter settled; Scott arranged this free time to relax, even as he ignored Cleveland's renewed complaints about the body count left in the wake of the Dodges' deaths.

Several quiet days had slipped by. For most Tulsans, swimming, ballgames, celebrations, and picnics transpired against abusive heat, an onslaught of insects, and Oklahoma's lack of rain. For Scott, the enigma of Hiroshi Ishikawa's murder and the attempt on his own life occupied the preponderance of his conscious hours. Fielding no longer buzzed around Wyatt's home or office in search of his alleged spy at Douglas Aircraft. The Tulsa police and the FBI had gone quiet. Neither outfit contacted him. Nothing got resolved. To Wyatt, it seemed things had been papered over.

Poor Hiroshi, Wyatt opined. It would have been interesting to see him again, ask him how he was, and find out some details of his life. If he worked for MacArthur's Japanese baseball tour of America, Wyatt could've taken him to see a ball game at Texas League Park. He might even have been able to smooth things enough with Ray Snider to get an exhibition game for Tulsa. Those gentle thoughts of might-have-been, of baseball games, and reacquaintance after fourteen years slipped behind a black screen of unanswered questions.

Murder, attempted murder, and any ridiculous association of Sleener with Hiroshi tapped at his brain like a deranged woodpecker on a concrete bridge support. Scott added and re-added pieces. He calculated. He multiplied. He divided. The Pythagorean Theorem didn't connect. Isaac Newton never formulated this calculus. His head ached with such frustration that he hoped Evie would interrupt him again.

A gunshot broke through the afternoon air, partially fulfilling his wish. Sixty yards north, the lush leaves of a boxwood hedge flew apart. Wyatt instinctively jumped from his spot and sought cover.

"Scott! Watch out, Scott!" came a call across Philbrook's grounds.

Behind the bridge, Scott drew his nineteen eleven and surveyed the grounds where sunlight and tree shade grappled for supremacy. Pierce dashed into view across the gardens and grass, running toward him. Gun drawn; Pierce eyed the hedge toward the property's border. Nothing came from the bush Pierce had apparently fired into.

"I think he ran." Pierce closed ground on Scott as he neared the bridge. "I didn't see anyone, but I saw a gun barrel pointing your way."

He waved his pistol. "Those bushes…" He pointed his gun more specifically toward a set of shrubs. "Bushes, right over there. They moved after I shot."

The idyllic landscape belied the warning Pierce declared. Leaves fluttered from the warm south wind. Too much daylight for cicadas or crickets, a jaybird clicked and jeered. Honeysuckle perfume fronted the scent of a few hot-weather flowers. Wyatt saw nothing that hinted at a phantom assassin.

Scott gave up on scanning the lawn and plied Pierce for information. "I gather your being here is not a coincidence."

"No. No coincidence." Pierce lowered his pistol to his side. "Fielding has me watching you."

"Fielding thinks the crew that killed Hiroshi haven't given up on me, right?" Scott holstered his nineteen eleven. "Those folks connect me with Hiroshi."

"Something like that." Pierce glanced past Scott and across the expanse of the museum grounds. He slid his gun back into its holster. "I get marching orders, not the why-fors."

Looking across the grounds for movement, Scott addressed Pierce without eye contact. "What happened after you shot?"

"I saw those bushes move." Pierce pointed his finger this time clearly toward the hedgerow made up of boxwoods. "They rippled further down the line, too, but I never caught sight of a shooter."

Scott glared at the distant shrubbery. "From over there, he'd have to run along the fence to hide from sight, then around the north side to make the parking lot."

Acting on his deduction and without a further word, Scott raced around the south side of the Philbrook building. Pierce instinctively followed. Wyatt's athletic body widened the gap with Pierce, who labored up the incline from the eastern grounds to the west entrance. Scott made the parking lot in time to see a dark sedan speed out of the gate, turning north into the surrounding neighborhood.

With Pierce following, Scott sprinted for his LaSalle. He rushed into the Caddy, opening the door and closing it a fraction of an inch short of his trailing foot. He flipped the key, stomped the starter, and gunned the engine, firing his LaSalle to life. Pierce arrived, huffing a little, and made it into the car through the passenger side. The Caddy screeched out of the parking lot, jolting Pierce back against his seat before he could shut his door.

"That dark sedan..." Scott leaned forward, scanning for the car as he swerved through home-lined streets. "...followed me before." The red Caddy screamed north, pursuing Wyatt's would-be assassin.

"I guess I'm lucky Fielding had you watch me even though I'm sure he set me up as bait." Scott kept focused on the streets as he pushed harder. "Know this, Pierce; it's my show. You can sit, watch, take part, even help, but you do what I say or jump out right now!"

Pierce chuckled at Scott. "Sure, boss." After Scott made a squealing left turn west, the CIA operative commented further: "You think you can sneak up on him in this inconspicuous fire engine?"

"I just want to catch him." Scott's intent remained on the chase. "I don't care if he knows I'm coming. I want reckoning, and this is my chance."

Even with the car out of sight, an odor of spent fuel with a twinge of oil guided Scott to turn north through avenues lined with prominent homes beyond Philbrook. The LaSalle arrived at a neighborhood crossroads. Both riders checked for intersecting traffic, even though Scott barely slowed. He caught a glimpse of the sedan a block west, turning onto Peoria Avenue. Pierce, seeing it too, pointed while Scott gunned the red convertible through a sliding left turn, heading toward Peoria. He floored the gas, causing the car to buck and bounce on the imperfectly poured cement surface.

Superfluous cars speckled the major artery of Peoria as the LaSalle's right turn brought it into the flow. The fleeing sedan almost hid within the rolling vehicular detritus. Abandoning its northern path, the suspect car hung a left, heading west on Twenty-first Street. After a long block flew by, the pair held tight, making a horn-blaring left turn, daring oncoming cars to slow or crash as they reached the junction of Twenty-first Street and Peoria Avenue.

Safely through the busy intersection, catching nothing worse than honked horns and unheard expletives, the pair scanned Twenty-first Street heading west. In the distance, the sedan flowed among daytime vehicles. It passed through routine traffic approaching the Arkansas River. Cars veered off onto Boulder Avenue then Riverside Drive, depleting those between the suspect vehicle and the chasing detective and spy. A smattering of cars remained between the pursued sedan and the stalking LaSalle as Scott and Pierce reached the U.S. Highway One Sixty-nine bridge that connected Twenty-first Street on the east with Twenty-third Street west of the river.

"He's crossing the river!" exclaimed Pierce.

"Westside, for whatever reason," observed Scott.

As Scott and Pierce sped onto the bridge, very few cars ran between them and their mysterious quarry. Wyatt pushed harder, his speedometer whirling higher just as the dark sedan cleared the bridge on the west bank. Both cars roared past the crossing, continuing north along Quanah Avenue through the thinly populated west side of Tulsa. The single remaining car between them slowed and pulled into a parking lot, forcing Scott to apply the brakes and lose ground. When the way cleared, he pepped the LaSalle, narrowing the gap once more. The sedan slid, making a hasty exit onto U.S. Sixty-four.

"You have any idea where this guy's going?" asked Pierce.

Scott swung his LaSalle over to follow. "Mannford, Enid, California; west is all I can tell until he makes another turn."

The sedan picked up its tempo. The change caused Pierce to shift in his seat before he spoke. "Fox has caught your scent."

A single pickup truck, packing tradesman tools of its driver – an upside-down wheelbarrow, a stubby cement shovel, and a double-hole hoe propped on its tailgate – rumbled past heading east in the oncoming lane. Once the truck passed, empty asphalt stretched to the horizon along the oncoming lane. Scott pushed harder. Underbrush, immature elms, and thickets flew by on either side. The powerful Cadillac engine propelled the convertible to close in on the sedan.

"The license plate; he covered it," yelled Pierce.

"Won't do him any good. I'm not reporting him to the cops." The portentous tone and implied threat came through clearly. "We'll deal with him."

Pierce jerked, seeming surprised by the 'we' in Scott's declaration. "Better figure out who it is and if he's just some tool for a bigwig. Professional quality shooters usually do not execute murders for themselves," instructed Pierce.

"I will get answers if I have to crush his balls," barked Scott.

The dark sedan slowed, approaching a fork that went north to Keystone or west to Mannford. The car veered left toward Mannford. Just seconds behind, Scott, Pierce, and the LaSalle followed. There were no oncoming cars, but the road twisted violently in the hilly country, providing short vistas. The sedan would slide from view until the Caddy made the next bend.

After rounding a sharp, hilly curve, the culprit car braked to a skidding, squealing stop. The passenger side wheels fell onto the soft gravel shoulder. It lay like a predator in wait. Scott jammed the LaSalle's brake pedal to the floor, resulting in a screeching slide toward the suspect auto. The Cadillac's rear fishtailed but stayed on the blacktop roadway.

The sedan's driver, a clean-cut, stocky, Slavic looking man, leaned out of his window. His right hand leveled a silenced pistol at the red Cadillac. A pop, a whoosh, and a thumb's worth of spraying glass from the LaSalle's windshield proved the guy meant business. The bullet had lanced almost perfectly equidistant between Scott and Pierce. It had flown under the rearview mirror and over the front seat before lodging in the backseat upholstery.

"Son of a bitch!" Scott blurted out his anger.

Wyatt reached inside his coat for his gun. Pierce didn't move but stared cold-heat at the shooter's face. While Scott and Pierce focused on the shooting figure, a second shot punctured the driver's side front tire. The shooter pulled his arm and upper body back into the sedan. Scott produced his Colt but did not bring it to bear with the windshield blocking his aim. Pierce continued to stare with his mouth gaped open. The gunman, safely back inside his sedan, engaged his gears and accelerated away. The car shimmied and fought its way back onto the road surface, throwing gravel from the right rear tire in the process. Wyatt flung open his door and aimed his nineteen eleven at the diminishing outline of the car. A hill and a curve ended any hope of a round striking his target.

"I think I know who that is," claimed Pierce, still carrying the dumbfounded look he conveyed since he saw the shooter poke his face out.

Scott wrenched his head around to glare at Pierce. All but burning holes through him with his eyes, Scott replied, "You know him from your *work?*"

"Yeah. I'll know for sure once I dig that bullet out of your backseat."

Scott shifted his attention and glared at his flat tire. "If not, a guy playing in your spy game, the bastard must have stock in Goodyear the way he keeps ruining my tires."

Pierce climbed over the seat, pulled a knife from his pocket, and went to work carving up the backseat fabric around the bullet hole. Still grumbling, Scott headed for the rear of his car. Before he popped the trunk lid, he peered across it, watching Pierce digging into his upholstery. As he released the lid on the LaSalle's trunk, it blocked his view of Pierce's mischief. Inside, a jack and the newly repaired rear tire, now serving as his spare, greeted him. His sour mood worsened. He didn't know the guy, but he had grown as mad at him for his two ruined tires as he had for the attempts on his life.

* * *

Scott dropped Pierce off at his car on a side street near Philbrook before nursing the wobbly LaSalle to the Peters Brothers Sinclair station. The damaged red Caddy limped in front of the mechanic's bay, seeking help. While he waited, Wyatt fumed a little and stared at the bullet hole in his windshield. Zip Peters, the younger of the two men, emerged from their tiny office. In his late forties, Zip had rough, weathered skin, brown from his time in the sun. He wore a ball cap that hid his crew cut head of stubby chestnut hair, unlike his brother, Spike, who wore one to cover his bald spot. Both men usually wore their unofficial uniforms of khaki pants, work boots, and a light blue shirt with the Sinclair insignia, since that's whose gasoline they sold.

As Zip approached, Scott thought it took a near miracle and all the Peters brothers' patching talent to make the first shot tire hold air. That same tire, mounted on the driver's side front, allowed Scott to hobble back to Tulsa. He deemed the latest Goodyear victim to be a fatality that the brothers could not resurrect. Scott envisioned a new tire in his future but held hope for the windshield.

Zip made it to the driver's side and nodded to Scott. "My repair's up front, I see. I'd like to think you ran over a nail or somethin' is why." The younger Peters glared at the windshield. "That round hole in the windshield makes me think different though."

"Ran into more trouble, Zip. Old spare's in the trunk."

"You lookin' to have us repair it?"

"I suspect it's a goner." Wyatt threw up his arms and offered Zip a fat, sardonic smile.

"Have to check with Spike, but I doubt we got a tire that could fit this classy Caddy." The mechanic and pump jockey eyed the windshield.

"Not sure about cleanin' your windshield without splashin' your dashboard."

"I can see through bug guts, but wind whistling through that hole is a worry."

"Not sure there's a repair other than taping over it." Zip stretched over the hood and ran his finger around the hole. "Lemme' get Spike from under the Chevy in the bay, and we'll mull over what's what and what can be." He pulled his lanky frame back to vertical.

"Sure thing, Zip. And if Spike is too much in the middle of something, tell him it's okay."

Zip smiled. "Oh, he'll wanna' see you, Wyatt. More so when I tell'em you got shot up again." He strolled back into the office, presumably to go into the mechanic's bay and retrieve his brother.

Alone with the Tulsa sun burning him, Scott waited. A metallic rumble cued him to look at the bay door. It drew up, revealing Spike's legs. As the chain ratcheted the door higher, a bluish tinted Chevrolet up on their rack showed its side panel. Zip, manning the chain, remained hidden behind the wall of the garage. Spike pulled his cap up and wiped his brow before fixing it neatly back. Working on an engine and not confronting his customers, Spike wore a tee shirt rather than his long sleeve Sinclair option. The door made it to its peak, allowing Spike to step lively toward Scott and the LaSalle while he wiped his hands with an orange rag.

Fairer than his younger brother, Spike carried freckles across his nose and splashed on his forehead. He smoked Camels when he kept himself away from the station's gasoline pumps. Apparently feeling safe, he threw the rag over his shoulder and pulled his pack from his rolled up left sleeve. Spike sucked a cigarette from the pack as brother Zip emerged from the garage bay. With a lighter from his hip pocket, Spike fired up his smoke.

He blew fumes out of his nostrils as he addressed Scott. "Zip tells me you got yourself shot up again."

"Can't keep a secret from you, Peters brothers." Scott grinned.

Spike reached his right arm over the convertible's door. "Other than almost gettin' shot, how the hell ya' been, Wyatt?"

Scott gripped the clean, rough hand as firmly as he received. "Been fine, Spike. Just a run of bad luck with some nitwit that enjoys shooting tires."

"Seems like he might've wanted you too, or he's got awful poor aim hittin' that windshield," remarked Spike Peters after he eyed the hole.

Zip came to his brother's side. "Like I tol' ya,' doubt we have a tire that'll fit."

"Could dig around in the back pile of tires. Slight chance we could light on something," offered Spike.

"Won't make us a nickel, but your best bet'll be Oklahoma Tire," advised Zip.

"Yeah, Zip, I thought that'd end up being the spot." Scott pushed his hand over the steering wheel and pointed at the hole. "You don't have any great new Sinclair miracle that could fill that hole?"

Zip snorted a little laugh. Spike tried to be serious, but his advice had a grin behind it. "Wad a bubble gum probably better than any miracle I know."

"I need to do something. Besides costing an arm and a leg, I bet I'd have to wait weeks for Cadillac to send a windshield." Scott looked at the brothers. Both nodded their agreement with his grim forecast.

"August, shouldn't rain, so we could cut some cardboard and tape over the hole." Zip made his proposal to Spike, leaving Scott as a spectator.

"Best bet for now," agreed Spike. "Is she running all right other than holes from bein' shot up?"

"Hits on all cylinders, thanks to you guys." Scott gave a thumbs up with his pitching hand. "I'll drop by in the fall for plugs and a tune-up."

"Fair enough," replied Zip.

"Need gas?" asked Spike, making the best of the situation.

"Might as well. I'll pull in by the pump for ethyl."

"Sure thing. That red baby swigs the high octane and nothin' else," agreed Spike.

"I'll run get tape and close that hole." Zip dashed back toward the office.

Spike stepped back as Scott started the LaSalle and angled it near the pump for its premium lead feeding. Wyatt cut the engine. Spike freed the gas cap behind the license plate. He rang up the pump, pulled the nozzle free and began filling the LaSalle's tank. Zip disappeared through the office door.

With his hand still squeezing out gasoline, Spike stared at the backseat with the immense hole Pierce left from digging out the shooter's slug. "Damn, Wyatt. I thought you got shot up. The back seat looks like somebody gutted your upholstery."

Scott shook his head at Spike. "Cut out the bullet where it stuck."

Spike shuffled nearer Scott, stretching his gas-pumping arm to get his body closer for conversation. "Kinda' messy job. Won't look classy with tape on that."

"No. When I get some time, I'll have the seatback redone."

Zip came flying from the office with a roll of mechanic's tape and a piece of cardboard.

Spike watched the pump wheels spin. "Your baby's thirstier than you let on."

Scott glanced at the pump. "Well, Spike, fill'er up is fill'er up."

Zip set to work on the windshield. He ripped four pieces of tape, each one stuck to a different finger. With a five-inch square of card-board pressed against the bullet hole, Zip locked one corner down with tape. He applied another strip to the opposite corner. Wyatt and Spike watched the dark patch grow. Zip pushed the last piece of tape down before strolling to the Caddy's front and popping the hood.

Hearing the gasoline gurgle up the input pipe, Spike pulled the nozzle. He stopped the pump with the rotating digits reading four dollars and thirty-two cents. Zip checked the oil dipstick. Satisfied, he restored it to its place in the engine and eased the hood closed. Scott pulled out his wallet to fulfill his part of the transaction.

Spike came back to Scott. Before he could pronounce the price, Scott handed him a five-dollar bill. "Don't bother with the cents, Spike. You two take care of my red honey better than I do."

"Just what we're supposed to do, Wyatt," said Spike.

"It is," agreed Zip. "Hope that patch holds. Best I got now." He came back to his brother's side. "This baby deserves excellent treatment."

"Zip's right." Spike stroked his thumb across his chin; the fiver crushed in his fingers. "You better get the guy that did this to her."

"And before he gets you," added Zip.

"Believe me, fellows, that's top of my list." Scott looked away from the brothers at the bullet hole repair in the windshield. It prompted his inner detective to search under an unlikely rock. "Doubt it will happen, but if you guys service a dark sedan, black, maybe navy, with a stocky, foreign guy driving, call me."

Zip didn't move. Spike pocketed the five and gawked at his brother. "Week or so ago, right Zip?"

Breaking out of his trance, Zip managed to nod. "Yessir, foreign for sure."

Spike pointed to the street and swept his finger toward the pump for regular. "Guy came in, took some gas. Had a map on his front seat and still asked how to get over the river."

"Weren't no German." Spike seemed to conjure the details of the event. "Somethin' from Europe though."

"Could that foreigner have been Russian?" asked Scott.

"Never met any Russian, but coulda' been," answered Spike.

"Could've for sure," agreed Zip. "Had an oddball tattoo on his left arm. I couldn't guess what it's supposed to be. He leaned on the door window when askin' about crossin' the river."

"I remember that tattoo. Funny squiggly thing." Spike zigzagged his finger through the air. "Sombitch was cheap too. Got eight cents in change and sat there spreading pennies out, counting them."

"You guys don't have any idea where he went on the westside?"

Both shook their heads. "Sorry, Wyatt." Zip shrugged his shoulders.

"We don't think much a' Ruskies. If he ever comes back, we'll call the cops," added Spike.

"Cops won't be able to do anything if it's the one I ran into. If you see him, call me," advised Scott.

"We can do that." Spike looked at his brother.

Zip nodded and voiced his plan. "After I check under his hood, I suspect he'll have starter trouble till you can get here."

"That's a good plan, Zip. You two play dumb, tinker under the hood, and call me. I'll come running." Scott ratified their plan with a sly grin.

"You betcha," agreed Spike. He backed away from the LaSalle and stood tall.

Zip drew back with his brother. "I'll call around for a used tire. Even if you get a new one, that patch job won't last."

"We'll check with the dealer about getting you a windshield too," added Spike.

"Thanks. I doubt that Russian comes back, but if he does, you boys try nothing. He is deadly dangerous," warned Scott.

"We'll follow your plan," agreed Spike.

"Just don't get this baby shot up no more!" scolded Zip.

Scott started the LaSalle. "I'll do my best, fellas." He pulled out, offering a quick wave as he merged into traffic.

Even though he left without a tire, the windshield hole was closed, he had a full gas tank, and some surprising information. Scott still needed to make it to his office. He wondered if he needed groceries. He knew the liquor cabinet needed attention from the bootlegger. Life wouldn't let him hide from the mundane even with an assassin stalking him.

* * *

Back in his apartment after the strange, if not harrowing, afternoon, Wyatt Scott sat on his couch, leaning forward toward his coffee table with a drink in hand. He swirled Cutty Sark whisky that flowed around, over, and between the ice cubes in his glass. The amber fluid communicated soothing, cool, and apt for his purpose—trying to consider why he had garnered the lethal attention of someone that ran in Pierce's and Fielding's spy game. Wyatt swallowed the earthy refreshment just as the buzzer for his front door sounded. He didn't move. He glowered at his door. It sounded off again. Despite his severest scowl, it went off a third time. At the insistence of the impudent doorbell, Scott downed the last sip of his drink, sliding the glass across the coffee table. He abandoned his couch and strolled to the entry. He opened his front door to find Mrs. Campion, suggestively dressed as usual but wearing a mask of worry rather than her usual leer.

"I need to speak with you about Waldo." She pushed her way into his apartment and gawked around the living room. Without slowing, she whirled back to face Scott. "Offer me a drink, and let's talk."

Scott stepped to his bar cabinet. Despite the one on his coffee table, he pulled a pair of glasses from the cabinet. He poured two fingers of tawny whisky into each glass. He held one toward Mrs. Campion. "Ice?"

"Soda water is all I need," she replied while fidgeting with her purse.

Scott put her drink under the soda canister and shot a stream into the pure Scotch. He extended the drink. She grasped it, then meandered toward his coffee table. He dumped two melting chunks of ice in his glass and toted it to his wingback chair. He kept his eye on Mrs. Campion but did not speak to her or press on what she wanted.

Mrs. Campion dumped her purse on the coffee table near an ashtray and a box of wooden matches. She paused, contemplating the items but ignored them in favor of pacing the length of Scott's living room and back. She imbibed one swallow in each direction without looking at her glass or showing any enjoyment from the sips. Scott sat in his armchair and observed her take her round-trip across his living room.

"Waldo wasn't much, but he was my brother," sighed Campion.

She posited her lament as a statement of fact. Scott detected the twinge of guilt lurking in her inflection. He had followed the pacing but eschewed a reply to her declaration in favor of sipping his whisky. She started a second leg toward the kitchen before stopping short.

"Albert wants to wait for the police, but there's more going on than Waldo blackmailing people; I know it." Charlotte Campion blurted out her frustration with her back still to Scott. "When the FBI men came to our house, Albert had two lawyers there." She pivoted around to face Scott. "I told them the truth: that I knew nothing of Waldo's escapades." She paused a moment to consider Scott before resuming her travels and her story. "They wouldn't give me anything. The Tulsa cops telling me it was that crazy Indian oil heiress doesn't hold water now."

"I'm surprised the FBI visited you. Did they say why they came?"

"Not really." Mrs. Campion paused her pacing. "Most of the time they spent huddled with Albert and his lawyers. I figure they were snooping into his business." She swallowed a long drink and returned to the sofa. "If all his international trade is on the up and up, I'll be surprised."

"Your husband is protected. The U.S. government has a stake in what he does, and I believe they need it to continue."

She put her glass down near Scott's old one. Mrs. Campion rummaged in her purse and pulled a pack of cigarettes from it, then slid one into the corner of her mouth. "Do you have a light around here?" she asked, oblivious to the paraphernalia directly in front of her.

Scott pointed toward the matches and ashtray. Mrs. Campion spied them this time. She pulled a stick from the box and popped the match head with one of her long fingernails. It sparked up, and she lit her Chesterfield from its tiny blaze. She shook the flame out and tossed the spent match, not quite making the ashtray. She pulled on her cigarette and sighed out more frustration than smoke.

"Well, will you find Waldo's killer for me?" She posed like a magazine ad, with her left hand planted on her hip and her right elbow tucked in so that her lit cigarette lingered near her cheek.

"That's why you're here?"

"Yes." Apparently taking offense at Scott's question and its unstated implications, Mrs. Campion dropped her pose in favor of an incredulous stare. "You're supposed to be a private detective, and I want answers." Recovering some of her equanimity, she took another smoke. "You know I have money."

"It wasn't Ruth Brown," offered Scott as a start.

"I, too, came to that conclusion." She puffed once more. "Still, that is something. You must know more. It's there when you say it wasn't her." Her expression shifted. A tiny blush of hope warmed beneath her makeup. "You're confirming that there are others involved."

"The story runs deeper than your brother, Waldo. You are right about that." Scott looked into her eyes. "And I do hope to find his killer."

"I can pay you handsomely," she said with a lilt of hope and gratitude in her voice.

"Waldo is a tangent to something else, something bigger. He left word for me a few hours before he was killed. He had something on his mind other than a fast buck, and I think that is why someone killed him."

"You've been looking into it on your own?"

"Let's say his murder is one of the nagging loose ends I feel compelled to tie up."

"Then find out." She reached into her purse and pulled out several high denomination bills. She extended them to Scott. "Here, I want you working for me. I don't trust Albert with his government friends. They deal in shadows where poor Waldo will be lost," opined Mrs. Campion.

Scott noted the change in her look. She showed concern, interest, and maybe affection for her dead brother. He mulled over this fresh side of Charlotte Campion but did not reach for the money. He sipped his drink instead.

Mrs. Campion laid the cash on the coffee table. "I trust your honesty." She inhaled deeply and exhaled loudly. "I trust *you*."

"You don't know me well enough to make that judgment, but you might be lucky with your guess." Scott projected his purposeful, cynical persona. He knew he was on the up and up with Mrs. Campion, but he still wanted all those in Sleener's orbit to feel uneasy.

"Then you're going to work for me and find Waldo's killer?"

"I'd find his killer without working for you. I won't be beholding to anyone in this mystery. The deep truth is what I want to uncover."

"Call it what you want. Take my money and use it to find the son of a bitch!" Her anger and resolve burst out with her declaration.

Scott would take her case. He was already on the case. Her earnestness made accepting her money simpler. He leaned forward. "Waldo's little book. Have you had any new thoughts or ideas on it?"

"Other than your mention of it, I never knew or heard of any such thing."

"Pity. That damn book has secrets." He shook his head and sipped down another gulp of his Cutty Sark, clinking the ice against the glass as he did.

Mrs. Campion shrugged. "We all do." She smiled for the first time. It appeared to be a second cousin to a smirk, but there was sufficient smile to count.

She worked her way around the coffee table, then stashed her lit cigarette on the edge of the ashtray. She scooped up the money, bringing it to Scott. Campion grabbed his empty, non-drinking hand and stuffed the bills into his palm. Scott held the bills. She held her gaze on him.

"Thank you, Wyatt Scott, for looking into my brother's murder." She leaned down. "Thank you for being a decent man."

Scott calmly took another swallow of his Scotch while she loomed over him. He slid the money into his front trouser pocket. Her new demeanor put him ever so slightly off guard.

She pulled his drinking arm and glass away from his mouth and leaned in. "I appreciate your help more than you know." She kissed him. He did not take part.

His front door banged open. Evie Hall dashed through the entryway, carrying an official-looking manila envelope. Momentarily shocked by the scene, Evie recovered her sardonic disposition as she walked toward Scott. "I see your clientele has improved financially. And apparently the service has expanded too."

At once embarrassed, Mrs. Campion retreated to the refuge of the couch. Spying her forgotten cigarette in the ashtray, she grabbed it. After a quick puff and a gaze at Scott, she rested a guarded eye on Evie.

"What have you got, Evie?" Scott held out his hand for the envelope.

"Something from your government buddy." Evie extended the packet.

She slipped Mrs. Campion a slow, searing perusal. Scott took the object, and Evie shifted her attention to him. She slapped her left hand to her hip and scanned Scott, then Campion, and back again. Miss Hall glared at the pair with the expression of a displeased Sunday school teacher.

Scott opened the envelope. He slid out the top half of a black-and-white picture with a note paper-clipped to it. The note read, 'Campion's office ASAP.' The photo held the image of the Russian who shot up Scott's car. He pushed the photo and note back down into the envelope.

Mrs. Campion scooted to the side of the couch nearest Scott. Evie noted the movement and crossed her arms. Campion glanced her way, then revived her attention on her P.I. host. Evie took a half-step forward, scowling spicier than before.

"So, what's cookin' with the old chippy?" The absence of an account of the scene grew to be more than Evie could handle.

"Watch who you call a chippy, little girl!" Campion whirled toward Evie, flourishing her irritation with the insult.

"Balls and strikes. Balls and strikes. I call 'em the way I see 'em!" exclaimed Evie.

Scott left his chair for Evie's side. The brewing catfight did not appeal to him, and he needed to see what Fielding wanted. "Thanks for bringing this, Evie. Did he say anything?"

Evie calmed a bit and directed her reply to Scott. "Just to get that envelope to you right away."

"Okay, Evie. This is a big help. Beaucoup thanks for rushing it over." Wyatt patted her shoulder.

Evie nodded. Campion puffed away. Evie glared at her.

Campion pulled the cigarette from her mouth. "Shoo away your errand girl, Wyatt. I want to make sure you're on my side and not those government men."

"Go climb your thumb, sister! You're ruining the decor." An irate Evie moved toward Campion.

Charlotte Campion sprang to her feet. The wealthy society wife wiggled her fingers and nails like a mountain lion protecting the entrance to its den.

Scott grabbed Evie by her shoulders. "Head home, Evie." He aimed her body to face the door. "Mrs. Campion is leaving too." He glared over his shoulder, blistering Campion with his eyes. "I'm going to this meeting where I better find some answers."

Evie departed but checked her back twice, striding down the hall. With a head flip, Scott signaled Mrs. Campion to go as well. He waited for her to pass before pulling the door closed.

CHAPTER 16

Spies in Tulsa

Fielding entered through the disproportionately high double doors of the capacious office of Albert Campion, who stood fretfully beside his desk. The CIA supervisor wore his orthodox navy-blue suit and his equally orthodox non-committal expression. His meager nod to Campion would have been considered a twitch by any less constrained human. Palms on either side of a far window, Pierce looked around to regard Fielding before continuing his surveillance of the street below. Campion performed a nervous shuffle, shifting his handmade wingtips in small circles on his plush carpet. His office, his business, his domain, but he acted like a rum runner at a temperance meeting.

Fielding stopped in front of Campion's desk and granted his wristwatch a transitory audience. Patience didn't seem to be a virtue cherished by any in CIA management, but even less so by Fielding. He glared at Campion, which caused an upsurge in the portly man's shuffling. His vest jiggled in harmony with the plumpness around his abdomen. Pierce maintained his high-rise vantage point, displaying little curiosity and less concern about the room's tenor. The side door, rather than the tall double doors, opened, causing Fielding to glance toward it.

Scott stepped through and spoke, "Okay, Fielding, what's going on?" He shut the door hard without looking at it and made his way across the carpeted expanse, leaving Pierce at the window, and stopping several feet short of Campion and Fielding.

Fielding motioned for Campion to leave. The cargo millionaire trod to his imposing main doors. He grasped one's handle and threw it open. For the first time, he seemed light on his toes. Campion swept through the door with an appearance of relief at his exclusion.

"I want to go over what went on," stated Fielding with an echo of his former military clout.

"Go over it?!" Scott shifted toward Fielding. "You know the guy. You know the shooter. Pierce as much as admitted it; so, come clean." Scott stopped just short of Fielding, glaring down more with insistence than animosity.

Pierce budged from his window. He approached the desk, his jacket still too tight for his body and bulging, holstered gun. Fielding shifted away from Scott and around the desk to sit in Campion's cushy chair. He sat with his former military demeanor, stiff and arrogant. Scott stood fast, following the former colonel with annoyed eyes. Fielding studied Scott. Scott glared at Fielding. Pierce sat on the edge of Campion's desk, and he too faced Scott.

"He's a Russian; Alexi Dimitrov," stated Fielding impassively. "Officially attached to the Soviet's Chicago consulate as an agricultural specialist." He cleared his throat. "In our world and in reality, he is an assassin."

Scott wandered to Campion's lavish bar but did not partake. "So, what is he doing here?" After asking his question, he studied liquor bottle labels as opposed to viewing the two spies.

"He cleans up loose ends that worry the commies," chimed in Pierce with a mixture of bravado and annoyance.

Ignoring Pierce, Scott addressed Fielding. "Colonel, what loose end am I, or for that matter, was Hiroshi Ishikawa?"

Fielding raised his right hand and pointed toward Scott. "That is the million-ruble question." He pulled his hand back and dropped both palms on the desk. "It gets worse factoring in Waldo Sleener."

"Maybe that Sleener guy had some dope about him and blackmailed Dimitrov," speculated Pierce.

Fielding narrowed his eyes at Pierce. His non-verbal reproach caused Scott to grin. Pierce slid from the desktop and skulked back toward his window retreat, leaving his CIA boss and the Tulsa P.I. to thrash out the Dimitrov enigma.

"The Soviets wouldn't kill over that," assured Fielding. "He's protected by diplomatic immunity. Anything he did worth blackmailing would get him sent home at worst. Even blackmail for espionage would just result in another operative taking his place." Fielding rubbed his chin before focusing on Scott. "If Sleener had anything on him, it has to be wider and more important than Dimitrov himself."

"Fine. I get it." Scott fiddled with a whisky glass. "You already know I'll keep digging into this mess on my own because I have been. What I do not get is why a secret meeting at Campion's office?" Scott dug at Fielding's true motive.

"Because I need something else," replied Fielding. "Something you can do which I cannot."

Pierce strolled from his window redoubt toward Scott. He held out his closed hand. When he opened the fingers of his fist, the bullet he dug out of the LaSalle's back seat rested in his palm. He offered the spent bullet to Scott. Wyatt studied it, then glared at Fielding.

"Scott, take the bullet," advised Fielding.

He stretched out his hand, palm up, and Pierce dumped the slug into it.

Fielding nodded his approval. "Now, Wyatt, you tell the FBI agents who visited you about the shooting. But leave Pierce out. You were completely alone in your Cadillac chasing the man you thought was stalking you." Fielding detailed his wishes. As an afterthought, he added, "And be sure to tell them you heard him yell in Russian."

Standing with the bullet in his palm and the question on his face, Scott asked; "And this will produce what exactly?"

"The FBI boys will match that bullet to our Japanese victim. Once they look at Russians, Dimitrov will be top of their list. After that, they'll move heaven and earth to get him for MacArthur. Hoover boys are always tickled to take the credit and land some headlines."

"So, this time you would rather they get him than you do?"

"We're looking, but if we don't get lucky, the Soviets will recall him," answered Fielding. "That would be worse."

Scott's puzzlement grew. "That's it? You guys are that afraid of him leaving the country?"

"Dimitrov is known, his diplomatic cover notwithstanding. The guy we want, the top commie, we can't find."

"Then you think the FBI can use Dimitrov to find your elusive top Commie?"

"Hell no!" declared Fielding. "They'd fuck up Stalin in a jail cell! We give them Dimitrov's scent, so they poke around. Our big guy won't know you or CIA has any role in his exposure. Dimitrov won't rat him out. Commies always figure that eventually we'll make a deal for one of our assets in a swap. This makes our unknown, big spy feel safe while we close in."

Scott returned the glass to the bar and grabbed one of Campion's decanters that bore the color of blended Scotch. He poured over two inches. "Okay. The FBI puts on pressure. You and I stay under the radar. What of it?"

"Our big guy has to make his own moves. No help from the Kremlin goons. Any slipup and we've got him." Fielding broke out one of his rarities, a smile, but he dropped it after a moment.

"Slip up?" Scott sipped his whisky. "What concerns are left for him?" Scott narrowed his eyes at Fielding and gulped the remaining Scotch. "Oh, I see, me. I'm still your goddamn bait."

Fielding remained expressionless. "Not that so much, but you would become an irritant. Our top man has to know that you have no government connection and that your involvement is personal. He might try to divert your attention, put it all on Dimitrov and, in so doing, give himself away."

"What about Pierce? If Pierce knows Dimitrov, then it's straight up Dimitrov knows Pierce. He saw him with me and tells this top dog all about me with Pierce. They'll probably figure that you're sniffing around too."

Fielding smirked. "I'll be shocked if Dimitrov contacts his handler, let alone his boss. He might run straight back to Chicago, perhaps back to Mother Russia. If not, the FBI guys can eventually find him."

Pierce chimed in. "Dimitrov doesn't want any part of us. We're not just bad for his stay in the U.S., but if Moscow becomes disenchanted with his performance, his health might suffer."

Fielding nodded and grinned. "Uncle Joe takes a dim view of failure and exposure." He walked across the office to confront Scott. "Now, you need to get this straight. For this event, Pierce was never with you. You heard the guy speak Russian. He shot at you with a silenced gun, just like before. Then, you, being the fearless and righteous detective that you are, had to pursue him to get justice."

Scott exhaled as much skepticism as he could muster. "Are you sure these FBI guys will swallow this bullet, the tall tale, me, the righteous detective, and all of it?"

"You met them. What do you think?" scoffed Fielding.

Scott juggled the bullet as he considered Fielding's ploy. He tossed it a little higher and grabbed the bullet out of the air. Wyatt slid it into the side pocket of his coat. He stepped to the large main doors. "Since you have this entire play blocked out, where are these Hoover boys staying?"

"Downtown. Adams Hotel," replied Fielding.

"Okay." Scott opened the door. He glanced back at Fielding. "I'll make a run at your FBI crew." He marched out and closed the door on the two CIA spies. Lacking any greater knowledge, he calculated that he'd try Fielding's scheme. His run-ins with the two smug FBI agents gave him little confidence that they could find the Russian or that he could garner any meaningful information from them. As he walked away from Campion's office, Wyatt tried to determine which set of government men actually cared about the country.

* * *

The ornate, eclectic, and baroque Adams Hotel almost, but not quite, blended in with the sundry Art Deco buildings dotting Tulsa's downtown topography. Inside the Adams, its decorative, cerulean tiled staircase enticed visitors to the mezzanine or its rooms above. Next to the elevators that abutted the inlay stairs, sat the lobby café. Not to be outdone in ornamentation, it sported terracotta, pastel blues and reds, granting it an assertion of the southern Mediterranean. Its white table clothes, on the dozen or so tables, gave it a clean if not antiseptic look. With more expensive and expansive rooms available for evening dining, the place had no customers save for Wyatt Scott, who waited for FBI agents while he sipped a Coke through a straw. After the solitary attendant left with an announcement that she was going out back for a smoke, Scott waited alone. His fedora rested to his right, guarding his soft drink from attempted theft or incursion on his space.

Agents Fleming and Phillips swept in and positioned themselves on either side of Scott. He acknowledged their presence by simply halting his cola suction for a beat. Fleming leaned on the counter just left of Scott and swiveled his head to view him on the same level. Agent Phillips oozed onto the stool to Scott's right. Flopping his arms on the counter, Phillips dented Wyatt's hat with an errant hand. Cooler than dry ice in January, Scott continued to suck on his paper straw.

"What have you got, Scott?" piped up Agent Fleming.

Wyatt pulled away from his drink. He dropped his hand into his left coat pocket and pulled the Dimitrov bullet out. "Some crazy Russian shot at me. I dug this out of my backseat." He slapped the bullet on the counter in front of agent Fleming.

From his other side, Agent Phillips chimed in. "How do you know he was Russian?"

"Because he yelled at me in Russian." Scott tilted his head toward Phillips. "In the OSS, I listened to Russians talk for two years. I studied it in graduate school. I know Russian."

Fleming tossed the bullet around with his fingers. "Forty-five. A little odd, though; could be Russian." He pulled back from the counter and reached behind Scott to pass the slug to Phillips.

"Yeah." Phillips also leaned behind Scott to take a gander at the chunk of lead. "I see what you mean. Not what you'd see from a Colt or Smith and Wesson."

After a quick sip of his Coke, Scott interjected, "As a topper, the guy that shot that had a silencer on the gun. That makes me figure he's the same guy that tried to shoot me the other night."

Leaning back on the counter and facing Scott, Agent Fleming continued his questioning. "We've been over this before, but do you have any idea why a Russian would want to kill you?"

"No." Scott smiled at Phillips, keeping him engaged before reverting to Fleming. "Other than knowing Hiroshi Ishikawa in Japan fourteen years ago, but that seems a silly reason," replied Scott.

"That does seem silly," agreed Fleming. He gazed at his co-worker. Phillips hesitated before nodding his concurrence.

"How did you run across this Russian in the first place?" continued Fleming.

"I saw the car snooping around." Scott sensed they wanted more.

"Big black sedan; new model. My friends drive nothing that well-appointed."

"Okay, you followed a black sedan," Phillips took his turn. "What was the tag number?"

"The tag was covered up. I'm guessing a local ticket didn't concern him."

"So, he spoke Russian, and he's a professional." Fleming jumped back in. "Whereabouts were you when he shot at your car?"

Scott swirled his straw in the cola. He knew he couldn't play cowed to this pair, but he could play reticent. "I followed him west across the river. Toward Mannford, well past Red Fork." Scott kept close to the true details, steering his story where Fielding wanted it to go. "Traffic thinned, and he made me. We came around a curve, and he jammed on his brakes, then shot when I slid toward him." Scott threw his hands up, adding physical theatrics to his performance. "Before I could grab my gun, he fired again and clipped my tire." Scott dropped his arms. "After that, he took off."

The two agents again pulled back from the counter to converse behind Scott. "MGB?" asked Phillips.

"Has that ring to it." Fleming continued the absurd pretense of talking behind Scott as if he were deaf and could read lips. "Let's get that bullet to Washington." Fleming stood after his suggestion.

"Right," agreed Phillips. "Better get some more guys in from Kansas City too," he added as he stood.

Fleming nodded. Both men began to leave, ignoring Scott as they did.

He spun around on his stool. "You boys let me know when he's going to shoot at me again." Sarcasm rather than Coke filled Scott's breath. "Okay?"

"Sure." Apparently not grasping the sarcastic tone, Agent Fleming continued. "In the meantime, you should probably make yourself scarce, Scott."

Wyatt had to stifle a chuckle. "You just find your loose Russian. I'll keep my eyes open and my back to a wall."

Fleming and Phillips departed. Scott sucked on his straw as he watched the agents walk away. He dropped a dime and a nickel on the counter. The counter girl, who had returned from her smoke, sat near the cash register, appearing as indifferent as she did bored. Scott retrieved his hat and corrected the crease that Agent Phillips had disturbed. With his errand for Fielding complete, Wyatt could not decide whether to go home or stop at the Tulsa Club.

Scott flipped a mental coin that might have had two heads on it and ended up at the Tulsa Club. The place was slow – a weeknight too late for after-work drinkers and evening diners. Even C. A. was missing. No piano music allowed tinny clinks from working silverware to ring through the sparsely populated space. Of the faces in the thin crowd, none looked familiar to Scott. Wyatt wandered to the bar, where John the bartender remained constant.

"Evening, Mr. Scott." John greeted him affably, as he always did. "Cutty on the rocks?"

Scott paused. The day had been hot. The evening remained so. A cool, cold drink might fit the summer night better than his drink of record. A gin and tonic, perhaps? Maybe a beer. A nice, cold beer might be good. "Sure, John." Wyatt surprised himself with his almost autonomic reply. Was it reflex or his distaste for change? The ice would make the whisky cool. The familiar taste would soothe his restless mind.

Scott slid his barstool such that the back did not force his view into the bar and its mirror but gave him an angled panorama of the room. Not being enthusiastic about crowds, the relative emptiness pleased him. His gaze lingered on the door. His mind played a game of who might enter. Many Tulsa elites could be on the list as well as his recent irritations; the Campions, Folgers, or Fielding. No one came through. The door never wavered. With no activity, his brain idled, and the game died.

Scott swiveled his stool back toward the bar to see his Cutty on the rocks waiting for his consideration. Apparently, John had moved not only with his usual efficiency but with inaudible stealth to deposit it there. Two reflexive sips cooled his tongue before he realized his thoughts were ticking back to his mysteries. He hadn't known any Russians. He saw a couple in Nome. There were several on shore leave in Anchorage, but he never interacted with them, let alone knew them. He had listened in on them. He had worked on Venona. Still, it was Brock who made the first breakthrough, and Fielding said they didn't crack it until late in forty-six, and he had gone home to Tulsa before then. What could Hiroshi, whom Scott had not seen since nineteen thirty-four, and he have in common that the Russians would want to kill them? Scott could not imagine any dangerous Soviet secrets that Hiroshi could know.

A long, conscious swig of whisky shifted Wyatt's thoughts to his involvement with anything Soviet related. He avoided Fielding, let alone Pierce, until after being shot at. Nothing he had done since the war came remotely close to Russia or any U. S. fellow-travelers. Could it be something of which he was never aware? The ballistic revelation about Sleener's murder offered a variable for his role to slip into the equation. The odd blackmailer had a sketchy character and seemed to have some communion with communism. Could the Soviets stretch his minor contact with Sleener into something dangerous to them? Having never talked directly with Sleener, let alone greeted him alive, the jump from him to Scott seemed a longshot but in a puzzle with no connections, he had to consider long odds.

An empty whisky glass brought his attention back to the present. "John, hit me again."

The bartender quit his mindless shuffling of backbar glasses and veered to take Scott's glass. He dumped the ice remanence in the sink, scooped new cubes into the glass, and set it back on the counter. A quick grab under the bar produced a bottle of Cutty Sark, and John poured liberally over the ice. "There you are, Mr. Scott."

"Thanks, John." Scott sipped. He felt like reminiscing. Japan had fine memories, but those would circulate around to the Hiroshi question, his involvement, and the whole damn Dimitrov quandary. Alaska held too many recriminations, sadness, and guilt to ever provide escape. A flood of fond moments with Janet zipped through before the inevitable transition to her leaving. He stared down at his glass and sipped again, hoping the taste and look of the amber liquid would promote a cheerful scene of moments past. The whisky level had sunk enough for the top cube of ice to be surrounded by air. Sadly, the drink offered nothing but the science of phase change and tangential commentary on his solitude.

"The F, B, I guys drive you to drink?" asked Fielding slowly, emphasizing each letter in the agency name.

Scott remained serene despite his surprise. Fielding took the stool on his left. Wyatt stared down at the bar while he replied. "Checking to see if I carried out your little plan?"

Fielding eased onto his stool. "No. You want to figure this mess out as much as I do. I had no doubt you would play along this time."

John moved to accommodate the new customer. "May I get you something, sir?"

"I am staying at the Mayo. I have a visitor tab here if you will check. The name is Fielding." He mused over a cocktail selection. "Gin and tonic."

"Yes, sir." John moved down the bar.

"Then why are you here?" asked Scott.

"No company reasons." Fielding took a step from his stool to fetch a small bowl of nuts farther down the bar. "I can't figure why Dimitrov would be interested in you. I keep thinking on it." He sat back down and popped two cashews into his mouth.

"You won't find an answer from me."

John brought the gin and tonic, interrupting the mutual puzzlement. "Gin and tonic." He set the glass before Fielding. "Just signal if you need another." John smiled and eased back down the bar to while away the boring night tidying his station.

Fielding barely sipped the drink before reconsidering his riddle. "Finding the connection for you or the Sleener guy falls outside the bounds of intelligence work and somewhere beyond sensible consideration."

"Whole compendium of improbable connections. Hiroshi couldn't hurt the Russians now. Sleener was a blackmailer, but he wouldn't know Dimitrov; you said the guy is based in Chicago. And I haven't thought about a Russian since forty-six." Scott pulled on an earlobe.

"Sleener has no overlap with the spy game. I hoped you had some info from him that put both of you in the MGB crosshairs."

"I never talked directly to him. Whatever interest the Soviets had in him, he never got a chance to tell me."

"They killed him before he could meet with you."

"I'm aware of that. The meeting had nothing to do with his telling me Soviet secrets. It was over his blackmailing of a socialite. I went there to pay him off." Scott turned to the backbar and stared at his likeness.

Fielding looked at Scott in the mirror. "Sleener, Hiroshi, then you."

"To be exact, it was Sleener, Hiroshi, me, then me again."

"No good reason, but they kept after you."

Scott downed the last of his Cutty. "The Tulsa police know about me and Hiroshi but can't square the combination either. Only Art Cleveland knows about the slug from Sleener matching. He told me he'd sit on that because it would make life harder for him as well as me."

"Because of MacArthur's baseball tour, the FBI will stay all over Ishikawa's murder." Fielding fished around in his pocket and took out a pack of cigarettes and a lighter. He performed the ritual of lighting one and blowing the smoke up in the air. "FBI probably doesn't have Sleener in its files. That bullet you gave them will be enough to point at Dimitrov, though."

"Fine. So, I wait for the FBI to stumble around and find Dimitrov if your guys don't find him first." Scott flipped the eyeball equivalent of his middle finger at Fielding. "And how the hell do I find out what this is about? What's going on? And why am I in the middle of it?"

"We ask Dimitrov." The spy minder slurped some of his gin and quinine.

"Kind of answer I'd expect from government operatives." Scott pushed away from the bar and stood.

"If you find an answer, Wyatt, I'd be happy to hear it from you." Fielding remained content to puff again on his cigarette.

"Yeah, sure." Scott signaled 'goodbye' to John with a quick flick of his wrist. "In the meantime, what do I do?"

"I'd stay away from Dimitrov if I were you." Fielding took another smoke without looking at Scott, then gulped more gin.

Wyatt walked away, stifling a dozen caustic comments.

CHAPTER 17

August Heat

The hot, dry breath of West Texas blew across the Red River, bringing grasshoppers and desiccation to the Oklahoma greenery. July had pummeled everything, but even it wilted under August's onslaught. Drought continued in Tulsa with August heat burning lawns and shoe leather beyond the awful levels of July. Temperatures stretched the tolerance of the locals who grew up with it, but northeastern Oklahoma broiled hotter than Hades for a Russian. Sweating through his undershirt as he sat at a kitchen table, Alexi Dimitrov glared out the small window above the sink. A simple cabin, his habitat, included a bed, the kitchen table with three chairs, a makeshift closet without a door, and an oil lamp for light. A wooden icebox sat on the floor with its ice door open, dry, and testifying to the cabinet's uselessness. The privy out back tossed flies and stench into the milieu. No gas, no electricity, and a hand pump for water set the cabin fifty years in the past.

The seasonally unnecessary fireplace stored a sturdy leather suitcase rather than logs. A trash canister held empty tin cans, a profusion of food scraps, coffee grounds, and a drained pint bottle labeled Smirnoff vodka. Two dirty dishes, a glass, a mug, a fork, and two spoons populated the sink. The countertop supported a clean mug, two glasses, and another empty pint bottle of vodka. Barely flexing the tautly made bed, an open aluminum case flaunted a high-caliber pistol, its noise suppressor mate, and three boxes of specialty ammunition.

Motor sounds from a car pulling up to the cabin stirred the Russian away from his stare through the side window. He grabbed the two clean glasses from the counter, placed them on the kitchen table, and took a seat facing his cabin's entrance. Its door swung open. A man hefting a grocery bag strode in.

"Brat shpion. Priyatno videt tebya snova," called out Dimitrov in his native tongue.

"Privet, tovarishch," replied his friend, continuing in Russian.

The man set his bag of groceries on the counter. He pulled out a new loaf of Wonder Bread, a package of Velveeta, two tins of Spam, then followed on with cans of peaches, peas, carrots, and a small tin of coffee. He folded the paper sack and left it on the counter. The visitor stepped to the table where Dimitrov remained seated. He drew a pint bottle of vodka from his hip pocket and deposited it with a thud in front of Dimitrov.

"Ty prines vocku, molodets!" exclaimed the excited Russian. He scrambled to his feet and grabbed the bottle.

"Po angliyski pozhaluysta," reprimanded his grocery benefactor.

"Yes, English." Dimitrov nodded. "Even American vodka is better than the Oklahoma moonshine. I thank you, comrade." He bowed, emphasizing his gratitude.

Dimitrov unscrewed the bottlecap. He poured vodka into his glass, then dispensed two inches into its twin. He pushed the vodka toward his guest. The burly Russian pointed to a chair. His comrade followed the suggestion, pulling the chair out and sitting. Dimitrov took his seat, then raised his drinking glass.

"Tost za nashu rabotu!" Dimitrov heard himself. "Oh, English, yes. To our work!"

Dimitrov took a huge swig. His guest raised his tumbler but merely sipped. While the other man lowered his drink and held it, Dimitrov poured another round in his own glass. He drank again.

"Ahhh," sighed Dimitrov. He peered at his benefactor. "How much longer?"

"We are not sure. If we cannot move you confidently, it will be several weeks." The spy supplier nursed his vodka with tiny sips.

"That is so long, comrade." The brawny Russian sighed and finished his vodka.

"Your blunder keeps you here. I will do what I can, while I follow the schedule. We will handle this. We don't want Moscow involved, and you don't either."

"I understand," lamented the Russian. "But it is so hot!"

"You have no one to blame but yourself!" The partner sharpened his rebuke.

"No one? I think there are errors by others, also." Dimitrov wiped sweat from his forehead, his nose, and his neck. "I cannot get cool."

"Swim in the lake behind." The man pointed over Dimitrov's head toward the back of the cabin and the lake fifty yards beyond.

"I did. The lake is hot."

"Endure. It is for our communist way."

"Da," replied Dimitrov, abjuring English for the mother tongue.

* * *

The wounded LaSalle lingered in its usual alley spot. While the Peters brothers' repair job stopped the wind whistling through the bullet hole, the blotch annoyed Scott's driving eyes. His new plan involved clear tape, double-wide, to block the hole on the inside. Two strips lengthwise and two across sealed it. Two more strips crossing to add strength finished his prep work. He peeled off the outer piece of mechanical tape and cardboard fitted by the Peters, then cleaned the road-facing glass with ammonia.

With the interior supporting tape in place, Wyatt readied his clever filler. He pierced the cap and squeezed almost the entire tube of model airplane glue into the hole. Before the glue could run, he slapped a cut square of laundry shirt cardboard, covered in Vaseline, against it. He ripped off two strands of clear tape and crisscrossed the square to hold it firm. The plan calculated that the outer patch could be removed as soon as the glue hardened. The interior tape, safe from weather, could remain until the tape lost adhesion. In the end, a minor spot of annoyance, a bug splatter in his peripheral vision, would remain rather than the titanic, irksome blotchy patch.

As Wyatt stood back admiring his masterpiece, footsteps behind heralded a visitor. He glanced up to see Art Cleveland approaching. The Tulsa police officer craned his head to view the LaSalle's infirmary poultice. He mixed quizzical eyes with a slight grin.

"Interesting patch job." Detective Cleveland bent down to inspect Scott's windshield work. He sniffed. "Smells like model airplane glue."

"It is. I thought it would block the hole without blocking half the windshield."

"Hmmm. Might work." Cleveland shifted to view Scott's patch from different angles. "I heard you got shot up again; not that you phone or let me know personally."

"I'm sure the Tulsa police stay well informed."

"Not so timely informed is my complaint." Cleveland pointed at Scott's fresh handiwork. "Besides the hole in your windshield, is there anything else you would care to tell me about that episode?"

"I don't know, Art. Unless the guy sends me a Western Union explaining why, your guess is as good as mine."

"You didn't see him?"

"No. Didn't see him." Scott thought the lie served Cleveland better than dragging him into the spy morass he was wading through.

"Wyatt Scott, shot up by ghosts." Cleveland tossed out a series of fake sighs and tiny head shakes of his disbelief. "Have those FBI boys come around to see you?" Cleveland glanced nonchalantly down the alley, at the LaSalle, and everywhere but at Scott. "They came by the department asking us about you. Morgan had words with them." He brought his gaze back around to Scott. "Not over you. They have taken over that dead Jap case completely. He told them that if they were so smart, they didn't need to bother the Tulsa department anymore. He left his own office before they could say another word."

"They came to my apartment. I figured they saw Morgan because they asked dumber questions than the first time." Scott smirked reflexively, thinking of Morgan. "Should be better for you, Art, if he has the FBI to be pissed at instead of you."

"Possibly. He dog cussed them after they left." Cleveland affectedly cleared his throat. "On that other murder, Morgan doesn't want to hear anything about Sleener." He focused back on Scott. "Just leaves the two of us who know the facts. I'm guessing just one of us knows what's really going on."

"I don't know more about Sleener's involvement than you do. Our bullet match gives a 'who' but not a 'why' in the mess."

"Sure." Cleveland's sarcasm dripped thick. "My guess is the same guy made that hole in your windshield. You know you could tell me *who*."

"Hiroshi Ishikawa factors in. Since the FBI took over, stay out of it. I would if I could." Scott stared Cleveland in the eyes. He wanted to convey the seriousness of the situation without revealing Dimitrov, Russians, or Fielding and the CIA.

"So, that's the way it is. You want me to dish to you, but the reciprocity ends with lunch." Cleveland glared at Scott.

"Art, you really don't want to wade into this mess. It truly is an FBI deal. It's international, brutal, and has no rules."

"The hell you say."

"I do. Be glad Morgan's off Sleener and won't ask questions."

"For better or worse, he's off that for sure now. A brand-new case has Morgan beside himself." Cleveland pursed his lips and bent his head a little. "It's a sad one. You hear about that young child found dead?"

"No."

"A little girl, just seven or eight tops. Old lady picking flowers nearby found her in a field south of Thirty-first Street. The kid was dressed up like she was going to church. Her hair curled, and she wore a pretty little dress with shiny new shoes. It didn't look natural, but there was no sign of physical abuse. Morgan's still waiting for the coroner to know if it's murder or not."

"That is sad, Art. Odd too," added Scott.

"Yes. It's hard for me to know what to make of it." Cleveland sighed. "Morgan is beside himself about it. He's taken it to heart. I've never seen him so upset, but this one has done it."

Before Cleveland could elaborate or Scott could comment further, Johnny Grayhawk strolled into the alley. "You don't have to answer his questions, Wyatt. Your lawyer's here now." Johnny grinned ear-to-ear.

"Well, Mr. attorney, your client is pure-ass gold when it comes to keeping secrets." No humor crossed Detective Cleveland's face.

"Oh, don't I know it." Johnny reached the pair and the front of the LaSalle. "My clever pal is patching his windshield with airplane glue. You didn't catch him sniffing it, did you?"

"Scott doesn't need that to act crazy. Has he told you what he's gotten himself into?" asked Cleveland.

"We're best pals, but I still have to fill in between the lines," replied Grayhawk. "I thought maybe Mike Barton would get more out of him, but that didn't happen."

"The retired detective Morgan replaced?" followed up Cleveland.

"Morgan couldn't replace Mike Barton's shoelaces," jumped in Scott. "Look, you two, I'm not trying to shade you. This whole mess makes no sense. I learned a little from Fielding, but it took me being shot at twice to find that little bit. I am leaving the whole mess to J. Edgar Hoover and his band of merry men." Scott threw up his arms to illustrate his dropping the case.

"I'm all for it if it keeps you alive," stated Johnny with a sincere face.

"Anything to keep the body count down around you, Scott." Cleveland pivoted to Johnny. "Do you believe you can glue a windshield?"

Johnny shrugged. "Never thought about it. If it does work, it'll look better than that mechanical tape blob he had on the Caddy before."

"Back seat's a mess too." Cleveland pointed to the tape Zip Peters slapped on the shot and slit seatback. "Looks like a Brooklyn bar repair."

"Yessir. I need my P.I. to fix up his automobile. That white-trash look will reflect on my classy law practice." Johnny winked at Scott.

"If you two are finished harassing me about my car, I will go pay some bills and see if I have enough money to make repairs."

"I'm already gone." Art Cleveland spun and walked away. He waved his hat without missing a stride.

"That glue notion might not be half bad," acknowledged Johnny.

"I hope it holds. I just couldn't stand that mess. It kept drawing my attention."

"It should keep until you get a replacement windshield." Grayhawk eyeballed the patch job. "And speaking of that..." Johnny shifted to face Scott. "...I met with Nathan Benjamin. Since you got Bugler off without Benjamin having to do any work, he gave my entire retainer back." Johnny grinned. "I guess old Nate is not as bad as I thought." Still smiling, Johnny added, "And with me getting back my four hundred bucks from Benjamin, let me buy you a new windshield."

"Not necessary, Johnny."

"It is, and I've already ordered it. Silly thing takes four or five weeks," groused Johnny. "What about the upholstery?"

"That I will take care of," declared Scott.

"Windshield didn't cost near four hundred. I can cover it."

"You've done too much with the windshield. Keep the rest as your reward for doing right by poor old Bugler."

Johnny acquiesced with a shrug. "Are you all right, Wyatt? Should I get the ball gloves to play catch?"

"Nothing to talk over. I don't know how or why I got involved in this."

"Your old shithead spy boss is how. I just hope you can get out of it with that head still on your shoulders."

"Me too, Johnny." Scott walked toward his friend and the end of the alley. "We'll play catch when this mess is over."

* * *

Scott hung up his desk phone after completing a chat with Spike Peters. Spike called to let him know that he and his brother had found a good used tire and inner tube for the LaSalle. After several days of driving on risky rubber, he figured to pick up the tire and ask the brothers for more details on Dimitrov's vehicle. Scott jerked his coat from the back of his chair and stood to put it on. He knew they could tell him the make, model, and any idiosyncrasies that the car might have. Before he could square his coat to hide his nineteen eleven, Fielding and Pierce paraded through his door.

"Wyatt Scott, my local man." Fielding drifted to the guest chair while Pierce shut the door and lingered just inside.

"Is that so?" Scott straightened his coat and buttoned it.

"It is now. I want you to work with Pierce to get Dimitrov."

"Look, I have somewhere to go. If you two jokers don't leave, I'll make you."

"Don't get testy, Wyatt. We're your customers here on business." Fielding reached inside his coat and produced an envelope. "You are our all-American boy; the secret weapon to unlock Tulsa." He slid it onto Scott's desk. "Here is your first official pay for services rendered to the U. S. government."

"What?" Scott picked up the envelope and withdrew a check made out to him from the U. S. Treasury. He read the insignificant details twice. It was real but still seemed phony.

"I told you we would hire you to investigate local characters. We believe Dimitrov is local." Fielding stood. "Another check will come next week." He glanced toward Pierce, then back to Scott. "I want you to drive Pierce around while you visit your contacts. See if any Tulsans have seen a Russian. Or, better still, know where one lives."

"Not sure this is enough money to spend time with Pierce." Scott tossed a scowl at Fielding's stocky gunsel but switched back to Fielding just before Pierce shot him the finger. "What makes you think Dimitrov is still around? A Russian would stick out like a bootlegger at a Presbyterian picnic."

"For enough money, some people will hide the bootlegger under the picnic table," reasoned Fielding. "We're sure he hasn't gone back to Chicago. The FBI boys have been searching all over. They've got marshals involved, asking questions. They've had state troopers in Kansas, Missouri, Arkansas, and Illinois set up roadblocks looking for foreigners."

"All that effort and no results, I gather. Tells me he's made it out of the country or gone to ground," reasoned Scott.

"My thinking, too." Fielding pulled on his lapels, straightening his suit coat. "But I don't believe he left."

"Since I want to find him as well, I'll bite on this deal. One stipulation." Scott stared at Fielding, then glared at Pierce. "He keeps his mouth shut. No better way to get folks to clam up than an outsider, government guy rubbing them the wrong way."

Fielding turned toward Pierce and cautioned his underling. "Just watch. Help Scott with Dimitrov but stay out of his way with the locals."

After a few seconds, Pierce delivered a slow, affirmative nod. He opened the door without waiting to be told. Scott watched him step into the hall. Fielding headed toward Pierce and the open door.

Scott pulled out his middle drawer, dropped the check in, and shoved it closed. "Are we ready to start this hunt for a Russian in a haystack?" asked Scott.

"At your pleasure," replied Fielding.

Scott headed for the door. "Then let's go. I have a stop to pick up a spare tire. Pierce can listen and learn. Dimitrov bought gas at my local station."

* * *

As Scott rolled into the Peters Brothers' Auto Repair and Fillling Station. Pierce manned the passenger side of the LaSalle. Noting the red convertible's arrival, both Spike and Zip ambled from the office to greet him. With the scorching weather, both gas jockeys wore white t-shirts rather than their long sleeve Sinclair standards. The younger Zip's larger biceps filled out his cotton tee, while Spike's rolled up smokes padded his left shoulder. They got to Scott's door, full of grins and ready to serve.

"Got that tire in the bay just waitin' on yer' hub," proclaimed Zip. "Already have the inner tube stuffed in her."

Spike kept his gaze on Pierce. "Who's yer' 'rassler pal, Wyatt?"

"Spike and Zip, this is Mr. Pierce." Scott waved his left hand toward the spy. "Pierce, these gents are the Peters brothers."

Pierce nodded. Spike abbreviated his nod to match Pierce's.

"Howdy, Mr. Pierce." Zip, being the more outgoing, touched his cap.

"I'll run grab your old spare to get the hub." Spike drifted back to the trunk and popped the lid.

"How you been, Wyatt? Haven't been shot up again, have ya'?" Zip grinned with his teasing. Abruptly shifting his expression to concern, Zip leaned close to Scott's ear. "Should I've kept shut about that?" he whispered.

"It's fine." Scott tossed his head toward Pierce, then looked back to Zip to let the pump jockey understand he could talk freely. "I've stayed clear of that trouble, Zip."

"That's good, I suppose." Zip Peters seemed to have a question, but none came forth.

Spike hefted the tire out of the trunk. He trundled it toward Zip, the ruined flat flopping along more than rolling. Stopping short of his brother's toes, Spike addressed Scott. "Let me get Zip out of yer' hair. He needs to help me pull this rim and get yer' tire on it."

"I'll get with ya,' Spike," reassured his brother. "Just thought I better check with Wyatt 'bout his gas and oil."

"Okay," replied Spike. He stepped closer to Scott. "How are ya' on gas?"

"I think good, but since I'm here, why don't ya' top it off." Scott glanced toward the gas cap.

Spike rolled the tire against the gas pump. "I'll get the gas started. Zip, you give the Caddy a look under her hood."

Zip saluted his brother and shifted to the front of the LaSalle. He looked toward Scott, then stopped. He stared at the refashioned patch on the windshield. Spike removed the gas cap and cranked the pump. Deserting the front of the LaSalle, Zip came back to Scott's door. Spike witnessed Zip's trot back to Scott while he shoved the nozzle into the gasoline pipe.

"What'd ya' do on that windshield patch?" asked Zip.

Before Scott could answer, Spike broke in. "Zip, why'd ya' leave off the oil check?"

"Look-see at that windshield, Spike. Wyatt's got a doozy of a patch now."

Spike peeked around Scott to view the bullet hole. "Hey, that is somethin'."

"Yeah. That patch is slicker than snot. How'd ya' do it?" quizzed Zip again.

"Model airplane glue," answered Scott. "I taped the inside and squirted the damn hole full of glue."

"I'll be," mused Spike. "That's some clever thinkin'."

"We'll remember that one," added Zip.

Gas started gurgling in the nozzle. Spike jerked the nozzle out of the LaSalle before any gasoline could overflow. He hung the hose back on the pump.

"Sorry, Wyatt. Almost had a spill toward yer' paint," reported Spike.

"No harm, Spike. Just get that spare fixed up for me," said Scott.

"Come on, Zip. We'll get that tire then do a check under the hood." Spike headed to the garage.

Zip leaned closer to Scott. "I was hopin' ya' got that damn commie." Disappointment tinged his statement.

"I'm still working on that Zip. Mr. Pierce here is helping out."

Zip looked over to Pierce. "Good luck to you too, then, Mr. Pierce." The younger Peters brother trotted off to help Spike air up the spare.

"Why have you got me at a gas station watching you run errands?" Pierce offered with half-question and half-complaint in his query.

"Dimitrov stopped here for gas. We can ask the Peters about his car."

"You and I saw the damn car. We already know what it looks like." Pierce scowled for punctuation.

"Look Pierce. These two guys know more about cars than anyone you'll find. They can remember details and tell us what we can expect from that car." Scott pivoted, leaning on his door to partially face the CIA agent. "You remember its make?"

Pierce spun to mirror Scott's pose. "It was black."

"Yeah, that's what I thought." Scott sighed. "It was dark. It might've been navy."

"Okay. Either way, we'll recognize him."

"If he ties a flag on the radio antenna that says, 'Dimitrov, Russian spy,' then yes. We can't run up beside every dark car in northeast

Oklahoma to look at the driver. The Peters will remember the make and model. Since they checked under the hood, they'll recognize the engine and what it can do."

As sour and skeptical as ever, Pierce stared at Scott. "Those two pump jockeys better be as observant as you claim. I don't need to be here wasting time with you."

"Take it up with your boss. He gave his orders." Wyatt peered across the downtown Eastside streets. A few Tulsa pedestrians braved the early August swelter. With that inflexible heat soaking the LaSalle, Scott checked the mechanic's bay door before he swiveled back to Pierce.

Sweat rolled out of the agent's hair, past his ear. Pierce ran a finger across his forehead and flicked the drops onto the pavement. "Scott, can you hurry those grease monkeys up? It's damn hot just sitting here."

"The brothers have an icebox." Scott shifted in his seat and opened his door. "Come on, Pierce. I'll buy you a cold pop before we head west looking for Dimitrov." Scott stepped out of the LaSalle and circled to its front.

The CIA man opened his door and eased out. Before he shut it, he took out a handkerchief and wiped his forehead. He slammed the door, engendering a scowl from Wyatt. Pierce drifted around the car's front fender on his way to join Scott.

"If I can put up with you, you can put up with the heat." Wyatt followed Pierce's progress toward him. "We're here to get info on Dimitrov's car, but we need that spare too. That son of a bitch ruins tires as a hobby."

Rattling from the bay door opening alerted both men to the Peters completing their work. Pierce and Scott halted their quest for cool drinks and waited by the gas pumps. Spike appeared first with the solid tire poised at his side. With the door fully open, he started forward. Without a tire to trundle, Zip caught and passed his brother to reach the LaSalle's trunk. He popped it open and stepped aside. Spike hoisted the spare up and in.

"You're all set," announced Zip.

"It's a good tire this time," added Spike as he slammed the lid.

"Thanks, boys. Let's go into your office." Scott pointed a finger in that direction. "I'll pay up, and you can add for a couple of cold pops. While we're at it, I'd like to hear what you can tell us about the Russian's car."

CHAPTER 18

Visitors, Too Many Visitors

When Scott pulled into the Sophian Plaza apartments, he checked his watch, finding it later than he thought, yet the heat remained stifling. Tulsa could be hot in summer; sometimes blistering. This year seemed determined to be the latter, although it could not compare to the one before he left for college. That nineteen thirty-six summer broke all records with dozens of dates recording over one hundred degrees, with one exceptional day reaching a broiling one hundred sixteen. He and his folks slept on their porch during those nights. Most of Tulsa had done the same. Backyards, even front yards, looked like sleeping dorms. Sheets, blankets, pillows, and people outfitted in flimsy clothing just short of getting them arrested speckled neighborhood landscapes. His nostalgic memory of that extreme heat made this evening cooler, at least in Wyatt's mind.

Scott parked his LaSalle, entered the building, and spurned the elevator in favor of four flights of stairs. He scaled the steps, reaching his floor, where the west flank supported his apartment. He strolled down the hall, reaching his door with little thought about the dimmer than usual passageway. As he reached to open his door, the hard metal tip of a gun poked his back.

"You will please enter without making movements." The accented voice declared its owner to be a son of Mother Russia.

Scott felt the gun barrel pull away from his spine. The man stepped back. Scott bent to unlock his door and saw Dimitrov in his peripheral vision. He jiggled his key and opened the door. He stepped across the threshold with the Russian spy close behind. Dimitrov shut the door as Wyatt flipped the light switch on. He stood by his bar and observed his would-be assassin. Up close, he noted the Russian's solid body; several inches shorter than Wyatt and built like an older, tougher version of Pierce. His face carried a slight twinge of Asian ancestry, making it likely that a great grandparent from Siberia coupled with Slavik and European Russians to produce his line. His clothing smacked of Sears and Roebuck and couldn't appear more American if he had sewn the stars and stripes on his shirt and worn a baseball cap.

The Russian pointed his gun towards Wyatt's coffee table. "Sit in your chair beside that couch."

Scott followed the instructions. He sat more delicately than his usual mode and kept his toes and the balls of his feet on the floor, ready to spring. Dimitrov made his way to the sofa. He kept his gun pointed at Scott as he reclined on its far side, away from Scott's chair. Wyatt stared at the gun barrel and its heavy silencer attached. He recalled Moe Berg's admonition after Jimmy Foxx slammed the long-ball at batting practice,

"Sometimes the *other guy* is a step ahead of you." Wyatt considered ways to get that step back.

"We understood you knew Ishikawa, but not that you work for C, I, A," declared Dimitrov.

"CIA?" asked Scott as guilelessly as he could manage.

"Yes. Your American Central Intelligence Agency," explained Dimitrov as if Scott were as naïve as he played.

The Russian scratched his gun arm with his left hand. Scott noted a tattoo in Cyrillic that claimed 'navy' with what looked more like a snake than an anchor below it. The odd squiggle must've been what Zip Peters spied. Scott refocused on the Russian's face. He looked him in his eyes. "Why would you think that?"

"You chased me with Pierce of the CIA." The Russian arranged himself on the couch, putting one foot up on its upholstery.

Scott stared for a moment at the offending foot dirtying his sofa before his rational mind realized its insignificance given the situation. "Do you know Pierce?" He reengaged the Soviet killer, even though he reasoned Dimitrov would know Pierce as undeniably as Pierce knew Dimitrov.

"As he knows me; by dossier."

Scott nodded at the simple, obvious answer. "Being shot at gives me a reason to deal with them."

"Da." Dimitrov nodded. "You worked for them during the war, no?"

"I worked with OSS and OIS during the war." Scott smirked. "And during the war, we were on the same side."

"In Europe, and only some of the time there, we were comrades."

Dimitrov waved his gun barrel like a pointing finger. "Not in Asia. Not in Alaska."

Scott couldn't tell how much the husky spy knew about him, Alaska, or any involvement he had with Fielding. The gun pointed at him notwithstanding, his curiosity emerged. "What did Hiroshi Ishikawa know that was so important that you folks killed him?"

"Ah, more curious than frightened. You *should* work for your country." Dimitrov cracked a self-satisfied smile. It lingered a moment before the Russian ripped it from his face in favor of his more stoic standard. "With respect to Mr. Ishikawa, that is the beginning of my problem. I did not perform as I should. I am a lowly servant of my government. My leaders do not tell me what was important about him, only my mission."

"I see. And they told you to kill me without a reason either?"

Dimitrov shrugged. He pointed the gun away from Scott and waggled it as an aid to his thinking. "No, I thought maybe you become a loose end, as they say in your American gangster movies." The Soviet spy wrinkled his brow. "You are very agile." He waved his gun back level at Scott. "I think you are my only failure."

"Don't lose heart. You're young; you'll get your share."

Apparently appreciating the sarcasm, Dimitrov smiled, perhaps even holding back a laugh. "I could have killed you when you left the Hotel Adams and those FBI."

"But you waited to kill me in my apartment?"

"I waited to ask you questions in your apartment." The Russian wet-works spy sighed. "I follow orders, but now I have questions about those orders."

Scott stared at Dimitrov. He stared back and scooted down the couch toward the end table. His eyes and the gun never left Scott.

"Things about you have become interesting, Wyatt Scott." Dimitrov looked away and picked up the picture of Scott, Brock, and Harris in Alaska. "A war memento photo, I believe. Who are these soldiers with you? Your comrades?"

"A pair of soldiers who died in Alaska during the war," answered Scott flatly.

"Both?" Dimitrov stared at the photo. "Hmmm." He pulled it closer to his face before letting his hand ooze it down to his side on the sofa cushion. "I found Alaska nice. My ship went to Anchorage."

"I thought it was a cold hellhole."

"Not Anchorage in summer nineteen forty-four. You were there with those friends and a girl."

Scott considered his single summer trip to Anchorage. "We saw a group of Soviet sailors." He retrieved the memory. "I didn't recognize you from that day."

"I remember my trip. Also, I did not place you there until now." The spy smiled. "We have lives in common."

"If you say so, comrade."

"To my questions. Why do the CIA men want me?"

"Because you killed Hiroshi Ishikawa and because you're a Soviet spy. That's pretty simple."

"Too simple, my friend." The spy peered down at the photo. "I think things are complicated. It started before the Japanese."

"That I know. You killed the blackmailer, Sleener."

"The man at Tulsa Union train station?" Dimitrov tapped his

finger on the picture frame. "He was my first assignment. You did not see me. Was it my bullet?"

"Yes. The FBI and CIA understand about your bullets. The CIA knows about Sleener. All of us wonder why him?"

"Ah. I, too, wanted answers. I am only here because I believed you possessed my answers."

"I am as lost as you are, comrade." Scott leaned forward in his chair. "If you have to kill me, you might as well go ahead; there is nothing I can tell you."

Dimitrov leveled his gun at Scott's chest. The gun and its wide, blunt silencer stipulated routine business. He held the elongated barrel steady. Wyatt wondered what he'd feel.

Dimitrov swung the barrel. He squeezed the trigger. A muted sound registered across the apartment. He smiled. "Now your sofa will remember me as your automobile remembers."

"That was dramatic." Scott stared at the gash through the arm of his couch and the slug's terminus in his wall. "Why my couch instead of me?"

"If it would benefit our Soviet Union, that hole would be in you, friend, and not a sofa." Dimitrov shrugged. "I have not heard from Moscow since before I killed the man at the train depot. My work is for Comrade Stalin and our party. I worry there is a problem."

"I no longer worry you?" asked Scott.

"Killing you now would serve no purpose." The Russian lowered his pistol. "I understand now. Wyatt Scott is not important to the Soviet Union."

"I tried to tell the CIA that, comrade Dimitrov."

"Call me Alexi. We are acquainted now." The Russian waxed on about the nuances of the situation. "We are in a strange play, comrade Scott."

"I don't see my role," said Wyatt.

"As it should be. You are the bystander; the one that does not know."

"That's puzzling. Where does it leave me?"

"I cannot guess. The Soviet Union does not care about you. As for me, I will not be moving back to my consulate. I will just...be gone." His voice finished with a nostalgic air of fatalism. Dimitrov raised the framed photo for another look. He stood and weaved around the coffee table. When he stepped close to Scott, he handed the framed photo to him. "Tell me about these friends as we walk to your kitchen for refreshment."

Scott accepted the picture. He left his chair and walked toward his kitchen. "They said both of them killed themselves."

Dimitrov followed close behind Scott. "What do you say, Mr. Scott?"

Scott slowed as he studied the wartime photo. "I say they were both murdered in Alaska. Someone shot the younger one."

The Russian followed in Scott's steps. "And the other?" asked Dimitrov.

"Alaska, the snow, the army, the war – one or more killed him," lamented Scott.

"Hmmm. I see. Yes, I understand." Dimitrov's inflection corroborated understanding.

Wyatt reached the kitchen entrance. His captor closed behind him. Dimitrov raised the silencer tipped pistol above his head and brought it violently down where Scott's neck joined his skull. Scott crumpled between his dining room and the kitchen. The framed photo slipped from his hands and struck the floor. It bounced, but the glass did not crack. The Russian stood over him for several seconds. He removed the silencer and slipped it and his gun into his pants pockets. He bent down on one knee and rifled through Scott's clothing. With nothing that interested him, Dimitrov picked up the framed photograph. He stood and stared at it before he sauntered back to the living room. The Russian positioned the picture back on the table next to the couch where Scott kept it.

In no hurry, Dimitrov rifled Scott's bedroom. As messy as he was thorough, he emptied drawers, scoured cabinets, and ransacked the closets. He brought one of Scott's shirts with him to the living room, where he draped it over the sofa's wounded arm like a laundered bandage. Cycling through every chamber, he didn't disturb the guest bedroom, kitchen, dining room, or bath. He worked his way again into the living room. After permitting relative order beyond the bedroom, Alexi Dimitrov departed Scott's apartment, leaving the door ajar.

* * *

Wyatt Scott stood on a pitcher's mound in his Athletics uniform. He twirled the white, stitched horsehide of a baseball in his right hand. With that hand behind his back and hidden from the batter, Wyatt gripped the ball. He maneuvered his index finger and his middle one to command a nickel curve.

The vague batter, his catcher hidden beneath his mask, and the obscure umpire awaited his offering. The stadium sat disconcertingly silent. Featureless faces populated the stands. Scott wound up. He took his long stride. He brought his hand and arm around in his throwing motion.

Wyatt's right arm, still gripping the baseball, flew toward home plate. Shocked and armless, Scott stood at the base of the mound. His catcher pulled his mask up on his head. It was Johnny Grayhawk, who strode forward to pick up the arm with the baseball still held by Scott's detached hand. He carried the errant arm in his throwing hand and confronted Scott at the pitcher's mound.

"Told you not to throw that damn nickel curve!" scolded Johnny.

Scott stared at Johnny, then at his detached arm. His fingers grasped a nickel curve grip firmly on the ball, even as his loose arm dangled from Johnny's hand. "My arm," replied Scott.

From behind and the right, Bugler moseyed up. "That nickel curve done ya' in, I see." He scratched his chin whiskers and shook his head as he looked up at Scott.

Johnny nodded his agreement with Bugler. The umpire marched to the mound in his blue suit, with the heavy chest protector remaining in place. The ump stopped next to Johnny. He removed his mask, revealing Hiroshi Ishikawa.

"Kommichiha Koutou." Ishikawa, the umpire, bowed.

"Hiroshi," replied Scott. "Arigatou, I guess."

Johnny looked at Bugler, who jumped in. "We don't speak Nip."

Ishikawa bowed again. "Sorry, Bugler-san. Wyatt-san speaks Japanese well."

From Scott's left, Colonel Fielding sauntered toward him in a full-dress army uniform. The eagle on his hat glistened from reflected sunlight. Wyatt stood with the assemblage as Fielding reached him.

"My arm came off," explained Scott to Fielding.

"Doesn't matter. You still need to break that Russian code!" As serious and dower as ever, Fielding crossed his arms and glared at poor Wyatt.

"But my arm," pleaded Scott.

"Stow it, captain! You lost your arm, nickel curve, and all." Full glare and no compassion, Fielding cocked his head toward the arm Johnny clutched.

"But I need it to pitch," protested Scott.

"You don't pitch anymore! Break that damn code!" bellowed Fielding.

"Scott-san, break the code." Hiroshi, the umpire, smiled at him.

"Break the damn code, you big lug," chimed in Johnny.

"But my arm."

Johnny Grayhawk shook the arm. "Wyatt!"

"Wyatt?" asked Bugler.

"Wyatt!" bellowed Hiroshi.

"Ichimu?" asked Scott.

"No. Not a dream. Akumu, Wyatt-san. Nightmare." Hiroshi wore his business suit. No longer an umpire, he smiled.

"Wyatt?" asked Fielding. "You're worrying me."

"Please wake up, Wyatt."

* * *

"Come on, Wyatt, wake up, buddy." A fretful Johnny Grayhawk hovered beside Scott's bed.

After playing a few rounds of focus, out-of-focus, Johnny's visage cleared for Wyatt. Streaked morning light poured through his bedroom window, closing down his irises. Scott rubbed his head with both hands to loosen the cobwebs. His head ached like a losing prize fighter whose corner had tossed in the towel three rounds late.

"Johnny?" Scott had trouble placing him in his apartment after his appearance in the one-arm pitching nightmare.

"You damn troublemaker! Of course, it's Johnny. Who the hell else would take care of your stupid P.I. butt."

"The boss called me this morning, and I came here too," broke in Evie Hall as she entered Wyatt's bedroom. "I got a pot of coffee going when you're ready." She took the opposite side of the bed from Johnny. Evie bent down, reached around Wyatt's shoulders, and hugged him. "I thought you were trying to croak on us. Or at least losing your mind."

The jostling stirred his headache to another level. It also blurred his vision until Evie let him loose. She stood grinning down at him. Her beaming face engendered a reflexive smile from Scott.

"Now that you're alive, I'll bring you some coffee," heralded Evie. She took a step, then added, "As long as you stop talking Japanese."

Evie dashed out of the bedroom before Scott could ask what she meant. He turned to Johnny, who had backed away from the bed, but whose stern stare persisted. "What did she mean talking Japanese?"

"You fired off a few Japanese words during some dream."

"Some dream is right." Wyatt decided not to impart the bizarre details.

"I was relieved to hear your rants even if I had no clue about what you were saying." Grayhawk sighed. "Doctor said you'd likely come out of it; just need to wait and keep an eye on you."

"How did you get here in the first place?"

"I dropped by to ask about your car upholstery. Your door was open, and you were on the floor. I got a doctor here, and we put you to bed." Johnny spread his arms toward the ransacked bedroom's strewn clothes. "Looked like a robbery, but since neither of us think much of the Tulsa cops, I didn't want to call them until you said so."

"You were right. We don't need the cops." Scott noted his ransacked bedroom with its strewn clothes and pulled drawers.

While Johnny nodded his understanding, Scott rebuilt the memory of the previous night. It appeared Dimitrov belligerently searched his apartment for something after coldcocking him. He concentrated on remembering their encounter and separating it from his pitching mound menagerie and its arm-losing nightmare. He had nothing the Russian could want. Still, Dimitrov thought it worthwhile to rummage around. A sharp head throb shunted his thoughts to a handful of aspirin and a glass of whisky. Before words could form, Evie came back. She carried a coffee mug with a hint of steam rising from it. He felt a smile at the corner of his mouth.

"Now that you're finally awake, you get coffee." She continued into his bedroom, arriving at the side of the bed.

Scott sat up to receive the welcome beverage. His head throbbed anew, and he noticed his vision drifted to a shade blurry. Evie handed him the mug. He took a slurping sip, noting his bare chest as he did. With his free hand, Scott lifted the white sheet covering him. He looked down at his frame. Undershorts proved to be his only clothing.

"Don't worry." Evie grinned ear-to-ear. "Johnny got you under the covers before I got here."

"Johnny thinks his job is watching out for me." Wyatt let the sheet settle back on his body.

"Somebody has to," said Johnny.

Scott gulped his coffee this time. "What's your excuse for becoming my nurse?"

"Such a tone." Evie cocked her head down at Scott. "Might show some gratitude, big boy, to the ginchy cookie nursing you back to health."

"Not what I was getting at, Evie." Scott knew how much she'd grown up in the last two months, way beyond her years and more than she should have. "Of course, I'm grateful. I just don't want you mixed up in it. You don't get paid enough to take these chances."

"Don't get paid enough; that's the God's truth, but I still stop for run-over dogs on my own time." She crossed her arms, underscoring her statement.

"Listen to him, Evie," Johnny added his concerned advice.

Scott chuckled as much as his thumping head would allow and grinned at her moxie. "Since you help injured creatures, there's some rye in that credenza in the living room. A pour in this coffee would be humane." He waved the mug.

Evie marched away. Wyatt heard his liquor cabinet open and close. In anticipation, he scooted to a full sitting position just as Evie waltzed back in with a liquor bottle in tow.

"Open bottle of Cutty Sark Scotch on top of your bar," remarked Evie. "Why rye?"

"Thinking balm is Cutty." Scott grimaced from the words vibrating in harmony with his head thumps. "Rye is medicinal."

Evie coughed out a giggle and tipped the bottle to pour rye into Scott's cup. "There's your medicine, then." She righted the bottle after flowing more than a dram.

"You're a doll, Evie."

"I am. I am a doll. You need to write that in your book and remember it, Wyatt Scott." Evie headed for the door, taking the rye with her.

"Evie," called Scott. He motioned her to come back. He pointed to the bottle.

She obliged and circled back to his nightstand, where she left the bottle for his future reference. "Since you're better, I'll head back to open the office."

"We'll both go," added Johnny Grayhawk. "The doctor just said rest to heal up. I say, stay out of trouble."

"Thanks again, both of you."

Johnny nodded and followed Evie as she made the door. Before going further, she ducked back in. The quizzical look on her face presaged her comment. "How did you get into this mess anyway?"

Scott smirked at the question. "I think I took a wrong turn someplace in nineteen thirty-four...or maybe nineteen forty-five."

Firing back a smirk of her own, Evie replied, "When you figure things out, send me a postcard." She left, closing the bedroom door.

* * *

A couple of hours and half a thousand head throbs after Johnny and Evie left, Scott abandoned his bed to tiptoe into his bathroom and secure a bottle of aspirin. He poured a few into his left hand. The exact count varied between unimportant and a blurred half dozen. He shoved the tablets in his mouth and spun the spigot on the cold-water tap. He bent his head down and slurped enough water to send the pills swirling down his throat. Dryer than a camel's tongue licking a sand dune, he gulped three more mouth's full to improve his hydration.

Scott tussled with a robe before wobbling into his living room. Its pleasant surprise was that Dimitrov had not ruined it like he did the bedroom. Even as he determined to push forward, he tiptoed to avoid the shock sent up his spine from his heavy heels striking the carpet. Getting through the kitchen door, his bonus sat on the countertop. Evie had left the coffeepot on.

While the first cup and its rye helper eased him back to reality, it did not palliate his head. Wyatt grabbed a fresh mug, filled it, and burned his tongue with a swig instead of a sip. He sucked in air to relieve his tongue and blew out over the coffee to cool down the brew. More judiciously, he sipped the infusion of over-brewed, viscous, and black-as-night Cain's coffee. His tiny but frequent sips lowered the cup's level by a third. He filled it back up to prepare for the arduous journey to his chair near the west window.

With awareness of both his head and the shifting liquid in the mug, Scott shuffled his way toward the wingback chair. He noticed that one of his shirts was hanging over the arm of his sofa. Neither Johnny nor Evie mentioned the bullet hole, so Dimitrov must have covered it. His head banged too stridently to dwell on the Russian's odd behavior. As he approached the coffee table, Wyatt shelved his original plan in favor of easing onto the sofa and set his mug on the table before lounging.

His west window offered a tableau of the day. While still morning, the blue sky and the Sahara-dry appearance of the sandbars in the river left no doubt that the summer heat would reign without interruption. It had been quite an eventful few days. Scott considered his plight as he reached for coffee. Cupping the mug in both hands, he slurped. That odd connection he sought among Sleener, Hiroshi, and himself worked out to be Dimitrov. The spy's circumspect conduct hinted at a reason, but that reason remained hidden. The spy seemed satisfied with their conversation; enough to let Wyatt live. He swallowed more coffee. The stimulant seemed to rouse his damaged brain. His aspirin dosing had eradicated the head thumping, leaving a steady ache as Dimitrov's tribute.

Scott's doorbell rang. A second later, the door opened, thankfully relieving Scott of the necessity of budging from his couch. Mike Barton crossed the threshold, his hat already in his hand. He waggled it as he saw Scott.

"Glad to see you up. I thought I better check on you after I heard you took a ten-count last night."

"Mike." Wyatt scooted up from his slouch. "Didn't expect to see you, but thanks for checking on me."

"Couldn't keep me away when you need help."

Barton strolled to the wingback chair, peering at Scott's bedraggled appearance. He dropped his hat on the table near the Alaska photo, then took a seat. Scott watched the process, knowing that a gracious host would offer refreshment, but in his condition, it would be self-serve.

"I've got coffee in the kitchen. You're more than welcome to grab some. Though, I am not budging."

"Thanks. Maddie poured a pot down me before I left for Tulsa." Barton cleared his throat. "I haven't talked to you, but I'm proud of you solving the Edwards murder and getting old Bugler out."

Scott almost smiled. Inside, he grinned wider than a young kid who just won a box of candy bars. "Thanks, Mike."

"Now, about last night." Barton glanced around the scene. "I heard your visitor left a mess. Not so bad now."

"Some mess in the bedroom. He left the biggest mess between my ears." Scott touched his sore head. "How did you hear about me?" The obvious question having just popped into Scott's battered brain.

"Johnny Grayhawk called me. He asked me to talk to you because he said you don't get on so well with the Tulsa police. He thought I could help investigate this while you recover" Barton smirked. "While he didn't say it, I also know that Johnny doesn't much trust the department either."

"I don't think the Tulsa guys can sort this out. The deep-down reason is off my radar scope too. The surface has to do with me, a Japanese named Hiroshi Ishikawa, and a blackmailer named Sleener."

"Oddball trio you've made your way into." Mike Barton scratched behind his ear.

"The tie-in comes about because the slugs from both of their murders and some potshots at me all matched," explained Scott.

"Holy Peter! Somebody wants to clip you along with two strangely different guys. Who?"

Scott didn't want to admit to being with Pierce when they spotted

Dimitrov. Even detailing the bare bones to Mike Barton would be hard enough. Scott washed away the foul taste of his omission with a large gulp of coffee. He put the mug back down and squirmed into a better position on the couch. "Last night, the guy told me straight out he had orders to kill those two, but he claimed I was a loose end he figured to clean up and not part of the planned program." Scott rubbed his temple after a particularly angry throb made its presence known. "He claimed that now I no longer mattered, that killing me would be a waste. I guess he slugged me to keep me from calling the cops right then."

"Why would an admitted murderer, who seems like a pro, whose face you saw, let you live?"

"Because the guy's a Soviet spy. He works out of their Chicago consulate and has diplomatic immunity."

"Oh boy. Full crap-show you've fallen into." Barton shook his head. "Wyatt Scott, Tulsa P.I. mixed up with Russian spies." He rubbed his chin. Barton kept a steady focus on Wyatt's eyes. He dropped his hand from his jaw to his lap. "I believe that story. The Russian didn't worry about you knowing him because you already knew him. Johnny told me your army boss came sniffing around. You're swimming with that CIA lot again. Why on God's green earth are you mixed up in that?"

"Retired, but still a great cop. You hit it. If the Soviets wanted those two dead, I still need to figure out why."

Barton sighed. "You believe this Russian killer; that he won't try again?"

"I do. He had other things on his mind."

"Wyatt, I advise you to get away from the CIA and quit the whole mess. But my guess is you'll keep on. Care to fill me in on the story?"

Scott smiled. "Long and odd story."

"Odd already. Give me long then." Barton leaned back in his chair. "But don't give me a snow job. Even if I don't like the facts, I'm on your side."

"Thanks for checking on me, Mike," said Scott. "No sense in you having to worry about spies." Wyatt kept his eyes on Barton through a lingering pause. "I'll keep this one on my private score pad."

CHAPTER 19

PEOPLE DIE

More than a week after Dimitrov's visit, and fully recovered from his head injury, Scott was weary of making further fruitless drives through west Tulsa with Pierce. They'd driven every road and asked anyone who would listen if they had seen a sedan that resembled Dimitrov's. From Terlton, Hallet, and onward north, Drumright and Cushing traveling south, with Jennings and Oilton in between, no reports of foreigners stopping at gas stations or buying provisions at grocery stores popped up.

Scott reported their hitless batting average to Fielding. The lack of progress frustrated Wyatt. Oklahoma's heat soured Pierce beyond his usual surly self, and despite his calmness, aggravation seeped from the twitching corners of Fielding's mouth. The man kept his stoic demeanor through three nights of complaints from Pierce and sarcastic barbs from Scott. Smart enough to see the rising problem, Fielding called a meeting where a day off garnered a unanimous vote.

Wyatt took advantage of the day and idled in his bathrobe. He vowed that this morning would be his. No closer to the motive of Dimitrov's boss for murdering Hiroshi and Sleener, Wyatt closed his eyes and forced the espionage hyena back into a mental cage. He felt exhausted. He craved to be lazy. On top of the spy-search frustration, three long days in a hot car with Pierce warranted a rest. Apparently, his doorbell didn't agree.

The irritating buzz filled his living room. Wyatt eased out of his chair and cinched his robe sash. Rapid knocks of knuckles on wood signaled more urgency from the nuisance guest. He didn't quite shuffle to his door, but it fell far from a confident swagger. He straightened his robe and ran his hand through his hair. As ready as possible for a surprise guest, Scott pulled open the door.

At his threshold stood an ashen faced Bugler. He held a newspaper. It shook in his unsteady hand. His eyes wet with disbelief, both corners of his mouth stretching down his chin, and a crooked Oilers cap foretold the end of the world.

"The Bambino's dead!" Bugler waved his folded paper as proof.

"Rough news," replied Scott as he saw the genuine hurt in his old pal's eyes.

"That throat cancer...says here in the World." He offered the folded paper up to Scott.

It came as a shock, even though everyone knew the inevitability of the news. Scott opened the door wide. "Come in, Eugene. I'll get us a couple of cold Cokes."

Bugler entered, hardly hearing his Christian name and its rare utterance. He removed his skewed Oilers cap. He shuffled through the door, allowing Scott to close it behind him. The old man hesitated, with his folded *Tulsa World* in one hand and his ball cap in the other.

Scott pointed toward the couch. "Have a seat. You can fill me in."

Wyatt watched as Bugler tested a cushion before accepting it as a seat. He dropped his ball cap on the next cushion before unfolding the newspaper. He ruffled through unwanted pages, then folded the paper to display what he wanted. The old fellow squinted at the headline, daring it to confirm what he had read more than once. Another notion pushed his eyes from the print, as Wyatt headed for his kitchen.

Bugler sprang to his feet. He cupped his hands around his mouth and yelled toward Scott. "Not one a' them bootlegger Cokes, Wyatt."

Scott acknowledged Bugler's plea. He grabbed two bottles of unadulterated Coca Cola from his refrigerator and pried their caps off in quick succession. He carried one in each hand back into his living room. "Plain Coke, Eugene." He handed one to Bugler. The old baseball aficionado stood and grasped it with both hands.

"To the Babe; greatest ever!" proclaimed Wyatt as he raised his bottle in salute.

Bugler dropped one hand and raised his Coke high. "The Babe!"

Both sipped their colas. The two men stood, each reflecting on the man and the game. Wyatt visualized the big man smiling in Japan. He had other memories, but that one held sway. Their shared silence persisted long enough for Bugler to take a self-conscious second sip.

"I imagine there will be a big send off for the Babe," speculated Scott.

Bugler nodded. "Probably like Roos-uh-velt or at least Gehrig." Bugler retrieved his newspaper. He ran his finger down a column of print. Arriving where he intended, he tapped the paper with his finger. "Says he'll 'lie in state' at Yankee Stadium today. That mean they're havin' his funeral at the stadium?"

"I believe they'll have him in his casket for folks to pay their respects. As many fans as admire Ruth, no other location is big enough. Baseball fans need Yankee Stadium for them to say their goodbyes." Wyatt crafted his explanation to meet Bugler's needs. "I expect his funeral will be in a few days at a church."

Bugler acknowledged the explanation with a nod. "Ought to bury him there. It's his home."

"It might be fitting all right, but I think there are rules that won't allow it."

"For the Babe, they oughta' break rules."

"You might be right, Bugler. Still, he will probably rest better in his own quiet space."

Bugler cogitated over his friend's opinion. He dropped his newspaper on the coffee table. He looked up at Scott with somber eyes. "Baseball won't be the same."

Scott met his look with empathy and his statement with agreement. "No, it won't."

Bugler picked up his hat. He ran his hands over it. He fiddled with the crown and shaping that had long since been set. "Don't know what to do with muh'self ta'day," he admitted.

Scott moved to his radio-phonograph console. He switched it on. Within a few seconds, static flared up. He signaled for Bugler to join him. "Why don't you tune this radio down the dial to see if there's a broadcast?"

Bugler meandered to the console.

"I'll get dressed and listen with you." Scott lingered, then pointed toward a knob.

Bugler took charge of the knob. He spun it slowly through static, music, soap operas, and more static. His slow twisting along the tuner spectrum brought scratchy, half-clear words that mentioned Babe Ruth. He twisted a little more, marginally enhancing the clarity.

Scott departed to his bedroom for slacks and a clean shirt. He pulled on some thin beige trousers, but his mind wandered as he stared at his laundered shirts. Thoughts of Lou Gehrig's death followed naturally after hearing about the Babe. But his cruel consciousness took side roads to Sleener and Hiroshi and those vexations. It didn't stop there. A quick flash of Harris sitting across from him in the Officers' Club swung through. Of course, the connections ran to the Quonset hut and poor Paul Brock. He grabbed a collared cotton print, shook it, and slipped it on. Wyatt consulted his mirror to see the fit. The shirt looked fine. The guy wearing it looked tired.

Scott wished for the summer tumult of nineteen forty-eight to be at an end. Tulsa had seen enough commotion and didn't need more. That went double for Wyatt. Even though he solved them, Cleveland was right; murders traveled on his path. He still had to find Dimitrov, deal with Fielding, put up with Pierce, and get through the dreadful heat. A little over six weeks until October, when cooler weather, the state fair, and the World Series could provide diversion and relief for Tulsans. He held onto those positive thoughts when he rejoined Bugler in the living room and the solemn broadcast he shared with his old baseball pal.

* * *

A car rolling up to the cabin roused Alexi Dimitrov from his seat on the bed and his dreams of cool weather. The spy in hiding circled past his kitchen table to open the cabin door. His comrade carried two full grocery bags, with a loaf of Wonder Bread barely contained on the top of one. Dimitrov held the door until his delivery man eased both bags down on the sink counter.

"Thank you, buddy." Dimitrov chuckled. "English, eh?"

"Da." The man laughed. "American English at that. Well done."

"Two bags. My stay grows longer?"

"We still do not know how long you will be here, comrade." The man unpacked the paper bag with the teetering loaf of bread.

"I am the servant of Mother Russia."

"Your work has been noted. You completed your assignment." The man withdrew a can of peaches before continuing. "I'm sure the complications will be resolved as soon as possible."

"Yes, those complications." Dimitrov smirked. "I recognize them now."

The man paused with a can of peas in his hand. "Oh, you do?"

"Are you Russian enough to know our saying: a word is not a sparrow: once it flies out, you will not catch it?" The steadfast spy let his eyes wander around the cabin. "Questions follow us; answers find us. Sometimes they do not come in order."

The supplier set the peas on the counter. He dipped back inside his sack and added canned corn to the countertop. "You have become a philosopher, comrade Alexi."

"No, a veteran of our world."

"We must do our part for Russia and the cause."

"I do not question that." Dimitrov returned his view to his patron. "We serve in different ways. Sometimes fate interferes with our service."

A tin of tuna became the next item set out. "Your service and mine move along. We cannot wait for others."

"I believe that is the problem," Dimitrov mixed a groan with throat-clearing. "I will be pleased when my hiding ends. This Oklahoma is too hot."

"Be patient. I have something that will help you forget the heat."

Dimitrov's contact continued setting items on the counter. The groceries accumulated with identical and similar products to his previous visit. After a few more cans, a slab of Velveeta, and a tin of saltine crackers, his first bag was empty. He tossed the brown bag into Dimitrov's trash basket. Delving into the second bag, he pulled out a box of Cheerios.

The communist provider reached into the bag again. "Here, comrade." He lifted out a quart bottle of vodka.

The cabin's resident beamed at the sight of a new, grand sized bottle. "Much better." Dimitrov rubbed his hands together.

The Russian's benefactor set the liquor on the kitchen table before moving back to the countertop and extracting a can of beets. For his part, Dimitrov grabbed the bottle and tore into the federal government seal securing its top. Holding the bottle down on the table with his left hand, he freed the closure with his right. Once opened, he didn't lift the bottle but shifted his full attention to the top of the exposed liquor. He sniffed at the open neck while nodding to his comrade. The other man, with his hand inside the grocery bag, nodded back.

Dimitrov hoisted his new large bottle and slugged down the alcoholic liquid. Bubbles ran to the inverted bottom of the quart bottle as he gulped. The spy closed his eyes, smacked his lips, and swallowed. His facial muscles relaxed. The corners of his mouth curled up, smiling from some rhapsodic paradise that only Russians feel from potato alcohol. He guzzled and drank and swigged, finally liberating the neck's aperture from his lips. As he drew the bottle away, a wide, blissful grin radiated from a contented Dimitrov.

"Za kommunisticheskoye delo," blurted out the man.

"Da," replied Dimitrov. "The communist cause!"

From inside his brown paper grocery bag, the man withdrew a pistol.

"Oh, so soon," said Dimitrov. He kept a stoic stare.

The gun fired. Blank-faced, Dimitrov stumbled back. He held fast to his vodka bottle. "YA znayu. YA znayu. I know it all."

A second blast sent another slug into his chest. The stocky spy fell backward onto the cabin floor. His momentum took the bottle down with him. Vodka splashed out, jetting across the floor. No longer capable of holding the bottle, Dimitrov's grasp failed, allowing the bottle to arc toward the dormant fireplace, sloshing vodka as it rolled.

The man swept the empty grocery bag onto the floor and walked around the table. He stood over the insentient Alexi Dimitrov. "Do svidaniya tovarishch," he bid.

The once benefactor, now assassin, triggered a third bullet, striking the downed Dimitrov low in his forehead. The dead man's head bounced just off the floor before dropping back amid a volcanic eruption of biological debris. Scalp, hair, skull, blood, and gray matter

patterned a bell curve from ear-to-ear. The man held his killing pose –
an impassive statue of murder in the spy game. After several seconds, he
lowered the pistol beside his thigh.

Still peering down at the dead wet-works spy, the killer tucked the
gun into his belted trousers. He backed up, stepping on the discarded
paper bag. He picked it up and began refilling it with some of the
groceries he had brought. Four fruit cans and the Velveeta fit the
bottom of the paper bag. He glanced at the spilled vodka bottle. Alexi's
executioner left it on the floor before finishing his bagging with the
Cheerios and the bread. He glanced at the cold fireplace and its resident
suitcase. A much longer stare bore down on the aluminum gun carrier,
which sat on the rigidly made bed.

Dimitrov's killer retrieved the gun case. He made his way to the
cabin door, cracked it open, and peered out. After his quick peek, he
pushed the door wide and took in a vista of empty countryside. He set
the case on the porch and returned to the counter. The killer picked up
his re-bagged sack of groceries and walked onto the porch. He grasped
the aluminum case and swung it to close the door. His job complete,
he left the hideout cabin and the physical remains of Alexi Dimitrov.

THE END

After reading SCOTT'S TULSA II, please pop over to Amazon or Goodreads to leave your thoughts or a full review. Your feedback means the world to me!

Join the community of readers! Visit my website (slchalmers.com) for behind-the-scenes insights, the history of 1948 events, places, and photos. Email (slc@slchalmers.com) for updates, specials, giveaways, or ask questions.

Social media with FB – SLsl Chalmers; Substack- slchalmers; X and others.

SCOTT'S TULSA III is coming in late summer 2026.

GLOSSARY OF 1948 SLANG

A

Above my pay grade – don't ask me

Active duty – sexually promiscuous boy

Ameche – to telephone

Armored heifer – Canned milk

B

Baby-doll - female appellation.

Bad business - trouble.

Bathtub – motorcycle sidecar

Black-and-white - police car.

Blivet - something unimportant or
    indescribable.

Blow a fuse - lose your temper.

Bonkers - crazy, insane.

Booger - brat, a rascal.

Bop - dance wildly.

Broad - a woman

Brush off - rebuff, snub.

Bum rap - false accusation.

Bupkis - nothing, zip.

Bust your (his/her) chops - to scold,
    chastise.

Buy the farm - die.

C

Can - jail or prison.

Chopper - tooth.

Chrome-dome - bald guy

Clip - to kill.

Cock-eyed - crazy, cockamamie.

Cold Fish - an unresponsive person.

Cook with gas - to do something right.

Cookie - guy or gal.

Crack open - to open a bottle.

Crack up - make laugh.

Crib notes - forbidden notes taken to
    an exam.

Croak - die.

D

Dead hoofer – poor dancer

Dish - pretty woman.

Doll dizzy – girl crazy

Dolly - girl or a woman.

Dome - head or skull.

Dreamboat - attractive person.

Drop - to kill.

Ducky shincracker - a good dancer

Dust off - to kill.

F

Fat-head - stupid or foolish person.

Fire up - start your engine.

Flap your lips - talk.

Flatfoot - policeman or detective.

Flip your wig - lose control of yourself,
    go crazy.

Fracture - to make someone laugh.

FUBAR - (acronym – F'd Up Beyond
    All Recognition)

Fuddy-Duddy – old-fashioned person

G

G-man - FBI investigator.

Gas - a great time, something hilarious.

Gat - gun (from Gatling gun).

Geezer - an old person

Glitterati -rich, famous people.

Gobbledygook – double talk, long speech

Gone with the wind – run off (with
    the money)

Gravy - easy money.

Grill - interrogate intensely.
Gumshoe - private investigator.
Gunsel - stupid thug who carries a gun.

H
Hairy - old, out-dated.
Hang up - quit.
Heave-ho - an ejection, throwing out
    physically.
Hen fruit – eggs
Hi sugar, are you rationed? – Are you
    going steady?
Hitch - to marry
Honcho - boss, commanding officer.
Honey - attractive female.
Hots - strong desire for a person.

I
In my book - in my opinion.
In the know - knowledgeable, aware.

J
Jitterbug - dance to fast big band jazz.
Jive - make sense, fit.
Johnson - The male organ.
Joint - A prison, jail.

K
Khaki wacky – boy crazy
Kibosh - to stop (something).
Killer-diller – good stuff
Knuckle sandwich - punch in the mouth.

L
Lettuce - money
lulu - something excellent, outstanding.

M
Meatball - a stupid or foolish person.
Megillah - tediously detailed account.
Moolah - money.
Motorized freckles – insects
Mug - face.
Mug - to make faces.

N
Natch - naturally, of course
Nerve - audacity.
No dice! - interjection of rejection.

O
Off the hook - exonerated, cleared
    of guilt.
Old lady - mother.

P
Patsy - a scapegoat.
Paw - Hand.
Peepers - Eyes.
Pistol - A dynamic person.

R
Rhubarb - argument, squabble.
Rock - a diamond or precious stone.
Rocks - ice.
Rub out - to kill.
Rug - toupee, a wig.
Run out of gas - lose interest.

S
Sappy - gullible, or overly sentimental.
Sauced - drunk, intoxicated.
Share crop – sexually promiscuous
Sing - inform or tattle.

Snap your cap – get angry
Souse - a drunk.
Spew - to vomit.
Spiffy - dressed up
Stompers – shoes
Swigger - a drinker.

T
Take a gander - look at, examine.
Take a powder - to leave.
Thingamabob - object without a name.
Through the wringer - tough questioning.

U
Unmentionables - women's underwear.

Up for grabs - available to anyone.

W
Wacky - crazy, insane.
Wad - money.
What's buzzin', cousin? – how's it going?
What's cooking? - What is going on?
Whistle Dixie - be mistaken.
Wolf - aggressively forward male.
Wrack your brain - think hard.

Y
Yuck - a stupid or foolish person.
    (He's a yuck.)